Praise for Valerie Wilson Wesley's Tamara Hayle Mysteries

"There's a richness of language in Wesley's writing, joined by a delightful sense of humor. She makes the mean streets of Newark come alive."
—San Francisco Examiner

"A major talent . . . Wesley's voice—laden with wit, style, and sparkle—is unique in mystery fiction."
—The Globe and Mail

"[Tamara Hayle] has a way with a wisecrack that is positively lethal."
—Washington Post Book World

"A wonderfully believable and independent sleuth who combines intellect

"Outsta   nanners."

"An engagi   er."

"The desperate search for a missing child makes Newark PI Tamara Hayle's eighth outing a chilling, thought-provoking read. . . . Wesley recounts Tamara's struggles with equal parts irony, compassion, and insight."
—Publishers Weekly on Of Blood and Sorrow

A Glimmer
of Death

VALERIE
WILSON WESLEY

KENSINGTON
PUBLISHING CORP.
www.kensingtonbooks.com

KENSINGTON BOOKS are published by

Kensington Publishing Corp.
119 West 40th Street
New York, NY 10018

All Kensington titles, imprints, and distributed lines are available at special quantity discounts for bulk purchases for sales promotion, premiums, fund-raising, educational, or institutional use.

Special book excerpts or customized printings can also be created to fit specific needs. For details, write or phone the office of the Kensington Sales Manager: Kensington Publishing Corp., 119 West 40th Street, New York, NY 10018. Attn. Sales Department. Phone: 1-800-221-2647.

The K logo is a trademark of Kensington Publishing Corp.

ISBN-13: 978-1-4967-2780-0 (ebook)
ISBN-10: 1-4967-2780-0 (ebook)

ISBN-13: 978-1-4967-2778-7
ISBN-10: 1-4967-2778-9
First Kensington Trade Paperback Printing: February 2021

10 9 8 7 6 5 4 3 2 1

Printed in the United States of America

For my sister-cousins
Joyce, Karla, and our beloved Janis

Acknowledgments

There is not enough space on this page or any other to thank the many friends who have supported and cheered me through this book and so many others. Thank you all for being there for me. My gratitude to Selena James, Wendy McCurdy, and the editors at Kensington Books, who believed in me enough to let me try a cozy. My continued thanks to Faith Hampton Childs, my friend and agent, who has been in my corner since I began writing. As always, my love and gratitude to my husband, Richard, for his good spirits and easy laughter when I most need them, my daughters, Thembi and Nandi, for their lean-on-me strength and gracious, loving ways, and my grandson, Primo, for bringing such joy into my life. And, of course, to Junior, the *purring* inspiration for Juniper, Dessa's cat.

Chapter 1

The office reeked of nutmeg. It tickled my nose, filled my mouth, forcing its way down my throat. Funny thing about nutmeg. A dash can spice up cocoa; too much can make you sick. Determined to ignore it, I focused on the real estate listings in front of me. Yet the smell wouldn't leave. I closed my eyes, trying to block this pain-in-the-neck, useless sixth sense, but it did no good. To me, Odessa Jones, nutmeg means death.

"You doing all right over there, Dessa?" asked Bertie Jefferson, the agent in the cubicle next to mine. At Risko Realty, only the owner, Charlie Risko, had an office. Everybody else worked in narrow, shoddy cubes that offered no privacy and little room for laptops, plastic cups, or computer printouts.

"Do you smell something, like, uh . . . eggnog?" I said, hoping I was wrong this time.

Bertie sniffed the air. "Eggnog? Naw, just the lingering stink of that nasty body oil Vinton greases himself down with every morning. You sure you're okay?" Bertie's eyes, framed by horn-rimmed glasses, looked brighter than usual.

I forced a smile. "Just discouraged."

"Don't be." Bertie smiled wide enough for me to spot a

speck of light sparkling on a gold-capped tooth. "Believe me, honey, good luck happens when you least expect it. Sometimes you have to make your own, need to smile through your tears till it happens."

Smiling through my tears was the last thing I felt like doing, though Bertie did a good job of it. She had reason to believe in good luck; she'd sure had her share of bad. After thirty years of working at the same place and married to the same man, she'd lost her job and man in one fell swoop: Her agency downsized; her husband walked out. Louella, who she called her "problem of a daughter," disappeared weekly, breaking her heart daily and forcing her to raise Erika, Louella's young daughter, on her own. Although Bertie adored her granddaughter, she swore the child bore no resemblance to anyone she knew—past or present—and stayed angry at Louella for reasons she never shared. Yet Bertie worked hard each day and carried her burdens *mostly* in silence. Like nearly everyone at Risko Realty, this place was Bertie's desperate snatch at sanity and middle-class respectability. Each sale (or promise of one) brought hope and a dream. Bertie had just sold a mid-six-figure Dutch colonial in a "better" part of town. At least for now, Bertie's dream had come true.

Risko Realty was a cut-rate real estate agency in Grovesville, an aging New Jersey town stuck between struggling Clifftown and affluent Bren Bridge, a once-upon-a-time "sundown town" that folks like me *still* avoided when the sun set. Like Goldilocks's favorite chair, Grovesville was neither too large nor too small. The winding, narrow streets were filled with people of various races, ethnicities, and social classes—much like the mix of folks in my office. Some thought Grovesville the perfect place to put down roots. Others considered it a brief stop toward a brighter destination—Manhattan was just two train stops away. A tasty blend of ethnic foods—jerk chicken, sushi, pad thai, and a twenty-four-hour diner—assured nobody went hungry. Crimes were few and far between, and citizens walked its streets (at a reasonable hour) with no fear. Five years ago, my late husband, Darryl, and I bought our small yellow house—a wedding gift to each other—on one of those winding streets and lived there happily until his sudden death last year. Those were the happiest days of my life.

"You've only been here, what, couple of months? No time at all. I might have a few rental leads for you," Bertie said, but I barely heard her. My mind was racing. The smell of nutmeg, grown stronger, was back.

I have what some folks call "second sight." I look like any woman in her early forties patiently waiting her turn in a beauty salon or checkout line. My round brown face, "cute" haircut (or so people tell me), and quick dimpled grin often remind strangers of a beloved sister or cousin, which I always take as a compliment. Six months before Darryl died, a streak of silver hair suddenly appeared on the left side of my head. Darryl jokingly told me to dye it blue, which I did, but now it's back, and I've decided I like it. It's distinctive, different, like other things about me. I can sense, smell, and hear things other folks can't. Hazy auras, sometimes with color, which my aunt Phoenix calls "glimmers," appear when certain people enter my space. I can "read" rooms and know intimate things about their occupants. When bad things are on the way, I sense them. Every now and then, other people's words tumble out of my mouth. (Thank God, that's not often!)

But I've grown to distrust and resent this "gift." Where was it last year when my life fell apart? Why did it give me no warning that Darryl would drop dead of an aneurism? Or that I'd be on the verge of losing our home? Or that D&D Delights, the catering business we started, would go bankrupt because I couldn't bring myself to cook? This "gift" had failed me in every imaginable way, and I was sick of having it. Despite what my aunt believes.

Aunt Phoenix, my informant on all things extrasensory, claims the gift is a family heirloom passed like a china soup tureen to those who deserve it. (As if anyone needs a china soup tureen.) She says my gift will grow stronger and more varied the older I get. (It's strong enough now, thank you.) I have distant cousins, Aunt Phoenix claims, who can wash dishes with the flick of a finger or trip a man going downstairs with the nod of a head. But my aunt does enjoy the occasional nip of cherry brandy from the flask she keeps tucked in her purse. I often assume her tales are flavored accordingly.

Yet despite my mistrust, I can't dismiss the gift altogether. It has warned me about risky houses and lying sellers. It has suggested the odd spice to jazz up rice pudding or tone down hot pepper sauce. I can't count on the thing but dare not ignore it. And here it was this morning, masking death as nutmeg.

"Hey, Miss Dess, how you doing today?" Vinton Laverne asked as he eased into the cubicle near Bertie. Nutmeg was overtaken by bitter lemon. Vinton was a short, wiry man older than me by a decade whose clothes aged him by two. His taupe three-piece suits, striped mohair sweater vests, and rimless glasses gave him the look of a stodgy bookkeeper about to retire. On my first day at Risko Realty, I'd noticed that he was surrounded by one of Aunt Phoenix's glimmers—mouse gray—as if it were inspired by his clothes and being. I'd gotten used to it, though, and barely noticed it anymore. According to Bertie, who had some goods on everybody, Vinton had been with Risko Realty for decades—through the deaths of Leon, the patriarch; his older son, Stuart; and into the reign of Crown Prince Charlie.

"Did you see Charlie yet?" Bertie asked Vinton as he turned on his laptop.

"Yesterday, just before you. Made my quota so he stayed off my tail. You did okay?"

Bertie grinned and pointed to a magnum of cold duck on her desk; it was Risko's idea of a celebratory award. "This is my lucky day, you-all. I got the wine and found these gloves cheap, cheap, cheap on eBay last week." She pulled out a pair of hot-pink leather gloves and waved them in Vinton's face. Bertie loved a bargain and at least three times a week displayed her latest online finds despite the quiet annoyance of the rest of us. "Take a look." She tossed a glove to Vinton, who slipped it on his thin hand.

"How come you got pink?" he said.

"I like pink!"

"Well, they do make a bold statement, I'll give you that. But they're so loud you can hear them arguing." Vinton cackled and tossed them back.

"You need to make a bold statement with the clothes you're always wearing around here. Half the time, you look like you're headed to the graveyard," said Bertie with more than a touch of malice.

"Well, there are *statements* left better unstated," said Vinton, not to be outdone. "I'll make my statements, and you make yours, loud as they may be. You meet with him yet, Dessa?" he said, changing the subject and turning his attention to me. I'd gotten used to the quarrelsome banter between the two of them and was glad not to be drawn into it. Occasionally, Bertie had a nasty, cruel streak that surprised me, and Vinton was often her victim. I was glad he'd answered back this time. Aunt Phoenix's glimmer told me he had a troubled soul, and I keep a warm spot in my heart for troubled souls.

"Not yet," I said. "His e-mail said he'd see me when he got in." My chest tightened when I thought about it.

"Sorry, shouldn't have mentioned it." Vinton must have noticed my expression. He threw Bertie a knowing glance. I slumped down in my chair.

Once a month, Charlie Risko met with each of us to discuss our status. The top-seller got the cold duck. Those with good sales got thin smiles. "Losers," who barely made enough for their desk fees, got a growl and were given a deadline of two months to cover what they owed for fees and insurance. He was also known to take out his .38 and playfully place it on his desk beside his motorcycle helmet, deerskin gloves, and latest issue of *Swank* magazine. He swore the gun was properly licensed, never loaded, and joked that he had friends in high places, implying he could get away with shooting somebody if he felt like it. I assumed he meant it to be funny, but it scared the heck out of me. You could never really tell what Charlie Risko was up to. He had an ugly sense of humor and was as unpredictable as he was spiteful. Since I was one of those losers he often referred to, I desperately studied the printout of rental leads (that might someday become home purchases) and wondered how much longer I'd have a desk in this crowded space. I prayed he wouldn't tease me with his licensed, "unloaded" gun.

Selling real estate had once seemed the perfect way out of my financial problems. I figured I could make my own hours, leaving time to shore up D&D Delights. After I got my real estate license, I imagined a small agency like Risko Realty would offer a quick, easy way to earn some money. I hoped that being surrounded by pleasant office mates would force me to leave the home I share with my cat, Juniper, and get through the loneliness that often consumed me. It seemed the perfect place to start my new beginning.

But "new beginnings" are never the beginnings you think they'll be.

When the front door to the office opened, then closed with a slam, I jumped, assuming it was Charlie Risko. It was Juda Baker, Louis Vuitton bag swinging gamely from her bony shoulder. She settled gracefully as far away from me and Bertie as she could get. Vinton promptly deserted us and sat down next to her.

"You see Charlie last night?" he whispered, loud enough for us to hear. "You okay?" he added. Juda gave a dramatic shake of her long blond hair.

From the moment I set eyes on Juda Baker, I sensed she kept secrets. I also knew she was a liar. For one thing, nappy, black roots peeked defiantly through her golden mane. There was nothing wrong with dying your hair. I did it myself when that silver popped out, but to claim your "natural" color was inherited from your Swedish grandmother when that was clearly not the case was a step too far. Her Louis Vuitton was an obvious knockoff, which made me wonder what kind of a fool buys knockoffs when the "knockoffs" have knocked out the real thing. Although these were small, innocent deceptions. I sensed there were more. Juda never spoke to me or Bertie. I assumed it was because she didn't want to be identified too closely with other black women, which annoyed the heck out of me and Bertie. This morning was no exception. Never know where someone's Nikes have jogged, Darryl liked to say, and in the spirit of my late husband, I gave Juda another try.

"Morning, Juda," I chirped from my cubicle. As usual, she ignored me. As usual, Bertie rolled her eyes and spat.

The screech of a motorcycle halting outside the building pulled my attention from Juda back to the front door. Everyone stopped what they were doing, looked up, and took a collective breath. Charlie Risko, his young wife, Tanya, hanging on his arm, strolled lazily into the office.

Risko was five foot six with a broad moon face and ruddy cheeks. The thin red hair underneath his helmet was cut in a mullet—short in front and on the sides, long in the back—and his pointed, ragged beard resembled a woodpecker's crest. Jeans, meant for a man twenty years younger and thirty pounds thinner, fit his wide behind like a sausage casing, while his snug T-shirt rode dangerously up his back, revealing flesh as pale as a trout's belly.

Tanya was tall and disturbingly thin, making up in youth and style what her husband lacked in both. Her black leather pants were as snug as a snake's skin, and stiletto-heeled boots shot her six inches above Risko. Tight turtlenecks of various colors covered her lean body from hips to neck and always peeked from under her black leather moto jacket, giving her a dangerous air, but her dreamy, heavy-lidded eyes and high-pitched voice gave her a little-girl's charm. When she spoke, she drawled out her words, as if unsure of them.

"Hey, Studebaker, how you driving this morning?" Charlie yelled to Juda as he ushered his wife into his office. "Seemed to be driving all right last night. Who haven't I met with? Mrs. Odessa Jones, right? Anybody seen Lane? Or that damned Harley? Tell him to bring his thuggish butt in whenever he gets here. I got something to say to him," he added, slamming the door behind him.

"Studebaker?" I mouthed to Bertie.

"Must have been some kind of pet name he gave her when they were going together back in the day," Bertie whispered back. "Makes you wonder what last night was about, doesn't it?" We glanced surreptitiously at Juda, who feverishly studied the listings in front of her. Bertie had once mentioned that Charlie fancied himself a ladies' man, and had slept with three agents in the office. Two had quit, and I was reasonably sure Bertie wasn't the third.

Studebaker. An old car, elegant in its day but long gone from the showroom. It was a cruel quip that made me wish I had the power of my cousins to lay this man flat on his fat behind with a nod of my head. But then, as if summoned by thought, the nutmeg drifted back—and I realized that my minor gift was all I could handle.

"Real son of a bitch, isn't he?" whispered Vinton, who left his spot next to Juda to settle back with me and Bertie. "He married that tart right around the time Juda thought he was going to propose to her. Nasty thing to do to somebody like J, sensitive as she is."

"Well, love does have its way," I said, unable to think of anything else to say.

"Humph." Vinton wrinkled his nose like an aging rabbit. "I know what love is. I don't know what they got, but it ain't love."

The pain in Vinton's eyes surprised me. Even without consulting Aunt Phoenix, I knew that love was the source of the glimmer that never left him.

Nobody, including me, shared anything about our personal lives with others in the office. Most of my coworkers knew I was a widow but never asked about my loss and I never discussed Darryl. My feelings were still too raw to share with those I didn't know. Vinton must have kept his pain inside him, too, and except for his spats with Bertie, never revealed much about himself. What about the others, I wondered. What hidden hurt were they keeping inside?

"Mrs. Odessa Jones!" Charlie Risko bellowed my full name from behind the closed door. Everybody stiffened and avoided looking at me. "Mrs. Odessa Jones, it's time for us to talk."

"On my way, Mr. Risko," I said, hating how obsequious

I sounded. *This repulsive fool can't bully me!* I said to myself but was whistling in the dark. My fate was in Charlie Risko's hands, and that scared the heck out of me. I gathered up my pad with my rental leads, took a deep breath, said a prayer, and went in to meet him.

Chapter 2

Charlie Risko's office was the same curdled-milk color as the larger room, but its leaded windows and exposed ceiling beams gave it an old-fashioned, distinctive charm. The room was twice as large as the one I'd just left, with a back door that opened to the alley outside, and a private restroom. We had to use the disgusting public bathroom down the hall, which was supposed to be kept locked but was routinely broken into, and I avoided it. Risko sat in a luxurious black leather chair in front of a mahogany desk flanked on each side by chairs covered in red velvet. I chanced a look at the motorcycle gloves, resting in the space where he was known to place his gun, and shuddered. Thankfully, the gun wasn't there. A third chair, straight-backed and cushion-less, was directly in front of the desk. He nodded toward it, and I sat down. The smell of nutmeg stopped me short. I took a breath and coughed.

Risko looked me up and down like a soiled suit on the cheap rack, then chuckled like the joke was on me. "Don't worry. I ain't going to demand the money you're going to owe me for your desk and insurance today. You got two months. Tell her what a nice guy I am," he said to Tanya, curled like a cat in the plush chair on his left. She glanced up lazily, answering with a kittenish smile. "This is private, baby. I'll get back to you in a hot minute." When she stood up to leave, he gave her a hard slap on her behind with a lecherous wink that made me cringe. "Hope that didn't offend you, *Mrs. Jones.* You ain't one of those churchgoing ladies, are you?"

I gave him an enigmatic smile, wishing again for my distant cousins' knock-down skills.

"I guess you know what this is about." He narrowed his eyes. His stare entered the marrow of my bones. "I have a rule in this place. As you know, I give people six months to make a sale. You're just about there. I can't carry you people forever. Can't have deadweight hanging around using the phones, typing on computers, drinking the Poland Spring . . ."

"Breathing the air," I mumbled, immediately regretting it.

He gave me a lopsided grin. "That, too, I guess. You got to get off your ass and make some money. Make *us* some money. Somebody buys the cake, I get a slice, Uncle Sam gets a slice, you get a slice."

More like a crumb, I thought but kept it to myself.

"So are we on the same page here, *Mrs.* Dessa Jones?"

If he was expecting a response, he didn't get it. I was too busy staring at the oaken beam just above his head. The nutmeg smell was coming from there; there was no mistaking it. Startled, he followed my gaze, then shivered like a wet towel had been slapped across the back of his neck. He quickly shifted his attention to a stack of papers on his desk. "Like I said, I'm just able to give you a month or so, then I'll need to let you go. Or show you my gun," he said with a smirk. "That will put some fire under you, right? Wish I could say the same for that bike-riding crook. No hard feelings?"

"Right," I mumbled.

"That's all I got to say. Get my wife back in here, okay?" he said without looking at me.

Something had spooked him, and it had to do with the

nutmeg. I studied the ceiling. Was a beam destined to fall down on him? That didn't seem likely. It was an old building and they'd been up for years. An earthquake, maybe, breaking the windows?

I glanced back at him. "Listen, Mr. Risko. I got a couple of good leads. I've made an appointment to show a two-bedroom rental next Monday, which looks like a winner, and I got more leads from Bertie and Harley. . . ."

He scowled. "A rental? That's no money. Don't mention that thug Harley to me again, okay?"

"Sure."

I wondered what was going on between him and Harley but knew better than to ask.

"My wife. Don't forget to tell Tanya, okay? Don't forget, okay?" He sounded like a spoiled kid begging for candy.

"I won't. Thank you, Mr. Risko," I groveled as I stood up.

"Call me Charlie. Everybody does." A boldfaced lie. Charlie was the last thing people in this office called him.

"Okay . . . Charlie, thanks again!" I forced out the words, said a silent prayer of gratitude, and fast-stepped out of the room.

Tanya Risko, grinning, was perched on the edge of the cubicle belonging to Dennis Lane, who apparently had just come in. Her high-topped boots casually touched his chair as she twisted a strand of hair, little-girl fashion, around her finger. Dennis studied her with a bored, tolerant smile. He was blond and clean-shaven, with long-lashed eyes and arched eyebrows, obviously shaped in a salon. I knew that because I'd spotted him in one down the block. Dennis's jeans, as tight as Tanya's leather pants, and his well-cut, studded denim jacket made him look like a rock star between sets with Tanya as his adoring groupie. *They were two peas in the same spoiled pod,* I thought uncharitably. Dennis scowled as I approached them. Tanya gave me a weak, surprisingly authentic smile.

"Mrs. Jones, I'm sorry Charlie was rude to you." She extended a hand too delicate for the oversized diamond weighing it down. "Sometimes he's mean. Even to me. Especially when he's having a hard day. Especially today. He didn't try to scare you with that stupid gun, did he? Half the time, it's not even loaded."

I shook my head that he hadn't, and she looked relieved.

"Every day is a hard day at Risky Realty," Dennis muttered, turning on his cell phone.

"Not every day, Denny. You know what happened two years ago. You were here then."

"What happened, Mrs. Risko?" I always put stock in significant anniversaries.

"Please don't call me that. It makes me feel old. Tanya, okay?"

"Sure, Tanya. What happened?"

"Stuart happened," said Vinton from his cubicle, his subdued tone strangely reverent.

"Stuart?" I asked.

"Stuart Risko, his older brother, happened. He killed himself two years ago today. That's what happened here," said Vinton.

"How?" I asked, my curiosity getting the better of me. Even as a kid, someone was always yelling at me to mind my own business. Pure and simple nosiness, Darryl called it.

"Hung himself," Dennis said flatly. "On one of those beams in Risko's office. Hung himself dead. Laverne was here that night, weren't you? Working one of his damned crossword puzzles. He had to cut the guy down. Glad I was late. You remember that day, don't you, Vinton? How you had to cut the guy down?" He said it with a sneering meanness that had no visible effect on Vinton but made me cringe. Why be so cruel with no reason? But I was right about the nutmeg;

it had something to do with those beams. Yet that was two years ago.

"Did you say something, Lane?" Vinton said finally, his voice barely above a whisper. He turned off his laptop, tossed a newspaper and a page of listings into his briefcase, and pushed his folding chair into his cubicle. "If the bastard asks, I'll be back later to follow up. Tell him that," he said.

Dennis Lane watched him leave. "Hey, man, don't forget that laptop. It's a nice piece of equipment. Well, pretty ladies, I got an appointment. One of many," he added, throwing Tanya a playful kiss as he stuffed papers into a briefcase. "Be good, Juda. Don't do anything I wouldn't do. And if you do, keep it to yourself. Tell your old man—I mean you, Tanya, not her—that we'll talk later about what he said. Okay? Don't forget."

Tanya nodded, strangely obedient.

Dennis Lane's request to Tanya reminded me of Risko's, which I promptly delivered. "He sounded kind of desperate," I added.

"He's always kind of desperate," Tanya said, with a lingering glance in Dennis's direction.

I didn't need the gift to tell me there was something going on between them. The uncomfortable silence that followed Dennis's departure told me everybody else knew it, too. I glanced at Juda, feverishly studying her listings, and snuck a look at Bertie, who put down her hot-pink gloves just long enough to watch Tanya switch into her husband's office. A look of concern and worry suddenly appeared on her face. I'd have to ask her about that concern when we were alone. It was hard to tell what any of these people really felt. I rocked back in my chair, asking myself once again just who these people really were.

★ ★ ★

When I took the job, I imagined I'd be coming to an office like the kind you see on TV—filled with lighthearted talk, good-hearted laughter, secrets kept and shared. It would be a place, I had hoped, that would help me get out of myself, somewhere I could escape the sadness that often hovered near—a comfortable space to cope with my lingering grief. But there was no warmth or camaraderie here—no shared drinks, birthday celebrations, holiday parties. Folks came in the morning, made calls on their cells, dashed out to lunch, and went their separate ways. People often got testy, like Bertie and Vinton this morning, and occasionally cruel, like Dennis's words about Risko's brother's suicide. But mostly there was just a tense, polite silence that hung over everything. I knew next to nothing about these people I saw every day, and they knew less about me. There were two exceptions, however: Harley Wilde and Bertie Jefferson.

Harley, always toting two latte grande coffees, usually came in late in the day. He kept one cup for himself and brought the other for me. The caffeine, along with his wide grin, always spiked my spirits. I didn't know how Harley got his name but suspected it was because of his bike, which he loved with abandon. He was a generation or two behind me and Darryl—too old to be a son, more like a younger brother. Yet I suspected he was like Darryl had been at that age, floating cheerfully through life as if some benign spirit was keeping an eye on him.

I resented Risko calling him a thug and was angry with myself for being too much of a coward to defend him. Harley was nobody's thug, whatever that meant. A playful soul lurked behind the dark sunglasses, worn leather jacket, and helmet that topped his short dreadlocks. Like my cousin Samuel, whose wits never healed from a stint in Afghanistan, Harley, too, had left the war with injuries: He had a slight limp and occasional bouts of PTSD, but he'd bettered himself, and managed to earn an associate college degree. He was quick to anger and quicker to apologize, and, according to him, had done some bad things in his young life. I never asked what they were, and he never told me.

Bertie Jefferson was nice to me from the first, probably because I listened to her when nobody else would. I chuckled when she told corny jokes and nodded sympathetically whenever she complained about Louella, her "heaviest burden." When I finally met her daughter, I knew what she meant. Aunt Phoenix's "glimmer" shadowed the girl like fog. It was deep purple, more blue than red, and I was grateful nobody else could see it. Despite the glimmer, Louella was a remarkably pretty girl with long-lashed dark eyes, curly hair, and flawless skin the color of milk chocolate. She'd been a beauty queen in college, and there were still hints of it in her graceful walk. Yet she was as wounded a spirit as I'd ever seen. When I was younger, I'd always assumed the glimmer was one of my aunt's cherry-brandy inspired imaginings until I saw it floating around an evil uncle at a family gathering. Uncle Tim's glimmer made my skin crawl; Louella's made me cry.

Bertie claimed that Louella, a high-achieving student athlete, had been "perfect" until she graduated from college. A few years later, she ended up pregnant with a baby, then strung out on OxyContin. Her habit pushed her out of her mother's heart and into places Bertie said she didn't want to know about. Bertie was overly protective of her granddaughter and prayed that she wouldn't end up like her mother. I didn't think Bertie had to worry. Erika, a distinctive-looking child with caramel-colored skin dotted with random freckles and gray eyes, struck me as an independent little soul who brought a smile whenever I saw her. I never asked how Louella got addicted, and Bertie never told me. I just knew that she'd thrown her daughter out of her house, and Louella had ended up spending time in a homeless shelter and occasionally on the street.

And it was from that street whence Louella came this lazy afternoon. Vinton, back from wherever he'd been, was typing feverishly on his laptop. Juda was talking seductively to somebody on the phone. Bertie was surfing eBay, looking for a bargain. Dennis Lane was still at lunch. The Riskos were doing whatever they did. I was drowsy and felt like a nap. I'd missed lunch—that nutmeg smell had killed my appetite. Harley was late with my caffeine fix. When the front door opened, I hoped it was him, but it was Louella. Her glimmer surprised me. The purple color was nearly gone, far less than it had been before, hardly noticeable if you weren't looking. Maybe whatever was tearing her down was losing its grip. Maybe something good was going on in the girl's life. I threw Bertie a smile, but her face was tight with anger. Whatever Louella wanted to tell her mother, Bertie didn't want to hear it.

Slamming her laptop closed, she stood up, screaming at her daughter. "Didn't I tell you never to come around here no more? Didn't I tell you . . . ?"

"I need to talk to you, Mom. I finally need to make things clear. You need to understand. . . ."

"I don't want to hear anything you have to say. You are a curse to me and your daughter. Whatever you think is going to happen never will!" Bertie shot out the words, and Louella ducked them like bullets. "Get out of here. You're not getting her back. You're not getting back in my life. You're not fit."

I assumed Bertie was talking about Louella caring for Erika—a running battle between the two.

"I can take care of her now," Louella said quietly. "I need her in my life. She's my child, not yours. She can heal everything, everyone. Everything will be better. Mom, I'm trying to make . . . amends. I'm trying to make amends. I understand how I failed and who failed me. I need to make amends!"

Her anguished words brought tears to my eyes; they didn't have that effect on anybody else.

"Ah! Amends! That magic expression," Vinton muttered from his computer. "The girl must be in some kind of twelve-step program."

"Shut up, Vinton, and mind your own damn business. Ain't nobody talking to you!" Bertie turned to face him in a rage.

"Put your business in the street, somebody's going to pick it up," said Vinton.

Cruelty is always contagious. Dennis had passed it earlier to Vinton, and now Vinton was passing it on to Bertie. Bertie hung her head, too weak to fight back.

"I can't talk in here, Mom. I don't want to," said Louella, her voice low.

"Then go on back where you came from!"

"I need to tell you things before they come back. I should have done it by now. I need to tell you everything that has happened, so you understand it all. Everything has changed now; it's a miracle. What has happened is a miracle."

Miracle. I wondered what kind of miracle the girl was talking about, but the glimmer was different; maybe something special had happened.

"There's no miracle. Just a nothing wanting to ruin my life," said Bertie.

"I need to tell you before they come back," Louella whispered.

"Before who comes back? Who are you talking about?" Bertie's voice was louder, harsher than before.

Who *was she talking about?* I wondered. *Tanya and Charlie? Harley? Dennis? All of them?*

"Why don't you listen to your daughter so we can get some work done?" snapped Vinton.

"The hell with you!" Bertie snapped back. Louella ran from the office and Bertie followed behind her. "The hell with all of you!" she screamed, then slammed the door.

But the door wasn't heavy enough to block the arguing, yelling, and crying that went on between the two women, and nearly an hour later Bertie returned, alone. She sat at a cubicle far away from everyone. Her head was hung low and she wrapped her arms around her body as if protecting herself from blows as she rocked from side to side. The glimmer that Louella had worn seemed to have settled on Bertie, who suddenly began to tremble so violently I moved closer to her, wanting to offer comfort.

"Bertie, you okay?" I asked. She stared at the table as if she hadn't heard me. "Can I do anything to help?" She shook her head, waving me away.

"Thank God that's over," Vinton said as he continued typing. Juda, her voice overly cheerful, made another call. They were pretending not to hear her. A stream of sweat rolled down my back. I closed my eyes to shut myself off.

Darryl teasingly called me Deanna Troi, an "empath" from one of his favorite TV shows. And empaths, according to Darryl and the *Star Trek* writers, absorb emotions, get overwhelmed by other people's problems, have generous hearts that open too wide, and grab everything around them. He was right about one thing: I do take other people's emotions—anger, sorrow, fear—and pull them into myself. A gift from the gift I suppose, although it skipped Aunt Phoenix; empathy was not her strong suit. It did, however, belong to my late mother, Rosemary, who Aunt Phoenix never tired of saying was too sensitive for her own good. Maybe I was, too. I remember watching my mother close her eyes and go somewhere inside herself when people were cruel, or angry, or things got scary. She left whenever she argued with my father, which was seldom. Or when Aunt Phoenix made her cry, which was often. When I'd ask her where she'd gone, she'd smile. I can't recall all the times she left me.

Shutting my eyes didn't work this time. I had to actually leave. I picked up my bag, slipped on my headphones, and walked away fast, putting as much space between me and Risko Realty as I could. It didn't help that it was October, the month Darryl and I got married. Most days, I managed to fight my looming sadness, but between the nutmeg, Risko, and Bertie's sorrow, everything was welling up inside me. Somehow, I got to the park where Darryl and I used to jog, found our bench, played Darryl's playlist, and despite the curiosity of a couple of kids, cried for the next ten minutes. The sun was fading but still shining. I could feel its heat on my face. I closed my eyes as I let it warm me. I made myself hear Darryl's voice telling me I'd be okay. I breathed in slow, felt better, took some turns around the track until it was dark and the sun was gone.

It was time to go back to the office. Maybe Bertie would still be there and we could talk; maybe Harley had finally made it in with my grande coffee. I knew one thing, though: I wasn't yet ready to face my empty house. I spotted a motorcycle parked down the street but couldn't make out if it was Harley's or Risko's and didn't feel like walking toward it to find out. The office seemed empty, which was fine, although Dennis Lane must have forgotten his laptop, which was still in his cubicle.

I pulled up a website and had cruised through about a dozen listings before I noticed the light shining under the door in Risko's office and realized he was still in there. Suddenly, he began shouting and cursing out some poor soul with such venom and hatred it made me cringe—and I don't shock easily. My empty house was looking better by the minute. Too tired and disgusted to stay and hear any more, I picked up my belongings and headed home as fast as I could.

Home is a neat Cape Cod with a tiny brick front porch and a backyard I plant with spearmint, basil, and thyme in the summer. There's a working fireplace in my living room with comfortable easy chairs on either side, and enough space on the rug in front for Juniper, my plump black cat, to sit on without getting singed. When I settle down at night to watch Netflix or Hulu, I sip a cup of chamomile tea or a glass of merlot (depending on the day) and try to be as calm as I can and at peace with the world. This was a merlot night.

As usual, Juniper greeted me at the door, hoping for a cat treat he knew I'd deliver. The vet had told me to cut down on the treats, but I'm a fool for my pet and he knows it.

"No more, you plump little creature," I scolded as he scrounged for more, then felt bad for fat-shaming him and gave him another, which he eagerly gobbled down. Juniper was good company. My only company, if truth be told, and I was becoming dangerously dependent on him. Darryl would *not* have approved.

Despite everything, I found myself thinking about Risko Realty, wondering what had happened with Bertie and hoping Harley's temper hadn't gotten the better of him. I knew I had to find other things—and people—to worry about, but it was hard to do. Darryl was the sociable one in our marriage who made friends for us both. I was the lonely planet depending upon his sun to connect and reach out. But the friends we'd made as a couple slowly slipped away after his death. A few acquaintances remained, like the owner of Royal's Regal Barbecue, and Julie Russell, who was in her early sixties and lived next door. She was recently divorced (an unpleasant, unexpected surprise) and mostly kept to herself. But I'd never really reached out to her. My only kin nearby was Aunt Phoenix, a mixed blessing. I finished off the last of some left-over barbecued chicken from Royal's Barbecue (since I rarely cooked anymore), poured a generous glass of merlot, and settled down to watch a movie on Netflix.

When the phone rang, I knew who it was but answered anyway.

"I know it's been a bad day, Odessa, but put down that wine. Best get yourself a flask of brandy to take the edge off . . . troubling times." Aunt Phoenix's gravelly voice was surprisingly comforting. "It's curry for me. Strong curry. More powerful than nutmeg, so consider yourself lucky." I didn't bother to ask my aunt how she knew what was going on or what I was drinking. "I miss that boy, too," she added, remembering it was the month Darryl and I married. From the moment they met, Darryl and Aunt Phoenix were fast friends, an utter surprise to me. "Did you play that number like I told you to?" she finally got around to asking.

"No, Aunt Phoenix, I didn't play that number like you told me to do," I said, mildly irritated, knowing that if I had, my major problem would be solved. Aunt Phoenix was known around town for her uncanny ability to choose winning numbers in the state lottery. She didn't win big but she won frequently. "I need to ask you a question about the glimmer. Can a person pass a bad glimmer on to somebody else?"

"Depends on the glimmer. Depends on the person. Don't you work at that Risko Realty place? Better turn on the news. I love you, Odessa," she said and hung up. Our conversations were always brief.

It was the lead story with lights shining hard on the place I'd just left. Charlie Risko had been shot dead in his office. The police were looking for leads. His killer was still at large.

Chapter 3

"Shame for a man to die like that, in his own place of work," said Lennox Royal, the owner of Royal's Regal Barbecue. I wondered if he was thinking about himself and his kitchen. "If you ask me, the wife had something to do with it. It's always the spouse," he added with a weary head shake. I hoped his past wasn't informing that, too. He knew what he was talking about, being a retired police detective; he probably knew his way around a murder case. But it was hard to imagine that Tanya Risko, with her sweet face and childlike manner, could shoot her husband in cold blood. Yet sweetness is known to hide sour; the prettiest flowers, from oleander to lily of the valley, are often the most deadly. And like everybody else who worked at Risko Reality, I had no idea of who the girl *really* was. I couldn't depend on the gift to tell me, even though it had tossed out the nutmeg yesterday. (I had to give it that.) "So what kind of man was he?" Royal continued as he filled an oversized saltshaker. I shrugged and sipped my coffee. No sense in talking bad about the dead.

I'd been sitting at Royal's counter for the better part of an hour. This was my second cup of coffee and third glazed donut. I was his first and only customer. His place was famous for barbecued ribs and fried chicken wings, not so much day-old donuts and coffee strong enough to stew your liver. But I was desperate and had nowhere else to go.

I'd awakened this morning with my usual Friday thoughts—thank God I can sleep late tomorrow, what to wear to work, where to go for lunch, what to buy for dinner—then sat up with a start. I wasn't going anywhere. Charlie Risko was dead. Risko's Realty was probably closed. I tried calling Bertie then Harley to get their takes on what had happened and find out if they were feeling the same way as me, but neither answered their phones. I left messages for each, hoping they'd get back to me. I desperately needed to talk to somebody. Aunt Phoenix was out of the question.

Stumbling into the bathroom then the kitchen, I slumped down at the square oak table Darryl and I had bought at a yard sale two weeks before he died. It pulled out to seat six and we'd planned to have dinner parties. One more thing that was never going to happen. I took a breath, closed my eyes, and made myself stop thinking. Risko Realty had given me somewhere to escape to each morning. My coworkers weren't friendly, but at least they were people—unlike the chubby little creature chowing down on the cat food I poured into his dish.

"What should I do, Juniper?" I asked, as if he could answer. Puzzled, he glanced up, licked his chops, then went back to his meal. "Thanks for nothing," I said.

I rummaged through the cabinets for an overlooked jar of instant coffee, not my favorite thing to drink. I usually picked up my morning coffee at the Starbucks on my way to work. There was nothing here. I slumped back into my chair. Nowhere to go. Nobody to talk to. No coffee to drink. Royal's Regal Barbecue suddenly came to mind.

★　★　★

"I mean, was he a good man, or thank-God-that-rascal-is-dead kind of guy? A man with some heart, or the classic SOB?" Royal asked again, noticing my attention had strayed.

"A capital S capital O capital B," I said, forgetting my reverence for the dead. He chuckled and I laughed with him, realizing suddenly I'd forgotten how good it felt to laugh in the morning. I'd never thought of Royal as being handsome but at that moment I did. He was always joking with customers about eating too much of his own potato salad and his need to get back to the gym, but nobody agreed with him, and I'd noticed Georgia, his assistant cook, and more than one of his female customers give him an appreciative eye. He was tall and well built, but not overly so. His slight beard was lightly sprinkled with gray, which made him look distinguished yet approachable, and he had a quick smile that was slow to disappear. His eyes smiled, too, and never hid his feelings—probably a dangerous thing for a cop, as was the warmth he showed everyone who entered his place. He quietly fed those too broke to pay, listening patiently to their promises of reimbursement. Sometimes they were good for it; most times they weren't. He was a good man, unlike the recently deceased. I could say that without hesitation. But laughing with him now, I realized it was the first time I'd laughed with a man in a very long time. I stopped myself and took a sip of coffee.

These days, I hardly noticed men at all, handsome or not. Noticing felt disloyal, like I was betraying my love for Darryl, which was silly, but I couldn't get over it. Cutting myself off from the world would be the last thing Darryl would have wanted. I hadn't been a nun when I married and had known my share of men, some with good hearts, some without. I'd had a disastrous engagement that ended a week before we were to get married and pretty much committed myself to living solo. Until I met Darryl.

"Whoever it is, man, woman, or both, is still at large,

right?" Royal asked, pouring me another cup of coffee and bringing me back to his place. "Need some milk in that? I know it's strong. I like it strong. Always forget most people like it, what do they call it, café au lait?"

That made me smile, too. "How come you say both?" I said, turning again to Charlie Risko's murder.

"If she's going to do it, the wife, it's probably with somebody else, unless he was abusive, knocking her around, then she'd kill him herself before he killed her. That's a different case altogether. Was he abusive?"

"I don't think so."

"If he was, that puts a different spin on things. Have you talked to anybody at work? When something like that happens, people can't keep their mouths shut."

"Not yet," I said, thinking again how isolated I was from my coworkers.

"Did she have something going with somebody on the side?"

I remembered how Tanya had looked at Dennis Lane, but that wasn't on the side. That was in plain sight for everybody to see.

"I really don't know," I said after a minute. Bertie had never mentioned anything like that, and she wasn't one to keep those kinds of observations to herself.

I checked my phone to see if she or Harley had called back, but neither had. But there was a text from Aunt Phoenix. Her texts were occasionally quotes from Maya Angelou, which I welcomed; more often they were the daily lottery numbers that she wanted me to play. Her eyes weren't what they used to be, and she was known to hit wrong numerals or letters. But I needed the money, so I decided to take a chance.

"Do you sell Pick 4 lottery tickets, Mr. Royal?" My question took him by surprise.

"Mr. Royal? How long have we known each other, Mrs.

Jones? Long enough to be on a first-name basis. Please call me Lennox. Lennox Royal. Sounds like a fancy china pattern, doesn't it? But it's the name my mama gave me."

"Odessa," I said, extending my hand as if we were meeting for the first time. "But most folks call me Dessa." My full name had come out before I'd thought about it. It sounded strange to say the whole thing. Dessa was usually how I introduced myself these days. Nobody but Aunt Phoenix called me Odessa.

Lennox gave me a slow, wistful smile. "I've always loved that name. It's a beautiful one you don't hear much anymore. My grandma was named Odessa. Put me through college with what she earned as a cook. She was the one who taught me how to barbecue. To answer your question, I only sell one. Powerball. So you a gambling woman? Not that I have anything against gambling women," he added after a beat.

"Not really. I have a family member who thinks she has an inside track."

"There is no inside track. My ex-wife was a gambler. Believe me, that inside track can run right through you and those who love you."

"Is that why she's your ex?" I asked before realizing it was none of my business. The man giving me his name didn't give me the right to jump into his personal affairs.

"That and other things."

The shift in his gaze told me the other things weren't about to be shared. I quickly changed the subject. "How's Lena doing? I haven't seen her in a while."

His eyes lit up at the mention of his daughter. "She's doing just fine. At school now. If you stay around here long enough, you'll see her."

Most nights Lena sat in a distant corner—earphones covering ears, hands grasping her iPhone—always staying close enough for Lennox to keep an eye on her but far away enough to feel safe. Lena, twelve years old, was on what's called the autistic spectrum. After Lennox's wife left, he retired from the force to run the restaurant and take care of his daughter full time. Lena looked like her father, except she must have gotten her mother's eyelashes, which were long, and her plump cheeks, which you wanted to pat except Lena was too old for that, and if you reached for one, she'd be startled and move away. We met Royal through Lena.

Darryl was a special-ed teacher who worked with autistic kids, and Lena was one of his students. Lennox would stop by the school every now and then to check on his daughter while I waited for Darryl to get off work. He'd mentioned Lena's father was a cop. I'd had a couple of bad experiences with policemen and wasn't sure what to expect. But no other parent was as patient or gentle with a child as Lennox Royal, which had impressed Darryl, too. Father and daughter had come to Darryl's funeral, Lennox Royal weeping but trying not to show it. Lena rocking back and forth, trying to find a safe space in a room filled with sorrow.

"You know that if the murderer, be it woman or man, is still out there, you could be in danger, right?" His question took me as much by surprise as mine probably had to him about the Pick 4. For an instant, I could see the cop. Businesslike, no-nonsense gaze lowered slightly, no smile visible, eyes demanding the truth and nothing but the truth. I looked for a sliver of a smile, hoping he was half joking; he was dead serious.

"I don't think so," I said. "I think I'd know if I was in danger."

"You never know when you're going to be a victim," he said, with a trace of condescension.

"I'm pretty sure *I* would," I said, thinking about the gift but deciding not to mention it. Common sense told me that Lennox *probably* was not a man who put stock in smells, sounds, and colors that foretold the future. He was practical, earnest. I sensed that much about him. Even Darryl had been doubtful about the gift when I finally got up enough nerve to tell him about it. *Better keep that one in the family,* he'd said with an amused chuckle. He was definitely not a believer. Until he met Aunt Phoenix.

"Just be careful," Lennox said, obviously concerned. "I know what I'm talking about."

"Well, there aren't many murders or murderers in Grovesville," I said after a moment or two of coffee sipping and donut chewing.

He paused before responding. He wasn't a sighing kind of man, but I could almost hear one. "Odessa, this isn't the only place I've worked. I was in Chicago for a while, and before that LA. I saw more anger, kids killing each other over BS like wearing the wrong color or something dumb like that, than I ever want to see again in life. I've seen my share of killings, let's put it that way."

"But Grovesville is—"

"People are people. You never know what demons they carry around. What's going to make them finally break."

I'd forgotten to put my iPhone on vibrate, and the "duck" ringtone, which I'd put on to entertain Juniper, honked its way into the silence that followed Lennox's recollection.

"Lena likes that one, too," he said, amused by the sound. "No matter how many times I hear it, I look for a duck. Always makes her laugh."

"I need to find something more appropriate," I said, quickly turning it off.

"Well, not necessarily. You'll always know it's your phone that's ringing. Nothing wrong with that."

"If you're under thirteen," I said, startled by the name that flashed on the screen. It was Tanya Risko, as if summoned by our discussion of murdering spouses. As soon as Lennox left to sign for a delivery, I called her back.

"Hello, Mrs. Jones. This is Tanya. I got your number from Harley. I know you-all are friends. I hope you don't mind me calling you like this. I need to tell you some things," she said in her singsong, little-girl voice.

"No, of course not." *Are you keeping the place open?* I was on the verge of asking, then remembered she'd lost her husband the night before. "How are you doing, Tanya? Are you okay?" I asked, noting how upbeat she sounded, considering the circumstances. "Can I do anything for you? Do you have family nearby?"

"My only family was Charlie, my late husband," she said with no emotion at all. "Everybody in my family is dead, just like him."

Hopefully not as violently, I thought, but said, "Is there anyone . . ."

"Dennis has been looking out for me," she said before I finished, then added awkwardly, "Dennis is like family, in a way. You know? He and Charlie were close once, too."

"Are you talking about Dennis from the office?" I asked in disbelief, recalling the dismissive ways he often spoke about Risko and how rude he'd been to Vinton. I couldn't imagine him offering real comfort to anyone.

"Who else?" She seemed surprised.

"It's good to have somebody close," I said, taking all judgment from my voice, but Lennox's words echoed in my head. If it had occurred to Lennox, it had to others as well. I hoped she had an alibi. And that it wasn't Dennis Lane.

"Well, I guess you're wondering why I'm calling, right? Well, it's because of the memorial service. When I get his body back, I'm getting him cremated, real private. I want to have some kind of service as soon as I can, you know. Tomorrow.

On Saturday. He'd want it that way. Charlie would. Then I'm opening up the office after that. Monday morning, bright and sharp, because we do a lot of business at the beginning of the week and . . ."

It took me a minute to break in. "You're opening up the office two days after the memorial service?" I didn't like Charlie Risko, but even he deserved more than two days of mourning.

"It would be okay with Charlie. He'd want what is best for me, and I just need to put everything behind me, Mrs. Jones. You know what I mean? I just want everything to be behind me." It sounded like she was crying, a little girl's scared cry, but then that stopped as abruptly as it started. I had no idea what she meant. I couldn't get rid of my grief over Darryl, but grief comes in all different ways for different people, and who was I to judge?

"You need to take care of yourself and do whatever makes you feel right," I said after a minute.

"That's what Harley says. He's been real helpful, too," she added with a sniffle. Harley again. I knew less about my young friend than I thought.

"One more thing. The office is a crime scene now, but that's over by Monday. The police came to my house this morning to interview me about Charlie. They said they wanted to talk to me while things were still fresh in my mind. I don't know what kind of things they're talking about. They asked if they could come to the office and interview every-body who was there the day Charlie got killed. Is that okay? You think that's okay?"

"They want to talk to us in the office?" I said, shocked. "They don't usually do that, do they?"

"I don't know. I've never had a husband murdered be-fore. I've never known anyone who was murdered before. But that's what they said."

How involved are you in this one? I thought, but said, "What did they talk to you about this morning?"

"Stuff about Charlie. Before we got married. And other stuff, too. They told me not to talk to anyone about it." She paused, as if taking a breath. When she spoke again her voice was strained and frightened. "They have Charlie's gun. He was killed with that stupid gun he was always waving around scaring everybody with. Even me. The one he swore was unloaded. Guess he was lying about that! They told me not to talk to anyone about it, about the gun."

"Tanya, are you sure you want to open things up on Monday?"

"I already told the cops everybody would be there."

"Then make sure you tell everybody to be at work. If someone doesn't show up, he or she might look suspicious. Do you need me to make any calls for you?"

"No." She paused, then went back to the memorial. "Charlie didn't have any family except for me. You know his brother was dead. They all said they'd come to the memorial. Everybody from the office. Even Juda. I'll remind everybody then. Do you think they'll all come?"

"I'm sure they will." *Out of curiosity more than anything else,* I thought.

"Do you promise you'll come? Promise. Us widows need to stick together."

I was struck dumb. Widowhood was not a club one joyfully belonged to.

She gave me the address of the church where the service would be held, and I promised again I'd be there.

Customers eager for lunch were beginning to come into Royal's and his quick smile welcomed everyone. Suddenly, he was busy, grinning and greeting customers like family. I tried to sneak out, but he spotted me from the corner of his eye and nodded for me to come over.

"Let me know what happens," he whispered. "And re-member what I said, okay?" He turned serious when he said that, and a frown darkened his face. "Take care of yourself, Odessa Jones. You don't know who killed that man or why they killed him. Until you know that, everyone is a suspect. You may know something that will put you in danger. You hear me?"

"I hear you." His warning sent a chill down my back that I didn't want to feel.

Chapter 4

I was in a sour mood the next morning. First, there was the prospect of attending the memorial of a man I couldn't stand. Second, my going-to-a-funeral light gray suit was stained with grape juice. The only thing I could find to wear were dark blue slacks and a white sailor blouse that brought to mind the drummer in a navy marching band. Third, my car wouldn't start.

Our six-year-old Subaru had been Darryl's domain. He routinely changed the oil, checked the tires, and added necessary fluids at the proper time. I checked the oil and tires when a warning light popped up but blissfully ignored the odd rumble or rattle that hinted something was wrong. I paid for it this morning. It had been fine the day before driving back from Royal's, but no matter how hard I pressed the accelerator, the car balked. If I hadn't promised Tanya—twice—that I'd be there, I wouldn't have gone, but now I didn't have a choice. I ended up taking an Uber, good money I didn't want to spend. Lucky for me, there was a bus stop nearby, and I could take a bus home.

Charlie Risko's memorial was held in a tiny, overheated chapel with dusty stained windows badly in need of hosing.

Tanya needn't have worried: Everybody showed up. It was a lucky thing, too. Except for an elderly church usher and the funeral attendant, who dragged in an oversized portrait of Risko and a small, sad wreath, nobody else came. There were no clients, lawyers, accountants, fellow Realtors, or others one would assume would pay their respects to a fellow businessman.

I made a mental note to look for any of Aunt Phoenix's glimmers, sparkling or otherwise. I assumed the gray aura that always surrounded Vinton would be visible, and it was; it seemed to have seeped into his bones. With luck, I just might spot something on somebody else. At least there was no nutmeg; if there had been, Vinton's bitter lemon would have knocked it out.

Bertie wore the same black blouse and skirt ensemble she'd worn every Monday since I'd been at Risko's. *Monday morning is my day of mourning,* she'd told me more than once; she had it right today. She'd added a bit of flash with the hot-pink gloves she held in her left hand. They were an odd-looking fashion accessory, which brought an exaggerated eye roll from Vinton, who sat next to me. She was also wearing mismatched shoes—one black, one brown.

"Must have dressed in a hurry," Vinton quipped more to himself than to me.

Juda, stylish in a Blackglama mink thrown over one shoulder movie-star style, swept down the aisle, only acknowledging Vinton. Her coat brought back painful memories. My mother, who died when I was in my twenties, had always been proud of her "furs" and had a similar one she wore on special occasions. When she died, she passed it on to Aunt Phoenix, who never wore it because, as she put it, she didn't like wearing dead animals. It was a petty, quiet resentment I held against my aunt.

"Trust Juda to dress for the occasion," Vinton whispered.

There were no auras, glimmers, or anything else hovering around Juda. It was as if she were a shell, throwing out nothing. I'd have to ask my aunt about that. She pulled the coat snugly around her shoulders, as though chilled, though it was as hot as a sauna in the small, close room. I remembered Charlie Risko's nickname for her and wondered if the mink had been his last gift or if the coat was her way of paying her last respects.

Dennis Lane sat next to Tanya in the front row. He wore one of his many trendy suits, classy enough to withstand the scrutiny of a snooty maître d', sexy enough to make a practical woman forget she was there on business. Tanya, in a cherry-red pantsuit, was a blast of defiant color. Her thick hair, usually bunched in a sloppy topknot, fell freely down her back, framing her thin face in a wildly tangled mess.

"Must have forgot to comb it," Vinton said cattily with a nod in her direction. "Looks like she jumped up out of bed, threw on a party suit, and made it here right before they propped up his picture."

"People grieve in different ways, Vinton," I said. "Allow her to mourn in her own style."

"Humph," he sniffed and furiously patted his forehead with a Kleenex. "Hot as hell in here. Just like the place Risko will be going."

I didn't know about Risko's final resting place, but Vinton was right about the heat. It was chilly outside but not cold enough for this. Somebody had turned the furnace to full blast and sweat dripped down the middle of my back.

"She's celebrating the memory of that old fool with every grace he deserved. None," said Vinton, glancing around the tight, hot room.

His catty comments were beginning to annoy me. "Everyone deserves grace, Vinton. Even Charlie Risko," I snapped.

Vinton turned and looked me straight in the eye. "You don't know what grace he deserved and didn't, Dessa Jones.

You didn't know him like some of us did, so keep your good thoughts to yourself."

His words hit me like a slap, reminding me once again that there was more to Risko Realty than I knew. They were "family," in their own way, with family secrets best kept to themselves. I wondered what they could be. Until that moment, I'd put Lennox's warning out of my mind. I shifted away from Vinton, suddenly cautious and unsure what to make of him. I was not part of the "we" who knew Charlie Risko's true nature, and I never would be.

The pastor, a balding, soft-voiced soul whose face beamed good works, came to the front of the church to formally begin the service. Apparently, the Risko family had been big-time donors, although Charlie had cut the money off. In light of that, the pastor's remarks were mainly a celebration of better times and deceased family members. He began by praising Charlie's father, who had established a fund for the church's maintenance (spent, I assumed, on the furnace blasting the heat waves). He spoke solemnly of the older brother, Stuart. Vinton, trembling slightly, dropped his head in remembrance. He turned next to the widow, offering this "grieving young woman" his best thoughts and condolences. Tanya, who was sweating like the rest of us, daintily patted her forehead with a handkerchief she'd snatched from Dennis's lapel and slipped her jacket off her bony, pale shoulders.

I was startled by what I saw. Her arms and shoulders were covered with purplish-brown bruises that traveled within an inch of her neck. I'd volunteered in a shelter that housed abused women, and I knew what I was seeing. Tanya must have felt my eyes on her because she pulled the jacket over her shoulders again, dropping her head as if ashamed. But it wasn't her who should have been ashamed; it was me. Guilt swept through me because I should have known, seeing the way she acted around him, so scared and obedient. I had been so overwhelmed by my own pain I couldn't see anyone else's. Tanya glanced at me, then at Vinton, who shifted his eyes away. "No turtleneck today," he muttered.

Did everybody know but me? Why hadn't they done something about it? Were they all complicit? I took a breath as I remembered those women I'd worked with and their vulnerability, wondering where they were now. Had they escaped their abusers, learned to protect themselves, gotten away? Had they killed their abuser before he killed them? *Was he abusive?* Lennox Royal had asked me yesterday. *I don't think so,* I'd stupidly said. *If he was, that puts a different spin on things.* And what was the spin? Was Dennis Lane Tanya's savior or another violent choice?

The minister read from Ecclesiastes 3, and, my eyes brimmed with tears. It had been read at Darryl's funeral by his best friend and was seared into my soul. I closed my eyes tight, trying to block that day from my memory although I knew I couldn't do it and that it would always be with me.

Vinton nudged me. "You okay, Dessa?" he asked. I realized I'd been trembling like he'd been before.

"Yeah, I'm fine," I said, touched by his concern.

As the minister was finishing his reading, Harley, late as usual, rushed into the church and took a seat by the door. Tanya glanced back, mouthing something to him. He nodded in return. Louella followed him in, her head bowed, surrounded by the glimmer of sorrow, still hardly noticeable. Bertie must have seen her, too, but didn't acknowledge her. I caught Harley's eye and shook my head like a scolding parent. Embarrassed, he shrugged, smiled shyly, and glanced away. I'd scold him later, I decided. He wasn't kin but we were friends and he looked distressed. I needed to find out what was going on. He must have sensed my concern.

"Hey, Dessa, want to go get a drink? I could use one after that," he said, grabbing my arm as I left the church.

"After what? You missed the whole darn thing!"

"Wow, I guess I did," he said with a teenager's shrug, charming and annoying. "Listen, I need to talk to you about something. It's important." I studied him, looking for a clue—glimmer or otherwise—but saw nothing.

"Someone say something about a drink?" said Vinton, coming up behind us and breaking into the conversation. "I'd like to come, too, if you don't mind. I could use one. You want to come, Juda?" he added before we could answer one way or another.

"Where are you going?" asked Juda, pulling the mink coat tightly around her for warmth.

"Taft's, knowing Harley. Come on, Juda. You know you don't have anything better to do, do you?" Juda glanced away, as if she was embarrassed.

"You going? Dessa? I'll go if you go," Bertie said, edging closer to me as if for protection.

"Where's Louella?" I asked her.

"Gone, I guess," she said. I thought I saw the glimmer of a yellow glow when I'd said her daughter's name but it quickly disappeared. Aunt Phoenix had told me once that a yellow glimmer could mean fear or anxiety. Then she'd quickly added that sometimes it simply meant the sun had hit you wrong. It was impossible to pin my aunt down on any of this stuff, and I'd stopped trying. Bertie was tough, with an edge that could turn mean. What or who was she afraid of? Could it be Louella? Did she know something about Risko's death?

"Sure. Come on, it might do us both some good," I said.

"I don't do much drinking."

"Neither do I."

"I trust you, Dessa," she whispered low, so only I could hear her. "You're the only one I can," she added, almost as an afterthought.

I squeezed her hand reassuringly, telling her she was right.

★ ★ ★

Taft's was a shadowy bar and grill three blocks away, the kind of place you go when you don't want to be seen in daylight. We crowded around a table in a dim corner of the room, and the waitress plopped down two bowls of stale pretzels. Harley ordered the first round of drinks, and before we could finish them, Vinton ordered a second. Dennis Lane waltzed in from nowhere, plopped down at our booth for a hot minute, and ordered a third, compliments of Tanya Risko. He finished his drink in a gulp and went back to wherever he'd come from.

"Wonder where the widow is," said Vinton, chomping on a pretzel.

"Wherever he went," said Juda.

"Charlie would have killed her sooner or later. She must have known that."

"I wasn't going to let that happen," Harley said, so quietly you had to be sitting next to him to hear it.

"You don't know that," said Juda. "You don't know him like I did. He wasn't always like that. He never touched me." She finished off her second drink and picked up the third, a bit of it dribbling down her chin.

"I didn't kill him, but I'm glad he's dead," said Harley, his gaze fixed on the table.

"He deserved to die," Bertie whispered. "He did terrible things. Knocking her around like he did. Bruising her body like that. My daddy used to do that, hit us until we were bloody, pound on my mama's face until she couldn't see straight. He deserved to die, too, but nobody killed him. Somebody should have. Harley, you say you didn't kill him, kill Charlie? You sure about that? You could have. You were the last person to see him, weren't you? I saw your bike outside when I left." Bertie's voice was calm yet accusatory. She took off her glasses, as if emphasizing what she'd just said, then slipped them back on.

My heart jumped. I'd seen a bike, too, but assumed it was Charlie's. Everyone stared at Harley. His eyes darkened as his jaw tightened.

"You think I killed him! Come on, Miss Bertie. You know me better than that."

"I don't know you at all," Bertie said.

"I wasn't the last person to see him alive. That would be the person who killed him. I hated the guy for all kinds of reasons, but not enough to kill him."

"We all did," said Vinton, suddenly philosophical. "For sins present and past." He finished off the last of his drink and dabbed his mouth with a napkin.

"Not me," said Juda quietly. "I didn't wish him dead."

"You should have," said Vinton.

Those last words hung over the table, as if everyone was ashamed of something they'd said. Pretzels were loudly chomped. Drinks were gulped. Nobody ordered another round. Bertie stared hard at Harley, and he stared back, cocking his head as if curious. I studied the faces of my coworkers, hoping for some glimmer that would reveal some hidden truth, but there was nothing I could see.

Suddenly, Juda stood up, stumbling against the table.

"Watch it, girl," Vinton said, catching her arm to steady her. "Come on, sweetie. Let's get you out of here. It's been a long, ugly day. You've got to get something to eat."

That was the cue for everyone to leave, and after a few awkward good-byes, everyone did, except for me and Harley, who lingered to finish his drink.

"Got a minute?" he said to me after the others had gone. "You feel like something else to drink?"

"Are you kidding? Do I look like I need another drink? You should watch yourself, too," I said, immediately regretting my words. I was his coworker, not his mother.

"I meant coffee," he said, with the old Harley grin.

"What's going on?" I asked as soon as the waitress brought our coffees and a fresh bowl of pretzels.

"I don't know why Bertie would say something like that. It was like she was accusing me of something she knows I didn't do. Why would she say that?"

"I have no idea," I said. It had struck me as strange, too.

"You don't think I killed him, do you?"

"No," I said quickly. "Why would you think that?"

"Do you think Bertie does?"

"She was in a strange mood, and she doesn't drink much. She was probably tipsy. Charlie's murder has touched us all."

He gulped down his coffee, followed by a handful of pretzels, and ordered a glass of water.

"If you're trying to get sober, coffee and water ain't going to get it. You'll just be a waterlogged, caffeinated drunk."

"No, I'm okay. Really. Thanks, Dessa, for staying around. For listening."

"You haven't said anything."

He sighed, something I'd rarely heard him do. "It's just this whole thing with Risko. It's bringing up a lot of crap I don't want to think about, stuff I'd tried to put behind me."

"Like what?"

He drank the water, sip by sip, then added, "Remember I told you there was bad stuff I'd done? It wasn't only me, it was other folks, too, and one of them is dead, and that scares the hell out of me."

For present and past sins, Vinton had said to Juda about things Charlie had done. How present was that evil?

"I take it there was something between you and Tanya before she married Charlie," I said, taking a leap.

"Yeah. I introduced them. We were all friends. Until everything went bad, got ugly." He stopped, glanced at his watch. "Look, maybe now's not the best time to talk about it, right after his death and all."

"Okay. Let's wait," I said, sensing his discomfort.

He nodded. "Let me walk you to your car."

"If I had a car. Broke down this morning. You can walk me to the bus stop."

"Bus stop! Come on, I'll give you a ride." He grinned his wide, contagious grin. "You trust me, right?"

"Are you sure you're sober enough to drive?"

"Dessa, you know me better than that! I'd never put your safety at risk."

"To tell the truth, Harley, I'm not sure what you'd do and how well I know you," I said after a minute, and meant it.

I'd ridden with Harley only once before. It was a short trip, just around the block. Hanging on like a tick, praying to every god I knew, I had to admit it was fun.

"I'm too old to be a biker chick," I said, bones cracking like castanets as I awkwardly climbed on the bike.

"Miss Dessa, don't let people define who you are. You can be anything you want to be!" he said with a reassuring nod. Maybe he was right.

I felt a giddy exhilaration as the wind hit my face and the bike sped me, safe and sound, back to my home. Harley took a look under the hood of my car, and determined all I needed was a new battery. He called a friend who worked for AAA and the two of them got it running with stern warnings that I get it serviced on a regular basis. He left before I could find out what this bad stuff was he wanted to talk to me about, even though I sensed he wanted to tell me. But when I saw him again, it was too late.

Chapter 5

A text from Aunt Phoenix came early the next morning. As usual, she got right to the point. My aunt wasn't one to waste words.

Sunday brunch. You cook. I pay. No eggs.

My response was equally brief.

Flat broke!

She answered immediately.

Check Bank Account

I was astonished when I did. She had not only paid for groceries but transferred enough money into my account to cover my mortgage for three months. My eyes welled with tears. God knows I needed it. I'd avoided going into the cash Darryl and I had tucked away in our 401ks, but each month money grew tighter, and Darryl's insurance money was rapidly disappearing. I'd managed to scrape together enough for this month's mortgage, but next month was looming near. Aunt Phoenix's loan would definitely carry me through. And I considered it a loan.

I didn't like borrowing money from my aunt because I didn't know when I'd be able to pay her back. Although she claimed her lottery winnings were plentiful, they were just that, "lottery winnings." She believed her good fortune would last forever. I wasn't so sure. As a matter of fact, I had the same doubt about her weekly windfalls as I did about the "gift" in general. They couldn't be trusted. My aunt was a woman on her own—a *senior* woman on her own—with, as far as I knew, no visible means of support. When Darryl was alive, we assumed we'd play an important role in her financial well-being, that she might be dependent on us someday, and that was fine with both of us. My feelings toward Aunt Phoenix were complicated, but Darryl adored her. His parents had died when he was in college, and she seemed to fulfill his desire for an elder attachment. I didn't have the same need.

My mother, Rosemary, had two older sisters, the eldest being Aunt Phoenix. Everyone called my mother Rosie, and she was known for her cheerful disposition and loving ways. I inherited her deep dimples, which some said gave my face a sweetness like hers. Even though the gift skipped her and landed in my lap, she was the family favorite, and when she died, there was a hole in everybody's world, especially mine. Where my mother was relaxed and friendly, Aunt Phoenix was mercurial and distant. My mother hated confrontations. Aunt Phoenix, as scrappy as a feral cat, loved a good fight. My mother never admitted it, but I always sensed she was fearful of her sister, as one can be of a bossy, controlling older sibling. For better or worse, she passed her wariness down to me.

My belly always got tight, as if preparing for an unpleasant encounter, whenever I visited my aunt. I felt it this morning when I pulled up to her tiny two-story house surrounded by shrubbery that bloomed with pink flowers in spring but was now as thorny as a briar patch. She loved to garden. Tomatoes and squash flourished in her backyard, as well as black-eyed Susans, her favorite flower. The yard was barren now, but she grew summer herbs in small clay pots in sunny windows. She lived in what might be considered a questionable neighborhood. Houses on either side had been broken into, but my aunt's was never touched, which didn't surprise me. Crooks knew who to mess with and who to avoid. Her front door swung open before I could ring the bell. That didn't surprise me either.

My aunt was what some folks might call a character. Even without the gift. She was a thin, wiry woman, agile and quick as a girl, who walked fast and talked in short staccato sentences, much like her texts, which she preferred to conversation. This morning she wore a flowered kaftan and slippers made from alligator skins. (She seemed to have no problem wearing dead animals on her feet!) She loved wigs of every imaginable color, style, and shape. Some were long haired, the kind you'd expect to see on a teenager, and others were short and conservative. She had one styled in a short blond Afro, and another with twists vaguely resembling dreadlocks. Several were 1950s pageboy; others were pixies à la Audrey Hepburn. In the summer, she wore a wide-brimmed sunbonnet, which brought to mind an elderly toddler. She was wigless and hatless today. Her dazzling white hair shone in the sun like a halo around her perfectly oval face and brown skin, as flawless as a baby's.

Aunt Phoenix didn't suffer fools gladly. She was known to turn off her hearing aid when she didn't want to hear something you had to say. It was an odd act of passive aggression from a woman who had no qualms about telling you off. She'd pulled it on me more than once, yet she seemed in a relatively talkative mood this morning, and the knot in my stomach relaxed.

"Hello, my dear. What's for brunch?" she asked when I stepped inside. I gave her a peck of a kiss on her cheek and caught a whiff of Chanel No°5 (of all things) that she wore on special occasions.

"Since omelets and quiche are out, I'm making crab cakes,

but I need to use eggs to bind them and for the muffins. Is that okay?"

"Must have read my mind," she said with a mischievous grin.

I followed her into her sunny, tidy kitchen, surprisingly updated for someone who didn't like to cook. The kitchen table was in a corner and just big enough for two, and she'd splurged on tableware today. It was set with a linen table-cloth, matching napkins, bone china, sterling silverware, and gleaming crystal glasses.

"This is beautiful, Aunt Phoenix!" I said when I saw it.

"Special occasion," she said with a wink.

When I began to cook, I realized how much I missed it. Cooking had always been a form of meditation for me, and I could lose myself in the mundane motions, no matter how difficult the recipe or meal. I loved a tranquil, silent kitchen, with only the hum of simmering sauce or the peace that comes with the rhythmic kneading of dough for bread.

Aunt Phoenix's kitchen was calm, just the way I liked it. She studied me, as attentively as an apprentice, while I mixed and shaped the crab cakes, placing them in the refrigerator to chill before frying them. I made the muffins, tossed together an arugula and spinach salad, then whisked my special vinaigrette dressing. I'd bought a coleslaw mix with cabbage and carrots (I wasn't up to shredding today) and blended it with good mayonnaise, a bit of sugar, lemon juice, and cider vinegar. Aunt Phoenix was partial to ginger so I'd bought a tin of ginger snaps for dessert from a specialty shop. Since she didn't touch coffee, I planned to serve the cookies with herbal tea; she had every imaginable flavor. It was a good meal, and I was proud of it.

I waited for just the right time to bring up the money to thank her. I also needed to find out more about the glimmers and what they meant. That moment came after we'd eaten our meal, and washed and dried the dishes. I brewed some Lemon Zinger tea for her in a tiny delicate teapot and poured some hot water in a mug for myself, adding two bags of oolong and lots of honey. We settled down in her white-walled living room, as spick-and-span as the kitchen, me on her stiff sofa covered in paisley print. She added a shot of cherry brandy to her tea and began rocking in her vintage bentwood rocker.

"How's Juniper doing?" she asked out of the blue, which startled the heck out of me. He'd just entered my mind because I'd forgotten to check his dried food dish.

"Fine, as far as I know." I wondered with a touch of anxiety if she knew something about my cat's well-being that I didn't.

"You're a very talented cook, Odessa. Time you got back to it," she said, taking a sip of tea. I yearned for a cup of strong coffee; the oolong wasn't cutting it. "Thank you for brunch."

I cleared my throat. "Aunt Phoenix, I'm the one who needs to thank you. Thank you so much for the money, for—"

"Stop right there!"

"I promise I'll pay you back. I'll just need a few months with, well, at Risko Realty." I stumbled over the words. "I promise . . ."

She turned off her hearing aid.

"Oh, for goodness' sake, Aunt Phoenix!" I said, not hiding my irritation. "You're like a kid who puts her hands over her ears so she can't hear her parents!"

She turned it back on. "Listen to me, Odessa. You're the only family I've got close. It's my responsibility to help you if you need it. And, my dear, you need it."

"What are you talking about?" I said in amazement. "You have other family. What about Celestine, in Pasadena?" She shrugged. I'd always suspected that Aunt Phoenix had something to do with the lack of communication between me and other members of my family, but I couldn't be sure. I knew she'd never admit it. She surprised me this time.

"As a matter of fact, I have reached out to Celestine, and she's coming for a visit. We're sisters and we need to spend more time together, and she wants to see you."

"Well, I'm glad to hear that, and it's about time. But what about those cousins you're always talking about, the ones who can wash a dish with a wink and fell a man with a sneeze? What about them?"

She smiled at that. "I do hear from them from time to time. Delightful girls, all of them." I had to take her word for that since I'd never met them. "Thanks to their gifts, they don't lack for much. They don't need my help."

"Good for them!" I muttered. She raised her eyebrow.

"Like I keep telling you, Odessa—" She paused for a dramatic moment, then added, "If you'd played those numbers like I told you, you wouldn't be in this fix! How many times have I told you to listen to your gift?"

Annoyed, I went into the kitchen to get us both more tea and considered adding some cherry brandy to mine as well.

"Like I keep telling you, Aunt Phoenix, I can't trust it," I yelled from the kitchen as I waited for the water to boil. "It's let me down too many times." I added hot water and another teabag to her teapot and freshened up my cup.

"That it has," she said in a quiet voice I could barely hear, an admission that surprised me.

I returned to the living room and we sat together in tense yet contemplative silence. Since we were on the subject of the gift, I decided to bring up the glimmer. She spoke before I could say anything.

"It wasn't that it didn't warn you, Odessa. You were just too wound up in happiness to hear it. The kind of joy you and Darryl shared makes it hard to listen to warnings, to hear bad things," she said, her voice as gentle as I'd ever heard it. "Sometimes one can't see or hear things because one doesn't want to."

"Did you know?"

She sighed without answering, and I knew she never would. If she'd known, she wouldn't have wanted to cause me pain, and what did it matter now anyway?

"The truth is, Odessa, death has the final say. Always. Even the gift can't predict that."

"What kind of a useless, stupid gift is that? How can death rule over everything? How can happiness make you deaf, dumb, and blind? Tell me that, Aunt Phe!" I said, sounding like a teenager and returning to the nickname I used to call her. My eyes filled with tears, and I blinked them away.

She sat next to me on the couch, taking my hand in hers. I'd forgotten how soft her skin was, how much her hands reminded me of my mother's. I swallowed a sob. She hugged me tightly, and the scent of cherry brandy mixed with Chanel was pleasant and comforting.

"I'm sorry. I wish I were more like Rosemary, as sweet as she was. Unfortunately, I'm all you've got. At least for now. But Rosie was far too sensitive for her own good. Taking in people's sorrows like she did, claiming them for her own."

I didn't like to hear her criticize my mother and pulled away. She took out a linen handkerchief that smelled like roses and was warm from being tucked deep in her bosom and handed it to me. I hadn't realized I was crying until I held it. Was it for my mother or for Darryl this time? For everything? Aunt Phoenix, uncomfortable with tender emotion, brought it back to where we'd started.

"You asked about the gift? None of this stuff is cut and dried, like mixing . . . muffins or boiling water. It comes, lingers, and disappears with no reason or warning. Sometimes it's so strong you can't ignore it. Like the nutmeg you smelled when that nasty man was killed. Then you have to let it in. Listen to it. But other times it's not.

"Smells are easy. Glimmers are something else again. Sometimes they're strong, sometimes not so much."

"Like with Uncle Tim."

"Don't mention that terrible man to me!" She chuckled and wrinkled her nose in disgust. We were on safe territory now.

"There's a guy at work whose glimmer I can see clearly. It's always gray. He seems very sad to me. And there's a young woman, the daughter of a coworker, who has been deeply wounded, but I don't know how or why. I can see a glimmer around her that breaks my heart, but it was nearly gone the last couple of times I saw her. What was strange was it seemed to have attached itself to her mother. There are others who don't have any glimmer at all."

"Or you don't see them or don't want to. You give the glimmer your own interpretation. A glimmer is not only what you get from somebody. It's who you think that person truly is. We do have the gift, but we also have our own prejudices and biases. We can be wrong. See what we want to see. Or not."

"Thanks, Aunt Phoenix," I said, trying to hide my disappointment. I was hoping for more.

"What you really want to know is if the person who killed that man will have a glimmer."

"Yeah, that's about it, since I see these people every day."

"A glimmer won't tell you that."

"What will it tell me then?"

"What you need to know."

"How will I know if I'm in danger?"

"You'll know. You have more going for you than just seeing glimmers. As our gifts go, that's a minor one. But you need to listen to it, let it in! Learn to listen to your gift. I'll help you as much as I can."

Although my aunt didn't turn off her hearing aid, I knew that was all I would get, and maybe that was enough for today. She gave me some mint and sage cuttings to cultivate now and plant in the spring, and I promised I would.

"I'll call you when Celestine gets in town. It's time you two got to know each other," she said. My mother had been dead for nearly twenty years, and I'd only spoken to Aunt Celestine twice since then. I didn't know why. If the sisters had some healing to do, it wasn't my responsibility. I had my own to do.

I put in another call to Harley and Bertie when I got home, but neither answered their phones. I wondered if they were avoiding me or simply had other things to do. Whatever it was, I'd see them both tomorrow.

But that night, with Juniper fed and happy and as I sipped my chamomile tea, I had to admit I dreaded going to work the next day. I was afraid to go back to the space where Charlie had been murdered because I didn't know what I would feel or smell. I didn't really believe in ghosts, but I knew that if Charlie Risko showed up tomorrow morning, I'd be the only person to see him.

Chapter 6

Except for late-as-usual Harley Wilde, everyone on staff sat impatiently in their cubicles waiting their turn. It was déjà vu, with cops instead of Charlie Risko holding court.

"Why the heck are they talking to us here instead of downtown?" muttered Vinton. "Do they actually think somebody is going to catch the spirit, fall down on his knees, and confess?"

"You never know," I said, but thought that would probably be about as effective as waiting for the glimmer.

"What makes them think one of us knows anything?" Juda said, directing her question at Vinton.

"Somebody might know more than they think. Just tell the truth," said Vinton.

"Trouble is, everybody's truth is different," said Dennis Lane, sitting by himself at a far cubicle.

"They have the gun, so they know who did it. That's the truth," said Bertie, who had just left Charlie's office and joined us. She'd come in early and asked to be interviewed first because she needed to be home to babysit. We'd finally gotten a chance to talk late last night. Her granddaughter answered the phone, a good sign that maybe Bertie and Louella had worked something out, but when we spoke, she was distant and eager to end our conversation.

"If they know all that, then why the heck are we sitting here?" snapped Vinton.

"Ask them when it's your turn," Bertie snapped back.

"They told you they had the gun?" asked Dennis. "What else did they tell you?"

Bertie shrugged. "Ask them when you see them. They're through with me. I'm going home."

"Are you coming in tomorrow?" I hoped she was.

"I got a lot of things on my mind, Dessa. Bad stuff I'm dealing with," she said without looking at me. A glimmer shadowed her face, then disappeared. Was it the same one I'd seen after that fight with Louella, or the flickering glow of Charlie's cheap fluorescent lights?

"Is everything okay, Bertie? Is Louella doing all right?"

"Yeah, as far as I know," she said, still avoiding my eyes. "They probably know who did it. That's what I think. And if they do, good for them." She slammed the door hard when she left, as if shutting out everything that had happened in the past few days. I couldn't blame her.

"So where is the merry widow? Shouldn't she be part of this sugar show?" said Vinton in a mock-cheerful tone.

"Shut up, old man! You don't know what the hell you're talking about," said Dennis, his voice raised and threatening.

"Need I remind you there are officers of the law in the next room? Watch yourself!" Vinton shot back.

Our collective gaze shifted uncomfortably to Charlie Risko's old office where the interviews were taking place, just like they had before he was murdered.

"Vinton, don't say anything else. You'll just make things worse," pleaded Juda. And our collective gaze shifted to her.

"They can't get any worse. Everyone knows what Charlie was and what he did. For all we know, one of us could be next," said Vinton, looking around uncomfortably.

"My vote is you, old man," said Dennis. "You should be next. But you had more reason to want him dead than anybody else, didn't you?"

"Except her," Vinton shot back. "You know that as well as me. Who is the one who gains from all this?"

I closed my eyes, put in my ear buds, and took myself to the park where I had escaped the last time these people plucked at my nerves. I made myself feel the sun on my face, hear kids laughing, feel the brush of fallen leaves around my feet. I made myself remember the wind hitting my face as I sped down the street on Harley's bike on Saturday. I could hear Darryl's laugh, and I smiled. Just like my mother would.

"Mrs. Odessa Jones." A pat on my shoulder and a gruff voice brought me into the present. A stern pair of eyes loomed above me, waiting for a response. "Would you come with me, please?"

The officer was young, about the same age as Harley, with a dirty-blond crew cut and lips I couldn't imagine smiling. I glanced once at my coworkers—no support from them. They were silently engrossed in whatever was on their laptop screens. Like a child gone wrong, I obediently followed the officer to the scene of the crime.

There was no blood, no nutmeg, no glimmer, no ghost. Nothing but two plain-speaking cops with no-nonsense expressions waiting for me to talk. I wondered how they'd found Charlie's body. Had he been shot in the back, cowardly running? Sprawled across his desk like a butchered piece of beef? Sunk deep into the same chair where he threatened, teased, and scared us all? The huge desk was empty now. The officers sat in the plush chairs on either side. They nodded for me to sit in the straight-backed chair between them. A chill went down my back as I recalled my last interview with Risko.

"Mrs. Odessa Jones?" the cop asked again, as if his partner hadn't gotten it right. His balding head and chestnut-brown skin reminded me of my father's, which calmed and relaxed me. Momentarily. I'm always nervous around the police. I hoped they couldn't tell.

"That's me," I said, a bit too relaxed, flirting with flippancy. Not smart, I realized, when he raised his eyebrow.

"I'm Detective Larkin; my partner is Officer Raye. Mrs. Risko, the deceased man's widow, was kind enough to offer the use of her office so we can avoid doing interviews at the station. We need to verify several facts that have been reported. This won't take long."

I nodded, eager to cooperate.

They began with basic questions: my home address, how long I'd worked here, how well I knew Charlie Risko. Questions quickly asked and easily answered. Then they got down to the real stuff.

"You were here the night Mr. Risko was murdered?" Officer Raye, with the blond crew cut, asked.

"Yes," I said, wondering how they knew.

"Tell me exactly how long you were here, if and when you left, exactly what you saw or heard when you returned."

I told them about the park, leaving out the reason why I left, and explaining that it was dark when I returned. Officer Blond Crew-Cut leaned close, staring at me like a suspect. "Do you often take walks in the park?"

"Yes."

"Why?" he asked, wanting to know more.

"I just, uh, just wanted to get some fresh air." That seemed to satisfy him.

"Was there anything special about last Thursday, something that stuck in your mind?" asked Detective Larkin, the senior officer.

"Well, it was the day Mr. Risko gave us our reviews. Everyone was always nervous about that. You never knew what he was going to say, if you were going to be fired or not."

"Was anyone fired?"

"I don't know."

"Anything else?"

"Well, it was the anniversary of the death of Mr. Risko's older brother. He hung himself here in this office two years ago."

The looks the men exchanged hinted that I should have kept that to myself.

"Was anyone here when you came back? Besides the ghost of Mr. Risko's dead brother?" Officer Blond Crew-Cut asked sarcastically, not hiding his amusement, which earned him a rebuking glance from his elder.

"Yes. Charlie Risko."

"What was he doing?"

"Talking to someone in his office."

"Who?"

"I don't know."

"Describe the other voice. Female, male, black, white, old, young?"

"I don't know, but I'm pretty sure it wasn't the ghost of his dead brother," I couldn't resist saying, then wished I hadn't.

"And *you* couldn't tell?" Officer Blond Crew-Cut's scowl said he didn't appreciate my crack. I noticed a pimple on his chin and focused on it.

"Mr. Risko was doing all the talking. I could hear Mr. Risko, but I couldn't hear what the other person was saying."

"There *was* somebody in the office when you left?"

"Yes." Hadn't I just told them that?

"When you came back from the park, did you see a motor-cycle parked down the street?"

"Yes."

"Do you know who it belonged to?" They were eager for the answer. I thought about Harley and what Bertie had said at the bar and focused on Blond Crew-Cut's pimple.

"I assumed it was Charlie Risko's since he was the person who was here."

"Why would you assume that?"

I shrugged my shoulders. Truth was, it could have belonged to anybody.

They exchanged glances again, then stared at me is if their stern gaze would shake out some stubborn truth I was trying to hide. "Do you know where your coworker Harley Wilde was and why he is not here today?"

"No." I shook my head for emphasis, widened my eyes for innocence, and stared directly into the eyes of the younger officer.

Detective Larkin, the senior one, scribbled something on his pad. "Do you know a gentleman by the name of Avon Bailey?" he asked, staring hard at me.

"Never heard of him."

"That's all we'll need today from you, Mrs. Jones," he said without looking up.

I hurried out before they could think of anything else.

"Mr. Lane, would you step in now?" Officer Blond Crew-Cut said as I was leaving. Dennis headed into the office. For the first time since I'd known him, he looked scared.

But his interview was short and must have been sweet because he had no trace of discomfort when he sat back down in his cubicle. He immediately got back to business, his voice charming and seductive. Juda was next and Vinton after her. Their interviews were brief, too, which made me uneasy.

"I feel like a drink," Vinton muttered when he sat back down.

"They don't really think one of us did it, do they?" said Juda.

"I think they might." Vinton's voice was hushed.

"Did you tell them everything you know?" Juda whispered, but her voice was loud enough for everyone to hear. Vinton shook his head as if warning her not to say anything else.

"Anybody know a gentleman named Avon Bailey?" I said. The question came out of nowhere, sounding like what the cop had asked me. Smells, sounds, glimmers. Other people's words tumbling out of my mouth seemed like the gift's latest manifestation making an unwelcome appearance.

"Why the hell would you ask us something like that?" Dennis bellowed, uttering the only words he'd said to any of us since he'd sat back down.

"I don't know!" I said, sounding pathetic. "I guess it was because the police asked me."

"He was one of your and Charlie's clients, right, Dennis?" Vinton said with a smirk. "Wasn't Harley involved with him, too? Him, along with you know who?"

"Leave it alone, old man. Leave it alone," Dennis said, his voice tight.

The room was silent, as if nobody had heard the exchange between the two, and suddenly everybody was busy, doing whatever they could to avoid looking at each other. But one question lingered in my mind: Who was Avon Bailey?

When the memo flashed on my phone reminding me of an appointment to show some two-bedroom rentals, I said a prayer of gratitude. So much had happened in the past few days, I'd forgotten about it. Charlie had scoffed when I mentioned it. Our last conversation was too painful to remember.

Scarcely aware of what I was doing, I tossed my belongings into my tote bag and headed outside, glad to be gone.

My clients were a young married couple expecting their first child, and so far we'd been batting zero. This was my last showing, and I didn't have much hope. It was a third-floor walk-up in a 1930s building that had seen better times. It was in an older, shabbier section of town most had written off years ago, but artists, students, and writers had recently rediscovered its charms, mostly because it was close to trains heading to New York and rents were affordable.

As if on cue, the moment the couple walked into the place the sun lit up the rooms like klieg lights. They both loved the "bones" and "character" of the place, and raved about the spacious rooms, good lighting, and high ceilings, invisible to both me and the landlord. Their excitement was contagious, and they seemed to carry a lightness between them, somewhere between sunshine and moon glow. Aunt Phoenix would call it a glimmer, but I figured it was simply the joy of being in love with no expectation of sorrow.

Their mood even touched the gruff, mean-spirited landlord, who easily agreed to reduce the rent. I *knew* this place would be good for them, and that their child would be blessed. I didn't need the gift to tell me that. Just in case, I made a mental note to ask Aunt Phoenix for a charm or a chant that could ensure that good things would come their way.

The bliss between the two of them was the very tonic I needed to finish out a demanding, unpleasant day. I hated to admit it, but I'd been shaken by my interview. I knew I wasn't a suspect, but I had a sense of foreboding that something disagreeable was on its way. I hoped it didn't smell like nutmeg.

It was going on six by the time my clients signed the agreement. Too late to go back to the office, but I didn't feel like going home and it was nearly time for dinner. Royal's wasn't a large restaurant but there always seemed to be space, even when the place was crowded. There was a booth near the back reserved for Royal's daughter, Lena, and three tables where couples could sit cozily. I settled down at the far end of the counter. I could hear Lennox in the kitchen supervising Tyler, who sometimes helped cook. I ordered a dinner special—barbecue chicken, a roll, coleslaw—from Georgia, the assistant cook who sometimes works behind the counter. She regarded me skeptically.

"You're too late for lunch, and dinner is running slow," she said impatiently.

"Sorry, I'll take whatever is ready." I was taken aback when she haphazardly tossed my meal on the plate. I smiled pleasantly, hoping to get in her good graces. And then the glimmer made its appearance.

I'd never noticed the slight shadow that appeared when Georgia was around. It was avocado green, which Aunt Phoenix would probably define as envy. It was hard to believe this young woman could be jealous of me. She was younger by more than a decade and far prettier. Did she think that *I* was interested in Lennox Royal? I didn't know what kind of relationship she and Lennox had, but ours was no threat to her. Unless she had other designs. I knew I was smiling too much, which I tend to do when I'm uncomfortable, but I gave another warm one to reassure her. She didn't smile back.

"Miss Odessa, always good to see you!" Lennox said, coming out from the kitchen. "How about a piece of pie for dessert?"

One of the problems with being a chef, even a part-time one, is that I know a good pie, biscuit, or donut at first bite. My mouth puckered just thinking about those hard little donuts I'd had on Friday. Royal's Regal Barbecue was obviously in need of a baker. Lennox did all right when it came to barbecue and chili, but baking was something not everybody can do. You either had a feel for it or you didn't. I had a feel for it; he didn't. Should D&D Delights expand its services to include baked goods for small establishments?

"So, Lennox, where do you buy your pies and cakes?" I asked innocently.

"Nowhere special. Varies from week to week. Sometimes Georgia will throw something together. If things get crazy, I'll pick up a couple of pies from Acme down the street."

Georgia, moving closer to where he stood, mopped invisible grime off the spotless counter.

"And Georgia's pies and cakes are always delicious, as are her lemon cookies," Lennox quickly added, sensing her interest. He turned to acknowledge her with a grin. Georgia nodded and moved away. When she went into the kitchen, Lennox leaned toward me.

"But sometimes things do get really busy in here. I hate to burden Georgia. Do you know a good baker?"

"I might. It's a small catering company, but I can check and see if they're ready to expand." I took a sip of water, realizing with a pang of anxiety what I'd just said. It would be a big deal for me to expand D&D. I didn't know if I was ready. Half of me was ready to venture out on my own; the rest of me still needed Darryl coaching from the sidelines.

"Let me know when you find out. I'll pay a good price."

"What's a good price, so I can let them know?"

He bent toward me and lowered his voice. "Pretty much anything they want me to pay. Georgia's a hell of a good cook when she wants to be and she's great at the counter, but her pies aren't what they should be."

"And this was the slice of pie you were offering me?" I said, half joking.

"Actually, that one's from Acme." He looked embarrassed, rinsed and wrung out a dishcloth in the sink, and then went to check on Lena sitting in her booth. "Tell me what's going on with your office murder," he asked when he sat back down.

"You read me like a cop."

"That's because I used to be one." He broke into a smile.

"How often do the police interview witnesses at the scene of the crime?"

He thought for a moment. "Depends on the suspects, depends on the crime." He sounded like Aunt Phoenix talking about the glimmer.

"The police interviewed our staff today at the office, in the room where Risko was shot. Does that mean they suspect one of us?"

"Could be. Like I said, depends on the suspects, depends on the crime. From the little you've told me, sounds like it was an inside job."

"Please don't tell me that!"

"Remember the warning I gave you," he said, turning serious. "I don't mean to scare you, but it's not easy to tell who is or isn't a killer. Your murderer may not know the rage is growing inside. Sometimes folks don't know they have a killer inside until it's out. I've known fighters, some of the sweetest guys you'd ever want to meet, get in the ring and the beast will claw its way out. Take Mike Tyson. Remember him? He loved those pigeons he kept on the roof when he was a kid. First fight he had was because somebody killed one of those birds. You never know what will bring out the devil in you."

"Not everybody has a devil in them."

"Yeah, they do. But it's got to get poked," he said with conviction.

I finished up dinner, and Lennox wrapped up an extra

chicken leg, some mac and cheese, and a slice of that dreadful apple pie, reminding me to get back to him about the baker. I promised I would.

When I walked in the door, Juniper greeted me with his usual beg-a-thon show for treats.

"At least I know there's no devil in you," I said as I delivered his request for Temptations, reading the list of ingredients and musing aloud, yet again, why these particular treats had such a hold on my pet. I picked him up, hugged him, and he jumped out of my arms, scampering to the pantry where I kept them. "Or maybe you do have the devil in you," I said, giving him a few more. He gobbled them up, looked for even more, then ran into the living room and settled down on his favorite cushion on the couch. I had no discipline when it came to Juniper, and he knew it. It was good to be home, though, cheered by my dear little pet, who always lifted my spirits. When I thought about the young couple that rented the apartment, my feelings soared even higher.

Do you know any charms to ensure happiness? I texted Aunt Phoenix, hoping against hope she knew some special kind of magic.

Are U Kidding Me?! If I did, I'd sell them she quickly texted back. I could always count on Aunt Phoenix to deliver a dose of reality. But even my aunt didn't dampen my spirits.

I brewed some chamomile tea and poured it into my favorite oversized china cup, adding more honey than it needed, then watched a rerun of *Downton Abbey*, escaping into the trials and tribulations of the British aristocracy, which had absolutely no connection to me or anyone I knew. I'd told Lennox I'd check with my contact about expanding their business, my "contact" being Darryl. "Answer me in my dreams," I whispered when I got into bed that night because he often would, and he did that night, in that place inside me where he still lived. *Time for D&D Delights to grow. Go where you're meant to, my love,* came into my thoughts.

I woke up, knowing it was a dream, but not yet ready to let his voice go. I had my answer. When the phone rang a few moments later, I let it ring a while before picking up. I knew who it was even before I heard his voice.

Chapter 7

Dessa, it's me, Harley. I'm in jail. Grovesville city jail. They picked me up for killing Charlie, said my prints were on the gun, said I shot him. There's not another person in this world I can call except you. I put you on my list. Hope that's okay. Can you come down here? I need you to do something for me.

I'd known it was him so the gift finally was earning its keep or maybe I had simply added stuff up: Bertie's bar chatter, Harley's absence, suspicious cops asking where he was—that, along with the anxiety black women get whenever the law starts asking questions about black men they know. And this was not my first rodeo.

When I was a kid, my father was picked up for a mugging done by a man twice his height with skin three times lighter. Darryl had been pulled over more times than I can count, always for that old dependable catchall: DWB (Driving While Black, for the uninitiated). A part of me had always feared Harley Wilde might end up in somebody's crosshairs sooner or later, and now it had happened.

The despair in his voice stunned me. I'd always assumed Harley had family and friends, and his plaintive cry for help surprised me. Was I really the only one he could count on?

And what did he want me to do? God knows, I didn't have any money for bail. Hopefully, he just wanted me to contact a family member, which he must have somewhere—a doting mother or loving aunt who kept an eye on him and stayed in his business, a best friend near his own age, a girlfriend he kept tucked away in his heart and never mentioned—at least not to me. He acted like a tough, go-it-alone dude, but I knew men who played that role and were anything but that. I was reminded again how little I knew about him. Maybe he *was* guilty. What if the police were right? Should I trust him?

Not everybody has a devil in them.

Yeah, they do. But it's got to get poked.

Had Charlie Risko poked Harley Wilde's devil?

There was no point in trying to sleep. I was up now, fully awake. I went downstairs to the kitchen and brewed some coffee, stronger even than the stuff I'd had at Royal's last Friday. With Juniper traipsing behind me hoping for treats, I went back upstairs to the spare bedroom that served as our home office. It was a room I seldom used, except to pay bills online when I had the money. A stack of unpaid ones faced me now, and I tried to ignore them. A couple of catalogs, which I also ignored, were piled on the side of the desk. I tossed them into a wastebasket to clear up space and settled behind the desk.

This had been Darryl's place where he wrote lesson plans, did research, and kept his notes and observations about the kids he taught. It wasn't large but had enough space for a couch, desk, chair, and a tall IKEA bookcase crowded with textbooks, teaching materials, and the dozens of cookbooks I'd bought over the years. The room was musty, and I opened a window to let in the cold night air, which chilled me until I got used to it. The good thing was it would keep me awake. I turned on the computer, an old Dell, constantly urging me to upgrade to Windows 10, which I hadn't bothered to do. Big mistake.

Apparently giving up his quest for treats, Juniper sauntered into the room and settled down on the couch for a nap. "What should I do?" I said to myself and the cat, even though I knew the answer: I had to get up tomorrow morning, go to the jail, and listen to what the man had to say.

I need you to do something for me.

Offering to pay his bail was out of the question; he knew that because I was always borrowing a couple of dollars from him. What did he want?

There's not another person in this world I can call.

Who would I call if I found myself in similar circumstances? Aunt Phoenix. I chuckled at the thought. I'd have to think hard and long about sending *that* text.

Said my prints were on the gun, said I shot him.

"How the heck did they get on the gun if you didn't shoot him?" I asked an absent Harley, surprised by the depth of my anger. Juniper, taking note of my tone, picked up his head, perked his ears, then jumped on the desk and trotted across the keyboard, as he always does whenever someone is getting ready to write. I shoved him off the desk and smiled at his antics despite myself.

"Okay," I said aloud, to myself, Juniper, and . . . Harley. "I'll need to ask you myself."

Darryl was a great one for googling. It was his essential source of information on anything from recent academic studies to determining the longest—or shortest word—in the world. I thought about that and typed the words *how to visit someone in jail* on the screen.

I stayed up for the next few hours researching jails, what Harley was facing, and what I had to do to visit him. He was in a city jail, not a state or federal prison, a lucky thing for him. He'd been arrested and still had to face arraignment, plead guilty or innocent, and then be scheduled for trial. Harley had known enough about incarceration to put me on his visiting list. Had he been down this road before?

I still had lingering doubts about getting involved. We were just coworkers, after all. I *really* didn't owe him anything. I could hear Aunt Phoenix warning me to *stay away*. Yet I could also hear Darryl (a kinder angel) telling me to help Harley out in any way that I could. I'd promised myself when he left me I would honor the kind of man he was. No. I didn't owe Harley; I owed my husband.

I studied the website of the city jail to find out when visiting hours were. I was in luck. They were from 1:00 until 3:00 tomorrow. I also noted the visitation rules: Call before leaving in case there was a lockdown. Dress appropriately—no halter tops, miniskirts, or see-through blouses. (They didn't have to worry about that.) Bring a driver's license. Be prepared to go through security. I fell asleep at the computer, crawled back into bed, and woke up the next morning at 10:00 a.m. By noon, I was in line with other visitors, family members, and friends all waiting to see loved ones . . . and otherwise.

We were led into a gray, windowless room about the size of a high school cafeteria. People sat on either side of me, avoiding the eyes of others as they spoke in hushed voices. Guards, solemn faced and unsmiling, watched each move we made. Some visitors had bought food and soda from the vending machines in the waiting room, which they arranged in front of them as if they were at a party. When we were all seated, the inmates were allowed to come into the room accompanied by vigilant guards.

Harley sat across from me. Neither of us spoke. All the light was gone from his face. Fear was in his eyes with no trace of the young man who once brought me lattes, drove fast on his bike, with a loud laugh or good word tucked inside him. He looked shorter, thinner, swallowed by the inmate clothes that hung off his body.

"Thank you, Dessa, for coming. I . . ." He stopped, his voice choking up. "I hope you don't mind me calling you, putting you on the list, coming to a place like this. I know we don't know each other all that well. I know . . ." He stopped again, and cleared his throat. "I didn't do this, Dessa. I didn't shoot that man. They're going to kill me for killing him and I didn't do it."

I studied his face, his eyes, seeking out any truth I could find.

"Do you believe me?" he asked, his gaze holding me tight.

"Did you do it?" I whispered, aware of the others sitting on either side of us, but they were involved in their own conversations, hungrily savoring the bit of time they had with those they had come to see.

"I was there, but I didn't kill him. He was a jerk, but I didn't hate him enough to shoot him."

"Then how did your prints get on the gun?"

He paused, leaning close to whisper, "Remember how he was always taking that damn thing out and slamming it on his desk, bragging about knowing folks in high places so he could use it and get away with it? He liked to see people look scared. He was that kind of a bully. You know that as well as I do."

That was certainly the truth, and I nodded in agreement.

"Well, he pulled that thing out when I was there this time like he was going to shoot me, then slapped it down on his desk. I've seen people get shot, killed, over nothing. You don't do that kind of mess unless you mean it. You don't threaten people just for the hell of it. I cursed him out, picked the gun up, and slammed it right down in front of him where he'd put it. He looked at me funny, then started laughing. I laughed, too, because he looked so damned foolish.

"Charlie Risko wasn't nothing but a clown, a BS artist.

We both knew there was no way he was going to shoot me or anybody else. He was nothing but a joke. I cursed him out again, and left through the alley door because my bike was parked nearby." He paused as if remembering something, and then added, "You know when you hear something and then you don't? Like a ghost whispering?"

"Yeah," I said. I knew about ghost whispers; they were right up there with glimmers.

"Well, I thought I heard him talking to somebody after I left before he slammed the back door, but I was so mad I didn't give a damn. I got on my bike and got the hell out of there. Might have been talking to himself, for all I know."

"Did you mention that to the cops?"

"They found my prints on the gun. They don't want to hear nothing from me. They heard I was the last person in the office at the end of the day. They don't want to hear anything else. They got their man and that's me."

He paused again, as if remembering something else, and then shook his head with a surprising, thin smile. "I've known that fool since I got back from Afghanistan. I came to work for him because I wanted to save some money to go back to school. My mother was dying. I needed more money than I was making; that's how I got involved with him and his crazy, dirty schemes in the first place."

"Crazy, dirty schemes?" I asked, puzzled by his choice of words.

"It was all show with Charlie, everything he did was show," he continued, not answering my question. "I knew killers when I was in Afghanistan. Real killers. Charlie wasn't a killer. He wasn't a threat to me or anybody else. He wasn't nothing but a spoiled rich boy playing tough in places he had no business playing. Dennis Lane was the one you had to look out for. He was the real thing. If there was anything Charlie should have been shot for it was getting the girls tied up in that mess he was running, dirtying them up like he did."

"What girls?"

He leaned back in the seat, sighed deeply, focusing his gaze back on me as he changed the subject. "I guess you want to know why I called you over here, don't you? I better tell you quick before I got to go. I need you to do something important for me."

Now I was the one to sigh. "Harley, you know I don't have any money. I . . ."

He shook his head, that old Harley smile peeking through. "Listen, Dessa, I don't know what's going to happen to me in here. The courts are backed up, and when they arrested me they said it might be a while before my trial. I'll plead not guilty, and they'll get me some kind of a lawyer. They'll probably put me on house arrest with an ankle restraint so I can't go anywhere because that's what they do these days. It's cheaper than putting you in jail until your trial. But I'm liable to lose my apartment and everything in it. I have a couple of things I need you to get for me."

"These things you want me to get, they're not illegal, are they?" I was only half joking.

"You know me better than that!"

"Do I?" I didn't expect an answer and didn't get one.

"I need you to get my mama's Bible and keep it for me. I gave most of the stuff to her reading club friends after she died. That Bible is all I have left from her. That and Parker."

"Parker?"

He smiled shyly. "Mom's parakeet. My mom's been gone about three years. She was allergic to fur so a dog or cat was out, and I wanted to get her something to keep her company while I was out riding. I moved her in with me the year before she died, and she brought Parker with her. I've gotten attached to him. He's social, likes to sing."

"Likes to sing?" I said doubtfully.

"Can he stay with you, until, well . . . whenever? There's some money in an old wallet in my bureau drawer. About four hundred bucks. Take that to cover his food and stuff. He doesn't need much, just birdseed and company."

Harley, with his fast motorcycle, black leather jacket, and irreverence didn't strike me as a parakeet kind of man. Nor the kind of man who would care for an ailing mother during her last days, nor be concerned about a singing parakeet and a Bible. What else didn't I know?

"Sure, don't worry about it," I said without half thinking about it. Then an image of Tweedy and Sylvester, aka Parker and Juniper, popped into my mind.

"An extra key is taped under my mailbox. Feel around for it. I tucked it in real tight."

"Anything else you want me to do?" I was in for a dime, might as well be in for a dollar.

He shook his head. "Hope I get a good lawyer or . . ."

He didn't finish the sentence and I didn't push him. Maybe I should have.

His jaw stiffened. "Somebody killed Charlie Risko. It had to be somebody we work with, who knew our history. Whoever it is, is still out there, so don't let anybody know we talked. Stay away from this, Dessa. From people in the office."

"I don't know how I can do that. I still work there."

"Promise you will," he asked like a kid.

"Okay, I promise. With a cherry on top!" I added on impulse. He looked puzzled. "Before your time," I added.

He reached across the divide and grabbed my hand like a kid might, and I thought about his mother, three years gone, and the son I'd never have. Then something happened between us that only Aunt Phoenix would understand. Suddenly, I *knew* Harley was innocent. He had a glimmer, as strong as the one of Louella's that had made me want to cry,

and as heartbreaking as Vinton's that made me sad. I knew it
with absolute certainty in that place between my head and
my heart I'd always doubted was there. It told me that if I
did nothing else in my life, I had to keep this young man out
of jail.

"You okay, Dessa? Looks like you've seen a ghost."

"I think I have."

"If it's Charlie Risko, tell him I'll kick his butt when I
see him in hell," Harley said, and we both laughed hard at
that because we needed to laugh at something. When visiting
hours were over, Harley gave me one last look before he went
back to wherever they took him, tossing me that old Harley
smile, if only for a second.

My bond to Harley had been like that coffee that jolted
me back to life in the afternoon; seeing the glimmer changed
everything. Going to jail for years would kill him for sure.
These few days had diminished his spirit. I needed advice—
free advice—and I needed it quick. I didn't know squat about
the criminal justice system, except I didn't trust it. I thought
again about my poor father. He would have gone to state
prison, except the guilty guy showed up out of nowhere and
confessed out of the blue. Sheer luck, the arresting officer said.
Although my aunt never said so, my mother and I guessed
the truth—that Aunt Phoenix had a hand in it. I didn't think
she'd intervene for someone who wasn't kin.

What if Harley got a lousy lawyer? How do you go against
the law to prove somebody's innocent? There was no way to
explain the glimmer. An image of Aunt Phoenix showing up
in court to testify for its veracity, in one of her wilder wigs
and alligator slippers, popped into my mind. We'd probably
all end up in jail. This was new territory for me.

I needed to talk to somebody who knew something about
the law. Who better than an ex-cop like Lennox Royal? I

couldn't just drop by Royal's Barbecue for no reason, particularly if Georgia was at the counter. But I did need his help. And, come to think about it, he needed mine with his lousy desserts. Besides that, I *needed* to cook. I hadn't cooked anything since brunch with Aunt Phoenix. I'd forgotten how calming it was. Baking, grilling, whipping, stirring—put things in perspective.

It was time to bake a cake.

I stopped on the way home to get ingredients for something quick, cheap, and impressive: classic pound cake punched up with 7UP, baked in a fancy Bundt pan and sprinkled lavishly with confectioner's sugar. Always my D&D's fancy cake to go to in a crunch. When the cake was done, I set it on a pretty doily and placed it in one of D&D Delights' silver boxes, along with business cards and a price list for cakes and pies, then dropped it off at Royal's right before the dinner crowd.

"So this is from that bakery you mentioned?" Lennox said when I set it on the counter.

"Actually, it's my catering business. My late husband and I started it together, and I've decided to expand it, take in small orders from local restaurants. I've brought you a sample. If you like it, I can take an order now. I'm keeping it small for the time being, but I hope to expand at some point," I said, pouring everything out in one nervous breath.

"Okay, let me see what you got." He cut a slice, took a nibble. The cake, as always, had the expected response. "Wow! I'll order three," he said.

He cut a slice for Lena, sitting in her booth, and then re-read the business card when he returned. "So what does the D&D stand for?"

"Dessa and Darryl."

He must have noticed the shadow that came into my eyes.

"I'm sorry. I should have known," he said, embarrassed, and then took another bite. A big one. "Are you sure you're up to this, Odessa? Running a small business is harder than it looks."

"I just need to keep it small, for the time being," I said, wondering if I really was up to it.

He nodded as if he understood. "If the rest of your desserts are as fine as this, you're going to grow very quickly. And you need to charge more money. Add in how much it really costs and don't forget your labor. Don't sell yourself short," he added, sounding serious.

He wrote me a check for the cake, adding thirty dollars as a down payment on two more of the same.

"This was a sample!"

"Dessa, a *slice* is a sample, a cake is a cake," he said.

"Not this time," I said, shaking my head in protest. "Consider this payment for professional information."

"Professional information? You don't need to pay me for that."

"I need to know how the criminal justice system works."

"There's a lot to know. Books and college courses are filled with stuff about that."

"I don't have time to read or attend classes. I need something now."

"Okay, but I'm not a lawyer!"

"You know more than I do." I paused a beat, then got to the point. "A friend of mine has been arrested for Charlie Risko's murder, and he needs my help."

He shifted his eyes slightly, as if not completely ready to share all he knew. "Yeah, I heard they picked somebody up for that murder. Real quick. Too quick. Word spreads fast, even if you're not on the force anymore. Guy worked there. I was right about that. How come you're so sure he's innocent?"

"I just know. . . . I feel it in my heart." Now was *not* the time to mention the glimmer.

He looked doubtful. "If you trust your heart, I'll take your word for it. But think about this: You strike me as a kind-hearted woman. Is your heart overruling your head? Is this person somebody you're, well, romantically involved with?"

"No!" I said firmly. "He's like a kid brother. Young enough to be my son!"

"If you were a teenage mother."

"A *young* teenage mother," I said, returning his smile. "But he's a nice kid, Lennox. And he's had some bad breaks. There are other people in the office who hated Charlie, who, I might add, used to beat up his wife. Besides, this kid is a vet. He served in Afghanistan. I trust him."

"A vet? Okay. I'll share what I know from a cop's perspective." And over the next half hour, Lennox Royal earned that cake.

"If he's accused of murder, that's serious as a heart attack and he needs a good defense lawyer fast," he began. "He has to get somebody smart who knows the system. If he doesn't have a record, he'll be released with conditions, electronic monitoring, and house arrest. A shyster will tell him to plead guilty to save him the trouble of mounting a defense. If the police have it in for a person and the evidence is there, it's hard to fight it."

"So he can get out?"

"He'll have his first appearance within twenty-four to forty-eight hours, and the judge will set his conditions."

"Can he clear his name before he sees the judge?"

"If he has a good lawyer, he'll hire a good PI. One who knows how to question people and how to get answers, somebody to squeeze the truth from the person who is actually guilty."

I nodded like I agreed, though neither me nor Harley had

the money to hire a lawyer or any kind of PI, to say nothing of a good one. "So how would a private investigator know who to question and which questions to ask?"

"Instinct. Intuition. Solving crimes can be as much art as science. Intuition and a hunch more often than not will lead to the truth."

Like the gift and a glimmer, I said to myself.

Lennox cut another slice of cake and chuckled. "Grandma Odessa used to tell me that a good cake goes right to a person's soul. You can't say nothing bad when you're eating, and this cake is *good*. Cake like this would squeeze the truth out of any lying soul," he said with a chuckle. He cut me a piece and put it on a saucer with a fork, and I took a bite. I had to agree; it was that good.

Strangely enough, as I was drifting off to sleep that night I recalled Grandma Odessa's words to her grandson, then remembered Aunt Phoenix's to me about "listening" to the gift. A thought came to me: Could the words of two wise women be the answer I was looking for?

Chapter 8

The brilliant schemes you come up with at two in the morning usually dull in the light of the day. Yet the more I considered combining D&D Delights with the gift, the more I thought it might work. At the very least, I could hone those "listening" skills Aunt Phoenix claimed I lacked. And I could start cooking again. I'd gotten so used to gobbling down takeout (ridiculous, considering my tight budget), I'd gained five pounds and (shamefully) ended up at Burger King more than once. I missed cooking for others—be it Darryl, the kids he taught, or the teachers we routinely surprised with cupcakes or gingerbread men. I especially loved making desserts, which offered me the guilty pleasure of licking batter from the bowl and beaters, even though Darryl warned that it contained raw eggs and salmonella.

But what to bake? I knew little about my coworkers, so I'd need to play it by ear. Vinton's cubicle was filled with beach shots from Atlantic City, Bertie's with school pictures of Erika, Harley's with biker magazines. Most were empty of anything that offered clues to their lives. Who were they when they left Risko Realty? I honestly didn't know. That included Harley Wilde, who I thought I knew better than the others. Tanya struck me as a chocolate chip kind of girl. Vinton, always in gray, probably liked a no-nonsense pound cake. Everybody else? I had no idea.

The next morning I drove up to Harley's apartment building to pick up the bird and Bible. He lived in a squat three-story building from the 1970s, well kept, with a touch of charm. Someone, probably a tenant, had taken the initiative to plant flowers, now fading, in the stone planters and around the hedges, and the walkway leading to the building looked newly paved. I was immediately buzzed in when I rang the bell, hoping for someone to let me in. Either this was a trusting building or a guest was expected. Harley's apartment was on the ground floor, so there was a good chance of running into a nosy neighbor. Sure enough, as I struggled with the key, the woman next door opened her door, obviously expecting somebody else.

"Miss, who are you and why are you going into Mr. Wilde's apartment?" she said, her eyes narrowing with suspicion. She was a plump, gray-haired lady, a decade shy of Aunt Phoenix, with caramel-colored skin and piercing eyes that looked me up and down, expecting an answer.

"Hope she's here to get that crazy bird! I don't know what kind of a meeting we can have with him squawking like that!" I heard someone call from inside her apartment. I peeped inside and saw a blonde woman of about the same age sitting on the couch.

"I take it that's not Alejandra," said a high-pitched voice from another chair.

"I'm Laura Grace, and I'm waiting for your answer," said the first woman, her manner bringing to mind my terrifying third-grade teacher.

"I'm Dessa Jones. I work with Harley, and I'm here to pick his bird up and care for him while he's . . . away," I said, stuttering like a nervous third grader.

"A friend of Harley's. How is he doing?" asked the tall blonde, coming to the door and towering above both of us. "We heard he's in trouble, and we're worried about him. By the way, I'm Margaret Sullivan, and you've stumbled into a meeting of the ARC."

"I'm Clara Berg, and ARC stands for the Aging Readers Club. We're all retired teachers. What do we do? We drink and we read things!" Clara Berg called from across the room, and everyone chuckled.

"She stole that from Tyrion Lannister in *Game of Thrones!*" said Laura Grace, with an exaggerated eye roll. "And nobody's drinking now because it's too early. Hazel Wilde joined ARC when she moved in with her son. He's a good boy, took good care of her, read to her when she was too weak to read. It would break her heart to see what is happening to him."

"And we don't believe he's guilty, not for a minute," said Margaret Sullivan.

"Maybe you'd better get him now," said Laura Grace. "The bird. He's at it again!"

She was right. As I opened Harley's door, Parker began to squawk, even louder than before. I hoped it was for lack of company and not his usual behavior. "I'm here to take you home, Parker," I said, closing the door, as if my words would do some good, which they didn't. He was a noisy little creature, and I hoped Juniper's better angels would beat out his natural instinct. If not, I'd have some explaining to do when Harley got out of jail. *If* he got out. I'd face that when I had to.

Harley's apartment was a tiny two-bedroom with the biggest big-screen TV in the living room I'd ever seen, close to a stereo and a video recorder. A coffee table piled high with books about motorcycles was in front of the couch. Parker sat in his cage in the middle of the room; it was not love at first sight. The bird was bigger than I thought he would be but not as large as a parrot. He was nearly seven inches

long from his beak to his tail feathers, which were lime green
and speckled with yellow and blue spots. His tiny, lidded eyes
took everything in, and his lethal little beak looked ready to
crack seeds—or somebody's finger—if he set his mind to it.
His cage was spacious, as wide as it was tall, and filled with
various bird toys including a mirror, a swing, and a ladder as
well as a watering bottle, half full of water. A bulky cover I
assumed was used at night to keep him quiet lay on the floor
near the cage next to four boxes of food—two of parakeet
pellets, two of seeds.

"Okay, we'll be on our way shortly, Parker," I said, with
the uncomfortable realization that, except for my brief ex-
changes with the ladies next door, the only prolonged conversations I'd had today were with animals.

I walked down the short hall and peeked into the smaller
of the two bedrooms, which was remarkably neat. The corners
of a well-made bed were tucked in and tight, probably learned
from Harley's time in the army. The other room was larger,
with two windows, a chest of drawers, a full-size mirror, and
an old-fashioned rocking chair. The Bible, which looked as if
it had been in the family for generations, lay on the bureau. A
photograph of Harley as a child was inside. He looked around
six and sat on a two-wheel bike supported by a man sport-
ing a proud paternal smile who bore a striking resemblance.
I wondered why Harley had never mentioned him. But he'd
never mentioned his mother either. Harley was a man who
kept things to himself; that could be either good or bad.

Parker's raucous squawking reminded me that I had a
job to do, and it was time to do it. I returned to the living
room and tried to pick up the cage, which was heavier than it
looked. The cover added three pounds, but it quieted Parker
down, something to remember when I got him home. Slowly,
after several stops and starts, I managed to haul the bird and
the bulky cage to my car and slide it onto the backseat. I rested

for a minute, grabbed one of the tote bags I kept in my car, and headed back inside for the birdseed and Bible. When I left the bedroom, a hint of lavender rushed past me like a whisper.

"I'll do what I can, Hazel Wilde," I said to whomever lingered here to protect her son. I felt a wave of well-being, as if my promise had been heard and appreciated.

As I was leaving, I noticed a stack of booklets on parakeet care stuffed haphazardly on the top shelf of an overcrowded bookshelf. When I grabbed the closest, the others fell in a pile on the floor. I grabbed one and skimmed its back cover.

Parakeets are small parrots. They are sweet, gentle
creatures that enjoy socializing. They love to learn
new tricks and words.

A sociable *talking* bird! Just what I needed. I tossed the book in the tote bag with the birdseed and Bible. When I tried to push the other books back where they belonged, a stack of old photographs held together by a rubber band fell on the floor beside me. Out of curiosity (and simple nosiness), I sat down on the couch and shuffled through them, then wished I hadn't.

Louella, Tanya, Dennis, Harley—all of them were partying hearty in someone's plush, elegant living room. All were in their early twenties, except for Louella, who looked barely out of her teens. I saw her as she must have been once— laughing eyes, clear pretty face, no trace of drug use. Half-filled or empty liquor bottles were strewn around the room as if there had been a wild, sordid party. Stacks of dollar bills were piled on the coffee table and sofa like props, so many they couldn't be real. They were all drunk, arms tossed loose and easy around one another, dopey expressions, eyes sleepy and glazed, unaware or unconcerned that someone was taking pictures.

Charlie Risko, in his aging glory, was in all of them, arms resting on the shoulders of each of the girls. Louella sat on Charlie's lap in several of the pictures, kissing his cheek, her arm around his neck. A younger man, built like a heavy-weight and wearing a large-brimmed hat, stood off in the distance. The brim was pulled down, but I could still see his eyes, and his gaze, wide and disgusted, was fixed on Louella. In another, Tanya sat on Harley's lap, planting a kiss on his forehead. In another, she snuggled close to Dennis and was nuzzling Charlie in at least three of them. I studied Louella's photo carefully before returning it to the stack, scrutinizing the face of the young man staring at her. He was younger than the rest, his expression more grimace than smile.

I stacked the pictures together again, pushing them in the back of the bookshelf where I'd found them, knowing I'd wandered into a secret place I had no business going. I knew who the girls were now, the ones Charlie had dirtied. But where did the money come from?—if it was real. The girls were in most of the photographs. Who had taken them? Why had Harley kept them?

The doorbell rang, startling me. Feeling guilty, as if I'd been caught doing something naughty, I rushed to get it be-fore it rang again. It was Laura Grace from next door.

"When you see Harley again, I want you to tell him I said to keep the faith. I used to joke with Hazel all the time about that because her name was the same as one of Adam Clayton Powell's wives. Tell Harley that the ladies of the ARC are looking out for him and we'll do anything we can to help him, and that he has angels in high places, okay?"

"Yes, ma'am. I'll let him know," I said obediently, think-ing that angels were *always* in high places, but I kept it to myself.

Parker was quiet when I got into my car, but it wasn't for long. When my cell phone rang—the honking duck ringtone—he went into a frenzy, thinking perhaps that a fellow feathered traveler was on his way. The call was from Tanya Risko, and her message was as frantic as it was desperate. She begged me to come to see her the moment I got to work, ending her plea with a cringe-inducing crack about "us widows."

It took me nearly an hour to get Parker and his covered cage out of the backseat of my car and into the house. Juniper watched my ordeal with interest but made no obvious moves. I parked Parker in the office on the second floor, close to the window, then checked his food and water and took off the cover to let in some air, which set him chirping again. Juniper, still curious, stood nearby watching. Only the promise of Temptations lured him back downstairs. Hopefully, Parker would be our houseguest no more than a few days. Hopefully, Juniper would mind his manners.

"Where the heck have you been?" Vinton demanded to know when I walked into Risko Realty an hour later. "All hell has been breaking loose around here!"

I stopped short. There was no nutmeg, but the windows were wide open, water was on the floor near the coffeemaker, and Juda's right hand was bandaged up. The door to Charlie's old office was open, and Tanya's desk had been moved to the center of the room where she could see and be seen by others. When she saw me come in, she gave me a desperate wave. I could see she'd been crying, not surprising for a young woman recently widowed, even one married to Charlie Risko.

"Mrs. Jones, everything is going wrong!"

"You want me to close the door?"

She vigorously shook her head. "That's what Charlie did. I want to be close to everybody outside."

I noticed all the chairs had been moved around. I settled down in one of the plush ones, and she continued. "Seems almost like Charlie is still here, getting even with us. First, the coffeemaker blew up. That's why all that water is on the floor. Then the carbon monoxide alarm went off, and we had to call the fire department and everybody had to go outside and leave the windows open, then Juda tripped on the rug and hurt her thumb and had to go to the emergency room, and then . . ." She gestured for me to move closer, then whispered, "I'm scared that everybody thinks I killed him."

I let her words linger, then innocently asked, "Why would they think something like that?"

"I don't know," she said, her eyes wide. "Maybe it's because of me and Dennis, or maybe because of . . . you know, me and Harley."

"Harley?" I didn't hide my surprise.

"I talked to him, and I know they arrested him."

So much for keeping Harley's secret. "What else did he say?"

"That he trusted you. That he was sorry. Sorry about everything."

"Everything meaning what?" I asked.

She shrugged, as if she didn't know or didn't want to talk about it. I gave her the benefit of the doubt because she seemed at this moment as young as she and Louella had been in those old photographs.

Dennis walked in, breaking into any further conversation we might have, making me wonder about his timing. Was the choice of an open door his or hers? "Mind if I sit in on this?" he said. Avoiding my eyes, she shook her head.

"I don't think there's much to sit in on, Dennis," I said with a forced, lopsided grin. I'm not a good liar but hoped my fake smile would hide it.

"So what were you-all talking about then?" he asked, not letting her—nor me—off the hook, which left me wondering just what he didn't want me to hear. "This whole open-door thing is a mistake, Miss Lady, you know that, don't you?"

It was her idea, after all.

Tanya visibly squirmed before melting into the kittenish girl that always served her well. I remembered those bruises that covered her arms.

I studied Dennis Lane, taking his measure and recalling what Harley had said about Charlie being a rich boy playing at being tough, but that Dennis Lane was the real thing, the one you had to look out for. Where was the glimmer when I needed it? Absent as usual.

"We were just talking about my new business venture," I said. Tanya glanced at me and nodded. I realized she was afraid of him.

"Can I be part of this business venture? Anything to do with business, I'll be helping Tanya out. She's new to the business world, and I've been around for quite a while."

I'll bet you have, I thought, and gave a dimpled grin. "Well, I don't know if you were aware of this, Dennis, but I am expanding my catering service. And Tanya has offered—"

"Catering?" he asked, as if he'd never heard the word before.

"You know, cooking." I snuck a look at Tanya, who nodded as if she knew what I was talking about. "Anyway, I wanted to try out some new recipes on the staff, and Tanya said that was fine. I'm going to bring a dessert sample over to her place tonight and to anyone else who would be kind enough to have me drop by," I added.

"As long as it's not going to be in the office. Mrs. Risko doesn't want this place smelling like a bakery."

"No," Tanya said, her voice firm. "Tonight is good, Mrs. Jones. Around eight? I love chocolate. Can you make something chocolate?" She avoided looking at Dennis, hinting there were things she didn't want him to hear. She wasn't a chocolate-chip-cookie kind of girl after all.

"Did I hear the word *chocolate*?" Vinton called from his cubicle.

"Close the door behind you when you leave," Dennis said. "You got to keep that door closed. We don't want everyone to hear your business."

"Fresh baked? Anything I want?" Vinton said when I returned to my cubicle.

"Right from the oven. D&D Delights is my part-time job. I'm trying to build up my client list. If I don't drop my desserts off, I end up eating them myself."

"Why don't you just bring them in here?"

"Dennis said Tanya doesn't want me bringing anything into the office. It's a workplace, not a bakery."

"Yeah, well, that's Dennis trying to be Charlie. His attitude must come with the territory, if you know what I mean." Vinton gave a lecherous wink I chose to ignore. But I wondered if new bruises would become part of that territory, too.

"Just give me your order and address and the date you want them. Has to be in the next few days, though."

"Home-delivered, home-baked goods. Better than Grubhub. I'll take chocolate chip cookies. I'm definitely in." Vinton jotted down his information and handed the sheet to Juda. "How about you, Juda? You up for a tea party?"

She shook her head without answering but gave me a quick, surprisingly warm smile that touched me.

"You sure? I only have about five nights open. After that, I have a contract baking for another office group." Lying was getting easier. Any later than that wouldn't do me or Harley much good. "Bertie, how about you?" I asked. She had come into the office while I was talking to Tanya.

She didn't answer at first, rare for Bertie. I wondered if she'd heard me. "You okay?"

"I'm doing fine," she said, too enthusiastically. "What did you say?"

"I'm going to bring you a dessert from D&D Delights; just tell me what you want."

"Doesn't much matter," she said, then added after a minute, "pound cake would be nice. I used to make them a long time ago, with all that butter and sugar."

"Maybe something for Louella and Erika. Do they like cookies?"

"Just cake, that's all."

"Are they both living with you now?" Maybe things were better with her daughter. The change of her expression told me they weren't.

"Just Erika," she snapped.

"What about Louella?"

"She lives wherever she lives," Bertie said with a forced shrug that told me she cared more than she wanted me to know.

"Give me your address and I'll drop it off," I said cheerfully, my cheer as forced as her shrug. Maybe being alone with me in her own space would give us a chance to talk. "Call and tell me when to bring it over so I'll have time to bake it."

She nodded, but I didn't think she'd heard me. Her mind had returned to wherever it had been. Pleased with my progress on the D&D front, I headed home, stopping to get buttermilk, butter, good cocoa powder, and extra baking soda for Tanya's chocolate cake, along with chocolate chips and walnuts for Vinton's cookies.

I was sure I'd closed the study door, but the closer I got to home, the more I started worrying about Parker and Juniper.

"Juniper," I called out as I opened the door, halfway expecting him to bound downstairs with Parker clenched between his teeth. "Juniper, where are you?" I usually don't have to call him twice, which gave me pause. He came bouncing downstairs, round little belly rocking from side to side, with no Parker in his mouth. But what was he doing upstairs? He usually napped on the living room couch or rug or on the kitchen table when he thought nobody would catch him. I took the stairs, two at a time, and gasped when I got to the top. The door was open. I ran inside, took a breath, and then relaxed. Parker was flying around in his cage, chirping cheerfully. All was well. Juniper, sneaking up behind me, eyed the cage and Parker with a jaundiced cat eye. I must have forgotten to close the door to the room when I left that morning. I couldn't make that mistake again.

In my rush to get upstairs, I'd left my phone on the kitchen table; the honking duck called me back down. Slamming the door behind me, I ran downstairs to answer it.

"Why are you out of breath?" asked Aunt Phoenix.

"No reason," I said. If I told her about Parker, I'd have to tell her about Harley.

"I got the numbers for you."

"They don't call it the numbers anymore, Aunt Phoenix, they call it the lottery," I said with a touch of impatience.

"Well, I call it the numbers, but whatever it is, you better play it. It's five oh four one. By the way, Odessa, remember this: Cats will be cats and birds will be birds," she snapped before hanging up.

Just what I needed to hear.

I checked the door again; it was still closed. Forgetting about Aunt Phoenix, I began baking Tanya's cake, a D&D special called the Wickedly Delightfully Decadent Devil's Food Cake. It sounded just right for a widow who wore red.

Chapter 9

I was sitting in Tanya Risko's living room eating my Wickedly Delightfully Decadent Devil's Food Cake (and it *was* wickedly delicious). I realized when I walked in that this was the room where Harley's photographs had been taken—same high ceilings, arched windows, polished wood floors. It was an old-fashioned, elegant apartment, probably passed down, like the business had been, from dead father to dead son to dead son, and now it belonged to Tanya. All of it. Yet there was no trace here of her or of Charlie Risko. Everything— couch, coffee table, floor cushions—looked as if it had been plucked and dropped from a Pottery Barn catalog. Tanya, sitting uncomfortably in black velour loungewear on the hard sofa, looked as if she'd been plucked and dropped here, too.

I watched her gobble down her cake, licking the tips of her fingers like a greedy child, and wondered who she *really* was. One moment she was a little girl, trying hard to please everybody, including me, with her deferential "Mrs. Jones" this and "Mrs. Jones" that, begging to be protected from whatever or whoever threatened her. The next she was the sexy kitten purring and curled up on somebody's lap—anybody's lap—if you believed those photographs.

She seemed to have no glimmer at all, nothing like the ones that could be easily read on Vinton or Louella. Yet as Aunt Phoenix said, just because I didn't see it, didn't mean it wasn't there. The glimmer was who I thought a person *truly* was; that was what counted. I knew nothing about Tanya, not how old she was, where she'd grown up, how long she had worked at Risko Realty, how she was tied to Harley Wilde. I knew from the pictures that she'd been friends with Louella once but not what had happened to that friendship. What did Bertie think of her? She must have known they knew each other. What would she think of those pictures? I remembered Louella's words the day Charlie was killed, about not wanting to talk before *certain* people came back. Those certain people were in that photograph, except the one man who stood off by himself.

"I feel like a pig, eating this cake all by myself," Tanya said as she cut herself another slice. "Aren't you going to have some more?"

I took a tiny bite. I'd tasted so much batter and frosting during the making, the cake itself was an afterthought. I hadn't made this one in a while, and my mind strayed to Lennox Royal for an instant. If he thought that 7-UP cake was good, wait until he took a bite of this one. I'd need to call it something different, though, leave out the wicked, decadent stuff. I snapped myself back to Tanya, took another bite.

"Why do you think people believe you killed your husband?" I asked. Her face went blank. "That's what you said in the office today, don't you remember?"

She abruptly stood up, brushed imaginary crumbs from her black velour, and went into the kitchen and returned with a quart of milk. "I said all that?" she asked, sitting back down.

"Yes. Because of you and Harley or Dennis, you said. Then Dennis walked in."

"Oh yeah." She turned her attention back to the cake.

"Did you make it from a mix? Pa Nettie, my pretend grand-father, always used Duncan Hines. He said it was the best."

"No. Homemade. Why are you scared of him?"

"Who?'

"Dennis."

"I'm not scared of him or anybody else," she said with a hint of defensiveness that told me she was lying. "I've been scared of only one man in my life and now that man's dead. I talked to Harley today," she added, plucking it out of no-where, then nibbling at the cake like a mouse, bit by bit.

"What did he say?" I took the bait.

She sighed deep, no little girl, no sexy kitten, but straight-forward talk, which I hadn't seen before. "He's scared. The cops think he killed Charlie."

"Do you think he did?"

"No."

"Did *you* kill Charlie?" The question begged to be asked. Her response surprised me.

"What do you think?" Her eyes turned bright with some-thing I hadn't seen before. Defiance? Where did it come from?

"I don't know, but you did say that everyone thought you did." She looked at me strangely, then gave a full-throated, grown-woman laugh, not the girlish giggle. I laughed with her.

"What would you do if I told you I had?"

"Run out of here as fast as I could!" I passed it off as a joke but wondered if she was telling the truth. Something was gnawing at her. I knew that even without the gift.

"Charlie used to beat me sometimes. Did you know that?"

"I guessed it."

"Was it that obvious? No, don't tell me. Mr. Nosy Vinton Laverne, who thinks he knows everything about everyone but doesn't know squat."

"I saw the bruises on your arms and back when you took off your jacket at the memorial."

She nodded slowly, acknowledging the truth. "Harley told me it didn't do any good to try to cover them up, that I should let the world see them for what they were, but I was too embarrassed. Ashamed." She smiled a crooked smile that wasn't one. I'd seen it before on the world-weary, scared faces of the women I'd worked with in the shelter.

"The shame was his, not yours," I said.

"Yeah, right. But it still hurt like hell. He knocked me around when he got mad, which was all the time. On my legs he used a belt but usually it was his hands. He had big hands for such a small man. Did you ever notice that? Ham hands on a pork chop man. It wasn't bad at first. I put up with him because of the stuff I got from him. Living here. The clothes. The money. I should have killed him, though," she added, her voice surprisingly thoughtful.

"But you didn't."

"I left it to somebody else to do."

Her words stayed put, hovering above us, me questioning Harley again, wondering what, if anything, he had to do with Charlie Risko's death, until she broke the silence.

"I hired a lawyer for Harley so he won't have to stay in jail until his trial comes. He's a good one, one of the best in the state. That was one thing Charlie always said: A good lawyer will get you out of anything at all, even if you did it."

"I've heard that, too." Charlie Risko and Lennox Royal had something in common.

She opened the carton of milk and took a swig. "Harley said some good things about you, Mrs. Jones. Said you got some stuff out of his apartment for him. His mama's Bible and her stupid bird. His mama didn't like me much. I didn't like her much either. I don't like birds or other people's mamas, except for one. Louella's mama. I like her."

"Do you know when Harley is getting out?"

"Soon as he can. He doesn't have any priors. I thought he did, but he didn't."

"Why did you think he had priors?"

"Something Charlie said, but he was probably lying. He lied a lot about people." She yawned, covering her mouth like a child. "All that chocolate must have made me sleepy. Sugar slump, Pa Nettie used to call it."

"You mentioned Pa Nettie before. He's your grandfather or father?"

"Pretend grandfather. He wasn't blood."

"He must have been a pretty good grandpa, warning about chocolate and baking cakes. Did he raise you up?"

"I guess you could say that. My mother died when I was born. Nobody would tell me how. I figured I must have killed her when I came out because nobody wanted to talk about it."

"But you don't know that," I said, noting the shadow that crossed her face.

"My grandma took me in but she was sick with cancer. Pa Nettie was her boyfriend. My grandma was white like my mother. I think maybe my father was black, but I don't know. Most people think I'm mixed, but you can't look at me and tell. Do I look mixed to you? I hope I am so I can have some part of Pa Nettie inside me, even though he wasn't blood."

"Everybody is mixed with something, so you're a little bit of everybody," I said, and her quick smile told me it was something she needed to hear.

"Pa Nettie being black didn't sit well with my grandma's people, so when she died, he took me in because they didn't want to see me. He raised me the best way he could. Died when I was sixteen, then I was on my own. I think part of me has always been looking for a mama." I saw a glimmer then but just for a moment, not as powerful as Louella's but sorrowful. About his death. Memories that still haunted her.

"You were lucky to have him."

She found and settled into a soft spot on the hard sofa, pulled her feet up, getting comfortable. "Maybe Pa Nettie might have been the start of my thing for old men. They never repulsed me like they do some girls," she said and chuckled. I thought about that needy child tucked inside her. "After he died, his woman friend was cruel to me. I didn't mean anything to her and she put me out. Then me and Harley got to be friends. He was the first man near my own age I'd ever been with. Same pretty brown skin like Pa Nettie, which is probably why I fell in love with him like I did. Then he introduced me to Charlie and that was that."

"Harley introduced you to your late husband?"

"It happened fast between us, me and Charlie. I guess age and money beat out looks and love, right?" She spoke offhandedly, as if it were funny. Repulsed by her words, I pulled slightly away.

"It's late, time for me to call it a night," she said, even though it was just going on ten. I assumed she was expecting company, Dennis Lane, probably, which made me ask her, "What's going on with you and Dennis?"

"Good friends. Mrs. Jones, you're as bad as Bertie, worried about me and Dennis."

I knew they were tied in ways I didn't yet understand. I wondered what Bertie knew. "When I was at Harley's place getting the bird and his mother's Bible, I found some photographs of you with Harley, Dennis, and Louella. They were taken in this room. There was money lying all around. Looked like you all were at a party. You-all have known each other a long time, right? How did you meet?"

She sat straight up, suddenly wide-awake. "You were snooping around Harley's private things?"

"They were on the bookshelf and when I got a book about the bird, they fell into my lap." Almost the truth.

"Why the hell did he save them?" she said, more to herself than to me. "They were a joke. Dumb kid stuff."

"They must have meant something to him."

"Why don't you ask him?"

"I will when I see him, but what were you all involved in?"

"Meaning who?"

"The people in the picture. You all looked young, real young. Except your husband."

"Late husband," she said, more loudly than she needed to. "Whatever it was, it's over now. Charlie's death put an end to *all* of it." She abruptly picked up the cake, her plate, and milk carton, and left, ending any other questions I might have had, and took everything into the kitchen. "Do you mind showing yourself out, Mrs. Jones?" she called out in her little-girl voice.

I didn't know what to make of Tanya Risko. Nor Harley Wilde, for that matter. Was I on a fool's errand, looking for a truth I refused to see? I needed to talk to Harley as soon as I could; he owed me some answers, if for no other reason than rescuing his noisy little bird. Tanya had said she didn't know when Harley would be out. Another question for Lennox Royal, who was rapidly becoming my source for anything to do with the law.

Before I went to bed that night, I wrote up a new list of D&D dessert offerings, adding D&D's Cinnamon Crust Apple Pie, Chock Full O' Nuts Chocolate Chip Cookies, and Chocolate Lover's Chocolate Cake (formerly the Wickedly Delightfully Decadent Devil's Food Cake). The next morning when I dropped off the list, Lennox ordered two cakes, chocolate and 7-UP, and a dozen cookies. He also gave me what he called a generous "good faith" deposit that I gladly accepted.

"What's going on with your friend in jail? Did he get a

good lawyer?" he asked as he poured us both coffee, every bit as strong as I remembered. "Need some cream?"

I poured in half a cup, turning mine into a *milky* café au lait. "Yeah, that's what I heard."

"Is he getting out?" A shadow of concern darkened Lennox's eyes.

"I think he is, but I'm not sure when," I said, wondering about the shadow I'd just seen.

"If he doesn't have priors the lawyer will get him out right after he's arraigned, but they'll put an ankle restraint on him so they can check on him when they want to. The problem is, those things aren't impossible to disengage from. If he gets out of it, he could be halfway to Canada before they find him. Just remember what I said about being careful. He may be your friend, but you don't know what is in his heart," he added, then changed the subject. "So when can I get those cakes? That so-called sample 7-UP cake you brought disappeared out of here so fast I didn't get another slice."

"I'll try for a day or two, if I can."

"That's a lot of baking."

"I love to cook. It keeps me company. Better than my cat, Juniper. Yes, Lennox, I'm a lonely old lady with a cat. And a bird, at this point."

"I don't know about being lonely, but you're certainly not an old lady by any stretch of the imagination," he said with an appreciative grin. "I get the cat, but the bird? Aren't they natural enemies? You don't strike me as a bird kind of lady."

"I'm keeping him for a friend . . . in jail," I added.

He rolled his eyes but didn't say anything.

"I know what you mean about feeling lonely. My daughter helps me fight the blues. I don't know what I'd do without her." He smiled but there was a trace of pain in his eyes, reminding me that it couldn't be easy raising her alone.

Georgia, overhearing our conversation, came over and

gave him a loose hug. "I keep telling this stubborn man that there's always a place for him at my table. Him and his daughter."

He gave her a thin smile, as if he'd heard it before. "And when you see how much we eat, you'll wish you hadn't offered," he said good-naturedly.

"This man thinks he's the only one who can cook around here. By the way, you're quite the baker," she said with a side glance and forced smile.

"Thanks. It's a good way to make some extra money," I added, knowing as I said it that there was no reason to tell her my business, except I felt like putting her at ease. I wasn't sure why. It's one of the things that annoy me about myself, always needing to put somebody at ease. She gave me a half smile and left to wait on a customer at one of the tables on the other side of the room.

"Maybe you should take her up on it," I said when Georgia was out of earshot.

"Yeah, maybe someday I will," he said without enthusiasm.

"Something good might come of it."

He gave a noncommittal shrug before awkwardly changing the subject. "Who got him the lawyer? That's usually a clue to somebody who knows something they shouldn't."

"The widow."

"The widow of the murdered man?"

I nodded.

"That puts an interesting spin on things. Were they involved before, your friend and the widow?"

"Yeah, I think they were."

He paused for a moment. "You have a tender heart, Odessa Jones, I know that much about you. They might have done this thing together. Maybe he killed the husband out of jealousy or because he didn't like the way he treated her or she convinced him to do it. I don't know, and neither do you. I would hate to think you've been roped into believing this man is innocent when he's not."

"Yeah, me too," I said reluctantly.

"Look, I don't mean to sound like an overprotective daddy, but maybe somehow you could arrange for us to meet. I was a cop for a long time and have a sixth sense about people."

I didn't think that would happen, but if it did, I hoped Lennox's "sixth sense" was better than mine. Settling comfortably on my counter stool, I thought about Harley's glimmer, dismissed it, thought about it again. "I honestly don't know what to make of Harley Wilde," I finally said.

"Keep your wits about you. Keep your eyes wide open. Promise me that."

"With a cherry on top," I said, and being *close* to the same generation, we both chuckled.

Chapter 10

I baked Vinton Laverne's Chock Full O' Nuts Chocolate Chip Cookies (praying he wasn't allergic to nuts) and a dozen for Lennox's daughter, let them cool, and stored them in my special cookie tins, which made me remember the day Darryl and I had bought them. It was a terrible afternoon, cold and rainy. We'd found shelter in a mom-and-pop store filled with everything from ginger beer to cast-iron skillets in need of seasoning. Darryl spotted them pushed behind a shelf heavy with rice, black beans, and lentils. They were stenciled with red and yellow tulips sprouting leaves and tendrils, an old-fashioned style that made them look more expensive than they were.

We bought as many as we could carry, stuffing them into the totes we'd brought and plastic shopping bags from the store. They'd be our unique cookie tins, we decided, filled with fancy selections of D&D cookies for particular repeat clients. By the time we left, the rain had stopped, the sun had come out, and the whole world was bright with sunshine. Then the rain started again, a sudden downpour that left us soaked as we made our way home. Darryl built a fire, and we cuddled in front of it, cozy, warm, and grateful to be home, grateful for each other.

I'd never used them. Never wanted to. I knew what Darryl would say, that they were meant to be filled with good things to eat, that it was silly to save them. What was I waiting for? He wasn't coming back. Our memories were what were important; nothing could take them away. These silly containers were just taking up space on the shelf. *Come on, Dess. So all you've got to remember me by is a cookie tin?* I smiled when I heard his voice in my mind. It was time to let go. Lena would love the tin. She loved intricate patterns and would be fascinated by the design.

Between baking, double-checking Parker's cage, and feeding and watering both animal tenants on my way to work, I was late.

"You looking for Vinton? Left early to work at home. If you sniff hard enough you can still smell that body oil. He left you this." Bertie handled me an unsealed envelope. I'd been worried about her mood and was relieved to see she hadn't lost her spiteful sense of humor.

"You doing okay?" I asked as I skimmed Vinton's note.

"Said you needed to read it before tonight. I guess you're still making those cookies and things for folks, right? To drop off at their houses and stuff, right? You got some for me?" I studied her closely, sure she'd had something to do with Harley's arrest. At the bar after the funeral she'd practically accused him of killing the man. She'd obviously read Vinton's note, which annoyed me, but I decided not to mention it.

"You wanted a cake, right?" She must have forgotten she'd told me.

"Yeah, that's right. I need something sweet to get me through everything that man's death has done to me," she said, sounding like the old Bertie.

"Done to you? What about Charlie? The man is dead!"

She took off her glasses and scowled at me. "You know what I mean, Dessa. Don't be cute."

I sat down beside her and unpacked my things. "How is Louella doing?"

"The same," she said, her face turning hard.

I switched on my laptop and waited a minute, then asked, "Did you know that Louella and Tanya knew each other before she married Charlie?"

"Yeah," she said, putting her glasses back on again and glancing away before I could see what was in her eyes.

"You know they arrested Harley for killing him."

"I'm not surprised."

"Really?" I said, even though I knew my suspicions about why the cops had picked him up were right. "Do you think he did it?"

"Somebody did. May as well have been him," she said offhandedly.

Later that evening sitting with Vinton Laverne in his living room I got nearly the same response when I mentioned the news about Harley to him. "No surprise there," he said, scrunching his lips. He took a gulp of the gin and tonic he was drinking and nibbled on a chocolate chip cookie. "Gin and chocolate, you should try it. They're good together."

"I'll stick to milk."

He chuckled to himself but there was no joy in it. "You sound just like Stuart. Only grown man I ever knew who liked to drink milk. Hell, he'd have it with steak if I'd let him."

I sank into the large overstuffed couch covered in gauzy blue-and-white chintz. The cream-colored walls were filled with large and small photographs of Vinton and Stuart, taken both alone and together. Mementos of their relationship were everywhere: jeweled seashells from Atlantic City and Bermuda, small and large crystals, souvenir cushions tossed on the matching side chairs and couch. But despite the clutter, the apartment had an old-fashioned, homey feel to it. More *House & Garden* than Pottery Barn.

He eased back on the couch where we sat, and grinned. "We bought this place together a few years before he died. He inherited that huge, beautiful apartment where the widow lives now. It should have gone to Stuart, but Charlie grabbed it quick, and Stuart didn't care. He let him have it. Anything to keep the peace."

"This is a beautiful place, too. Makes you feel . . . welcome," I added, unable to think of a better word.

"If you like chintz, and Stuart *loved* chintz. Me, not so much. I hated it at first. I like my roses and vines in a vase, thank you, but there was no arguing with him. Now this room is the most precious thing in the world to me. Like this smoking jacket. This belonged to Stu. Who the hell wears smoking jackets?" He grabbed my hand so I could feel the blue brocaded silk, then he took another swallow of gin and tonic followed by a cookie. "Did I hear that you lost your husband, too?"

"He died a year ago," I said quietly. I still found it hard to say. Vinton raised his drink in a toast, which made me smile.

"I don't know who he was, but he must have been a good man to have married somebody as sweet as you."

"How do you know I'm so sweet?"

"The dimples."

"I got them from my mother. They make me look sweeter than I am."

"Nice place to get them, from your mother. But you must have gotten other stuff, too." I nodded noncommittally, unwilling to go into the "other stuff."

Vinton continued, "All I got from mine was a nasty temper, quick wit, and a string of real pearls that I sold shortly after she died. I'm sorry about that now. But that was something.

I should be happy for that," he added with a self-deprecating smile. "But looks are important although they can be deceiving. Take the folks at work."

"Have anybody in mind?"

"Well, Juda, for one, but I love her like a sister so I don't want to go into that. I'll say one thing, though. Nearly everybody in that place has a look that deceives. Your dimples are the least of them." He took a gulp of gin, opened a silver cigarette case on the coffee table, and lit a Newport. "Another bad habit Stuart dragged me into, bless his heart. You're not allergic to cigarettes, are you?" His eyes filled with concern.

"Depends on who's doing the smoking," I said, which was the truth. "My aunt Phoenix occasionally lights up something and definitely inhales. I've never asked her what. At her age she can smoke or drink anything she wants to, including her cherry brandy."

He laughed out loud, a good-natured guffaw. "Cherry brandy? Sounds like my kind of girl. I'd like to meet her someday."

I paused for a moment then said, because it was true, "I would like to have known Stuart. Can you tell me about him?"

He went to the mantle filled with candles and photographs and picked up one of a muscular man with longish blond hair mixed with gray who was sitting at what looked like a bar in a hotel. "Here he is. He was a good looker, that was for sure. I took this in Atlantic City. We used to go there all the time before it got seedy. Won a lot of money, lost a lot of money, had a lot of fun. I haven't been back since he died. Too much pain, even now. I can't face it. I know that."

I nodded in agreement because I knew what he meant.

"You know what I said about looks being deceptive? When I first saw Stu I didn't know he was gay. I knew I was, and proud of it, too. Things are better these days, but in my age group there are still . . . shall I say, challenges," he said with a sad half smile. "I was gay, proud of it, wasn't sure he was. He hadn't come out to his family yet. When we fell in love, I felt like I'd died and gone to heaven. We both did." He took a drag off the cigarette, then snubbed it out, squeezed his eyes closed.

"But Stu always had a darkness in him. Got depressed easily. Most times I could pull him out of it; sometimes I couldn't and that scared me. Maybe because he was hiding such an essential part of who he was from everybody except me. But Charlie knew and kept finding ways to undermine him and use it against him. Charlie knew his father wouldn't have approved of us. But that wasn't the worst of it. Nothing like the worst."

Vinton's thoughts had gone back to Stuart, as mine so often went to Darryl. I let them go where they would, just waiting to hear whatever he wanted to tell me, and when he was ready he did.

"The worst was after his father died. The company went to Stu, like it should have. Like the apartment, like everything else his father valued. His dying words to Stu were about how much he trusted him. Old Man Risko knew his younger boy wasn't worth spit. The only thing he cared about was Risko Reality, which he'd built up from what his father had left him. And he left it to Stuart, but Charlie still had a piece of it because he was his son. And that was the worst of it."

Vinton looked directly at me then, letting me see something within him that I knew few people had seen. It was anger, unbridled and terrifying, that he kept well concealed.

"Charlie Risko killed his brother as sure as I'm sitting here drinking this gin. That's what happened to the love of my life. Charlie Risko killed him. I should have killed him to pay him back for that. But somebody else stepped in, did what I should have done, and I'll thank him till my dying day.

Charlie Risko deserved to die. Especially on the anniversary of his brother's death."

The glimmer that always hung around Vinton grew darker as he spoke. Angrier, scarier, as if his words were giving it power, and the words were nearly the same as Tanya's, that someone else had stepped in, taken care of things for him.

He mixed himself another gin and tonic. I told him to pour one for me, too. Red wine is usually the extent of my alcohol intake, but I knew we were headed into the kind of conversation where he didn't want to drink alone. I took a swallow. The gin went straight to my head. He peeked at me and chuckled.

"I like them strong," he said.

"I can see that." I took another sip. "Strong but good."

"You can get away with a lot when you sell real estate if you know how to stretch the boundaries, how to take a company's good name and milk it for all it's worth, turn it into dirt," he said.

I waited until he finished his drink and made himself another. I sipped at mine. "Did Charlie turn it into dirt by himself?" I said.

He looked at me for a moment, then grinned. "You're not as naïve as you look, Miss Dimples, are you?"

"I found some photographs in Harley's apartment that . . . puzzled me."

"Harley's apartment? What kind? Who was in them?" he asked, genuinely curious.

"I'd rather not say," I replied, then added, "he wanted me to get some stuff while he was in jail."

"Another one who has a deceptive look," he said, half smiling. "Let me just say this: Charlie Risko was a corruptor of innocents. But he wasn't the only one."

I nodded as if I knew what he was talking about, but actually I had no idea.

"Okay. Let me tell you who was in them. Harley, Dennis, Louella, bless her soul. The widow, Avon . . ."

"Who was Avon Bailey?"

"One of the innocents. Him and Juda," he said, finishing off his drink.

"Juda?"

"Actually not so innocent. She knew all Charlie's schemes. That was what she had on him and why she stayed connected. It meant something to her. Not much to him, though. He was that kind of man."

"What were his schemes?"

"They were cons, baby. He ran con games. The kind you need fresh faces for. Fresh young faces and firm young bodies that can fool you. Deceive you."

"Like Louella and Tanya. And Harley . . . ," I added.

He smiled a sly smile. "Harley knew the young faces because he was young himself. I'll leave it at that. The scams? Stu explained them to me on his better days. How Charlie dragged his daddy's business into the mud. Risko Realty had been around for three decades. People in town knew the old man and how honest he was. You saw that in the church, remember? When you said that name, Risko Realty, folks believed your words, knew you were honest.

"I'll tell you this: Having a pretty face doing your bidding makes it easier to get away with things. Especially when that pretty face doesn't know the half of what she's doing."

"And Juda knew all about that?"

"Charlie shared secrets with her. One little bit of him she held on to. Sad, isn't it?"

I nodded that it was. My sense of her, thanks to the gift, was right. She held secrets but they didn't belong to her. "Why did everybody stay with him so long?" I asked the question that had been on my mind since my first day. "Why didn't they leave? Why didn't you leave?"

"Charlie Risko had something on everybody," he said after a pause. "Every line you crossed, every mistake you made. Everybody had a secret, and Charlie knew them all. But the thing about lying, it drags you down with it. You may not have meant any harm, but when you do harm you pay with a bit of your soul, and that's what Charlie made people do, like my Stu. He paid with a bit of his soul. Those pictures you found? Charlie had copies, I'll bet. Of those and more."

"And what about you? After Stu died, why did you stay?"

He took in a breath and let it out slowly. "I wanted to find a way to get even. To make him pay for Stu's death."

"Did you find it?"

"Too late now," he said with a shrug and a cackle.

"And Dennis Lane?"

"You got to ask Dennis Lane about Dennis Lane. I try not to mess with him."

I left it there, watching Vinton sip his drink, nibble his cookie, his mind gone to other things. I wondered if he was thinking of the schemes or of Avon . . . the kid he wouldn't mention, or maybe about Stuart and how sad life was without him.

"You ever get so sad you wish you could stop living?" he said, breaking the silence. "You know what I'm talking about, because you've been through it. You ever get that sad?"

His anguish touched me more deeply than I wanted it to, and I answered him quickly because I knew that nothing would do but the truth.

"I loved Darryl so much that there are times I keep on living, trying to be happy, because I know he would want me to. Sometimes it's just making it through the day. Get home. Play with our cat. Have a glass of wine. But it gets better."

"Not for me. I wish I had the courage that Stuart had, to do what he did." The glimmer grew even darker than before, and I thought about alcohol and sorrow and what it could drive you to.

"I go to places that I know he loved, where we were happy together. Sometimes that helps," I said. I reached out, took his hand, held it until he pulled it away.

"Thanks for trying, Miss Sunshine," he said after a minute.

"Miss Sunshine!"

His smile was quick and sly. "Just felt right saying it."

The glimmer had faded back to its usual gray, still there but not gone. He seemed better, calmer. I hoped my visit had done him some good.

"Let me pack these cookies up and give back this beautiful tin."

"It comes with the cookies."

"It's too pretty just to give away."

"Not to those who deserve it," I said, which was the truth, because he did.

He nodded as if he understood, then added with a slit of a smile, "You don't know me quite as well as you think you do, Mrs. Dessa Jones." I caught a whiff of nutmeg as he closed the door, and that, along with his parting words, haunted me all the way home.

Chapter 11

I tucked Vinton Laverne's final words where all disturbing thoughts go when I bake—midway between the measuring and mixing. I had cakes to make before tomorrow morning, and it was late. I took eggs out of the refrigerator, softened butter in the microwave (praying it wouldn't liquefy), and combined all the tasks I could—greasing the cake pans, measuring the flour, sugar, baking powder, baking soda, and cocoa (for the chocolate cake), putting all the ingredients into separate bowls. Luckily, both cakes could bake at 350 degrees (although I had to keep an eye on the 7-UP cake). By midnight, everything was done. I set the cakes out to cool. I'd make time to frost and glaze them in the morning. When I dropped into bed, I was dead to the world. Nearly dead to the world.

Thoughts of Vinton, along with that whiff of nutmeg, and of Tanya, obviously hiding something, wouldn't let me go. Vinton's tone had been mocking, mean-spirited, verging on angry, when I left him. As for Tanya, she was clearly waiting for somebody with whom to share the rest of that cake—and something else. Dennis Lane. I should try not to mess with him, Vinton had said. What did he mean by that? Except for Juda, Lane was the one member of the staff I'd had few dealings with. I'd need to talk to him sooner or later, but the more I learned about the man, the more I dreaded being alone with him. More problematic, I'd need to convince him to talk to me. He wasn't the kind of man to be tempted by chocolate cookies or a cake. It might be wise to ask Aunt Phoenix for an herb or spell for protection; I needed a powerful one, although I knew she'd be suspicious since I'd never asked before. Then there was Miss Juda Baker, one of Vinton's innocents. Innocent of what? And Avon Bailey, whose name kept popping up.

I drifted off to sleep with his name on my mind, except "Avon" didn't take the form of a person but of a beauty product, the kind my mother used to sell. When I was a kid, she was the Avon lady, and I was proud of her. She'd let me try her sample lipsticks—pale pink and crimson red—nail polish and colognes that smelled like roses, always special to me because of her name.

In my dream, glass bottles of Avon products were stacked in front of me in a sparkling, crystal tower. Suddenly, it crashed to the floor. The shattering glass woke me with a start. From somewhere in the distance, a creature began squawking like a bird, then mewling like a cat. Half awake, I realized what had happened. I bolted into the guest room, expecting the worst . . . and nearly got it. I should have known the gift would have its way with me one way or another, that dreaming about my mother would foretell some future event. As Aunt Phoenix might say, I didn't listen.

The crash was Parker's cage hitting the floor. Juniper, the source of the meowing, paced guiltily in front of it; the cage door swung open ominously.

"Juniper! Where is Parker? What did you do with him? Where is he?" I yelled as if he could actually answer me. He gazed up at me, his huge green eyes staring innocently.

"What am I going to tell Harley?"

Juniper blinked once, then again, as if to say, "Your problem, not mine!"

"Bad cat! Bad, bad cat!" I screamed, as though that would actually make a difference. Aunt Phoenix's warning came back: Cats will be cats and birds will be birds. I should have listened. Yet again.

"I'm sorry, Parker. I'm so sorry!" I bawled into the empty room. As I looked around the room, I realized there were no feathers, bones, or other telltale signs of a dead bird. Then I heard Parker, perched on the edge of a ceiling light fixture, squawking away. I shoved Juniper out of the room, placed Parker's cage back where it belonged, and checked the parakeet books on how to get a runaway bird back into his cage.

I knew that Parker liked apple slices. One of the books suggested varying his diet, and I'd tried it the night before. I placed a slice in his cage, made sure the door was wide open, then sat at the desk, pretending to ignore him. He flew around a few times, perching on the window shade, on the edge of my desk, then landed in his cage and began nibbling the apple. I snapped the door closed.

There was no way, of course, to know exactly what had happened. I was just grateful the bird was safe. I knew I'd need to find another place for him until Harley could take him back—hopefully, he'd be able to. There was only one person I could count on. I called her early the next morning

"Didn't I tell you about cats?" Aunt Phoenix said when I explained my situation. "I don't like birds, but you're in luck. Your aunt Celestine is here, and she's always been partial to them. Bring him over, drop him off, and spend some time with us. And she has an important gift for you," she added.

"A gift?"

"I told you before that she wanted to see you."

"What kind of gift could she possibly have for me after all these years?"

"You'll find out soon enough."

I had to get Parker to safer territory. Going to visit Aunt Phoenix would also give me a chance to get more information about the glimmer—and the gift. Maybe even get some help with protective herbs or spells. Talking with two peculiar aunts was bound to be better than talking to one. I couldn't remember ever meeting Celestine, although I must have at some point. I'd frost and glaze the cakes, then drop them off with Lennox Royal later this afternoon.

Aunt Phoenix opened the door before I rang the bell. As usual. "Where's the bird?" She got right to the point.

"In the car."

"You left him flying around the car?"

"He's in a cage."

"What do I know? Better bring him in so he can get used to his new *temporary* home," she said, emphasizing the word *temporary*.

"Don't worry, as soon as the owner is able to take him back he will," I said, heading to the cage before she could ask more questions. Besides, she probably knew anyway.

I hauled Parker, squawking loudly and flapping his wings, into the living room, placing him along with his food, books, and toys on a desk in the corner of the room.

"Does he have a name?"

"Parker."

"Noisy little something, isn't he?"

"You kind of get used to it."

"He won't be here that long."

"Parker will be here as long as he needs to be," said a soothing, commanding voice from the kitchen. Aunt Celestine entered, carrying a tray laden with three cups and a pot of what smelled like rose hip tea. She placed the tray on the coffee table, then turned to Parker.

"Calm down and hush," she said; Parker calmed down and hushed.

If I hadn't known these two women were sisters, I wouldn't have believed it. Where Aunt Phoenix's eccentricities drew attention whenever she left the house, there was nothing odd about Aunt Celestine—at least in appearance. Her neat pink shirtwaist dress was a startling contrast to Aunt Phoenix's blousy white kaftan, as was her dark brown hair permed into tight, old-fashioned curls. Her flawless makeup, probably applied early that morning, brought to mind a woman in an AARP ad for successful retirement.

"I'm your aunt Celestine," she said in a prim, well-modulated voice. "I mostly remember you as a child, Odessa. It's been years since we've seen each other." She gazed at me for a moment, then grabbed me and delivered an awkward hug. "You have Rosemary's sweet spirit."

"And *she's* got the gift," said Phoenix. "Just doesn't use it like she should."

"She will, so hush!"

"That hush mess doesn't work with me. I'm not one of your damned birds," Phoenix said.

"Not yet, anyway," said Celestine. Phoenix threw her a scalding glance, then both women broke out laughing.

I realized this must be kind of a long-standing joke between them that I wasn't meant to understand. Was Celestine the mother of those distant cousins Aunt Phoenix often talked about? If that were the case, they wouldn't be "distant." There were still far-reaching branches of my unconventional family I had yet to meet. For better or worse.

"Have some tea, darling," Celestine said as she poured me a cup. It had been years since I'd been called "darling," which made me feel like a six-year-old child.

"Some for you, too?" she asked Phoenix, who shook her head, took out her flask, and poured a shot of cherry brandy into her cup.

Aunt Celestine scowled. "A bit early in the day for that, isn't it?"

"Mind your own business, sister of mine, and I'll mind mine," Phoenix replied in a singsong voice as she settled back in her chair and began to rock.

The three of us sat sipping our drinks, the silence growing heavy yet filled with emotion I didn't understand. I wondered how long Aunt Celestine's visit would be, and why it had taken her so long to visit. Or maybe she had come before, and Phoenix simply hadn't mentioned it. It was hard to tell with my aunt, who always told less than she knew. The sisters seemed so focused on their thoughts, I wondered if there was a silent conversation going on between them that I couldn't hear. Where had my mother, the baby of the family, fit within all this? I suspected she was closer to Celestine, who was nearer her age, but dependent on Phoenix, who was strong enough for both of them. What secrets did they share?

Aunt Phoenix broke the silence, reigniting my suspicion that she could read my mind. "One of the joys of having Odessa so near is that she reminds me so much of the baby," she said to Celestine.

"The baby being Rosemary. You know she didn't like being called that."

"I know, but Odessa is her baby, even though she's a grown woman now. And Rosemary was mine."

"Ours," said Celestine.

"And this one has her sweet spirit," Aunt Celestine said again.

It was time to remind the two of them that I was here—and alive—and not a *darling* child waiting her turn to talk.

I took a sip of tea. "I need to ask you both some questions.

About our family's gift," I said firmly. "I need to know more about the glimmer. And I need you to tell me the names of herbs that can protect me from evil."

They glanced at each other, then back at me. "Odessa, we've talked about the glimmer before. There's not much more *I* can tell you," Phoenix said patiently, like an adult talking to a willful child.

"But there has to be more. Maybe Aunt Celestine . . ."

Celestine held up her hand as if stopping my question. "Phoenix is the glimmer girl, darling. She has always been better at reading and seeing them than me. Smells are my thing. Sounds, sensations. I understand that you can smell. You may have gotten a little bit of everything. She must have gotten the gifts that were supposed to go to Rosemary before she left us," she said, turning to Phoenix.

"Or maybe Rosemary was gone before she could fully learn how to use them. She was so young when she went. It came so quick, so sudden," said Phoenix.

The two were lost in their thoughts again, this time of my mother. Sorrow filled the silence, and nobody was willing to break it. I studied them both, noticing their similarities, wondering again about my mother, beloved by both, whom I'd lost before I became a full-grown woman. Aunt Phoenix had been here for me then, and now there was Aunt Celestine. Was she here to stay or would she disappear? Would she be like the gift, coming and going as she pleased?

"Exactly what evil do you need protection from?" Phoenix said. "*Who* do you need protection from?"

"I don't know yet."

"There are many protective herbs, but they're usually used in your home, to protect you from evil," said Celestine. "Lavender, sage, even oregano. Eucalyptus will purify a room. Anything from angelica to vinegar can protect a room if you spread it properly. Even black pepper . . ."

"She's not talking about protecting a room. That's taken care of," said Phoenix. She was right about that. When Darryl and I moved into our house, she'd burned so much white sage we couldn't breathe for two days. "Who do you need protection from?" she asked again, her eyes fixing hard on me.

"I don't know yet."

"That's not very helpful." Celestine stated the obvious.

The uselessness of the gift, again.

"Is it the person who killed that man you worked for? His murderer is still on the loose, right?" said Phoenix.

When I didn't answer, my aunts exchanged glances, then focused back on me.

"Time to go get it," Phoenix said to Celestine, who abruptly left the room. She came back with a pale blue stone attached to a thin leather string and handed it to me.

"It's a blue lace agate. Protects against everything. Rosemary gave it to me before she died, and I'm giving it to you. It shouldn't have taken me so long."

"I'd say it's right on time. Odessa may not have needed it until now," said Phoenix.

"Yes, I did," I said, my thoughts on Darryl again, though I doubted it would have protected me from all that happened.

The amulet was heavy; the leather string around my neck would take some getting used to, yet it was a gift I could hold and believe in.

"When you wear it, chew some cloves," said Aunt Phoenix.

"Cloves?"

"For courage. Understand that the killer will be the person you least expect it to be," she added out of nowhere. "Don't ask me how I know, but I do."

"That could be almost anyone," I said, remembering Lennox's warning. Harley had warned me, too.

"Let's leave it at that," said Aunt Phoenix, putting an end to the conversation.

Celestine went into the kitchen to make more tea. Phoenix refilled her cup with cherry brandy. Leaning back in her rocker, she closed her eyes. I checked on Parker, who was chomping on what was left of the apple slice. And Phoenix's words stayed with me. It could be any one of them. Harley, Dennis Lane, Vinton, Juda—all of them or someone I hadn't yet met.

"Try some of this." Celestine came in from the kitchen with a fresh pot of tea and poured me a cup. "I added rose petals in honor of Rosemary. It sweetens it a bit."

I sipped it, taking in the fragrance and taste, remembering my mother, made real at least for today by my aunts. "How long are you staying, Aunt Celestine?"

"Until we get on each other's nerves."

"Will you come back?"

"Up to my daughters."

"Her daughters aren't *those* distant cousins," Phoenix said, opening her eyes.

"My husband's daughters. My stepdaughters. Strangely enough, we've grown closer since their father divorced me."

"Not a nice man," Phoenix said, shaking her head. "Had a glimmer like your uncle. I warned you, Celestine."

"Yes, you did." The sisters locked eyes, sharing some secret that they weren't about to tell me.

"And after you made that bastard all that money. With *our* gift," Phoenix said, shaking her head angrily.

"He won the lottery?" I didn't hide my shock.

"No. He played the market. Bought and sold stocks and bonds with *my* advice. *I* don't play the lottery. That's Phoenix's game," Celestine said with a sniff.

"You play the market; I play the lottery. We'll see who comes out on top at the end of the year," Phoenix said, with a look at her sister that told me they'd had this discussion before.

We said good-bye then, me and my aunts, me wondering about my cousins, distant and otherwise, and feeling connected to my family in a way I hadn't been before. I touched the agate for protection, feeling my mother's strength, sensing her spirit hovering somewhere near.

Chapter 12

It was three in the afternoon by the time I made my way to Royal's with the cakes I'd promised. The place was nearly empty, except a clearly in-love couple oblivious to their surroundings and sipping coffee at one of the back tables. Lennox sat on a stool at the counter rather than behind it, leisurely reading the *Star-Ledger*. Georgia must have taken the day off. I'd worn my mother's agate in case I had to confront Georgia's evil eye. When it came down to it, she was the least of the evil folks I was bound to run into. As far as I knew, she hadn't killed anyone. Yet I was relieved she wasn't there.

Lennox grinned when I placed the desserts on the counter.

"Good to see this, better to see you," he said, opening the top of the box containing the chocolate cake. "I'm going to cut us both a slice."

"For Lena," I said, handing him the tin of chocolate chip cookies. "Tell her it comes with an automatic refill."

"Thanks for thinking of her. It means . . . means a lot to me." He stumbled over the words, trying not to show he was touched but didn't do a good job of hiding it. I knew little about his relationship with his daughter, only what Darryl had told me, and less about the challenges of dealing with a special needs child rapidly approaching adolescence. But the weariness in his face some mornings let me know it was a struggle. Darryl had mentioned that Lena was on the autistic spectrum, but I didn't know what that meant. Darryl had dozens of books about raising kids with special needs. I wondered if they might be helpful to Lennox. At some point, I'd mention them.

"She's going to love this gift box, a cookie tin, right? Hey, Lena, got a gift for you," he yelled, then went to where she was sitting with her iPhone and laptop in her corner booth. He came back in a moment, a wide grin on his face. "She was fascinated by this with all these colorful tulips and leaves. You may be refilling this box more times than you think. Thanks, Dessa, you didn't need to do this," he added, his eyes warm with gratitude.

"I have a lot of fancy cookie tins to fill. I'm happy to find someone who will love them as much as I do." I'd found a place for them. At last.

"Tea or coffee?" Lennox asked from back behind the counter, as he brought out two cups and dessert plates. "I think I'll go with the chocolate this time." He cut a generous slice for both of us.

"Tea is good."

"Sometimes it feels good just to take off that apron, such as it is, and pretend to be a customer, particularly on a lazy day," he said as he removed his apron, sat down beside me, and took a forkful of cake. "Now this is some good cake! I'm giving you a check for two more of these," he said, finishing it off. "Mrs. Dessa Jones, you are one hell of a baker! But you know that, don't you?"

"It's always nice to hear it." I nibbled a bit of my slice. After Tanya's cake and all those tastings of frosting last night, I was just about chocolated out.

"Can you handle two more? And some cookies."

"The cookies are a gift."

He hesitated for a moment as if something was on his mind. "Dessa, you've been doing a lot of cooking for this place. Are you sure this isn't too much? I can cut back."

"You have been paying for it," I reminded him, not adding that I needed the money.

"I know, but I want to do something nice for you. Try to come up with something or I'll feel bad."

It was the opening I was waiting for. "As a matter of fact there is. I want you to tell me everything you know about cons."

"Cons? Do you mean like grifters, con artists, thieves?" He didn't bother to hide his astonishment, then added, only half joking, "Why would a nice lady like you need to know about people like that?"

Male chauvinism, even wrapped in the skin of a charming man, always gets my back up. "Do you mean, like, please don't trouble your pretty little head about it, my dear? Come on, Lennox, you sound like somebody out of a 1940s movie," I said, not hiding my annoyance.

"Wow, I didn't mean to insult you," he said, his back up, too.

There was a moment of prickly silence as we both tried to figure out what to say next.

"I . . . ," he began, and I interrupted him.

"I didn't mean to snap," I said, realizing we didn't yet know each other well enough to speak so freely.

"No, I'm sorry. I just meant . . ." He paused again as if trying to figure out something to say that wouldn't offend me.

"Charlie Risko was running a con," I said, finishing his thought for him. "And that may be what killed him. I need to figure out what it was."

He sighed, and gave me a slightly embarrassed smile. "Dessa, I don't mean to be condescending, but I really think you need to back off from this mess and leave it to people who know what they're doing. Remember that promise you made me with that cherry on top?"

"I need to know the basics," I said, more firmly than I needed to.

"Okay," he said doubtfully, probably not wanting to offend me. "Ask some questions, and I'll tell you what I remember from the academy. It wasn't all that interesting to me at the time. Major crimes, homicide, larceny was where I wanted to be, but folks should know about scams to protect themselves, if for no other reason."

"Tell me what I should know, just in case," I said with a hint of mockery.

Lennox didn't take it as a joke. "Dessa, this is serious business. If you think your dead boss was running some kind of a scam that resulted in his murder, you need to tell the authorities."

"I will," I said in the most earnest voice I could manage. This wasn't the time to share my reservations about the good will of the police. "What exactly is a con?"

Lennox relaxed a minute before continuing. "Basically, con is short for confidence game. You got to get somebody's confidence to run it. There's the short con and the long con. Both have a hook, a line, and a sinker. You hook the victim, feed them a line, then sink them."

"Like fishing."

He nodded. "A short con is the easy one. Aims to take only what someone has in his wallet. Takes place in about fifteen minutes. Ever seen somebody play three-card monte? That's a short con. They do it with cards, shells, anything. It's one of the oldest scams around. Been here since the fifteenth century, and folks still fall for it."

"Well, they say a sucker is born every minute."

"Anyone can be a sucker. Believe me."

"Even you?" I didn't conceal my disbelief and chuckled out loud at the thought.

"Even me. Let me explain it. You have a con man or woman, a shill or shills—the dudes or women who work with the crook—and then you got the mark. That would be me or you."

"Me?"

"Not if you listen closely," he said with a slightly patronizing tone that I chose to ignore. "Marks are also called gulls, short for gullible."

"And you think I'm gullible."

"Dessa, I don't know you that well. I didn't say that!"

"I'm not as gullible as I may seem," I said defensively. But I wasn't so sure.

"Listen, anybody with a good heart and a trusting nature can be played. Here's the scene: Let's say you're walking down the street and there are strangers gathered around a guy playing cards on a table. You stop to watch the game. But actually, the *only* stranger is you. You are the mark. There are usually one or two shills, and they're all waiting for you. Looks like a simple game, where the player is following the queen, or something under a shell.

"You stand there, watch for a few minutes, and see how easy it looks. So one of the strangers, actually a shill, bets money, wins once, and then loses, then wins again, and you can see what the dealer is doing. And you think, I can do that. I can follow that card or that shell."

"And you bet?"

"Right. And he'll let you win once. Get a taste."

"And the shills standing around say how smart you are," I said, beginning to see how this con was played.

"Right. It goes to your head. You put some more money on the table, and you start to lose. And lose. And lose. Suddenly, somebody will say, Here come the cops! And the dealer will fold up his table. The shills will disappear into the crowd. And you're left standing there broke, feeling like a fool."

"Humph," I said. "But if you hadn't been so greedy . . ."

"Everybody is greedy. Look how many folks play the lottery."

Aunt Phoenix quickly came to mind. "Sometimes they win."

"Mostly they lose." He was wrong about that, but now wasn't the time to tell him.

"Could you use property instead of cash? Any con that Risko played would have to use property backed by Risko Realty."

Lennox turned serious as his old profession reared its head. "They're not still doing it, are they? If they are, you need to report it fast."

"No. They stopped before I started with them. Now they're legit."

"You sure about that?"

"As far as I can tell."

"I hope you're right. Well, if it involved real estate it was a long con, which takes time and people and makes more money."

"Like what?"

He picked up the newspaper he'd been reading and pointed to a headline. *Millions Lost, Yearning for Love.* "Now this is a long con. A con man finds a mark, in this case a lonely person looking for love. He convinces her that he has a way for her to make some money, a fortune maybe, but he needs a down payment to smooth the way. Like help him get out of his country, pay a lien, whatever. And he'll throw in a bit of romance to sweeten things."

"You wouldn't think somebody would be foolish enough to fall for that," I said, shaking my head in disbelief.

"Well, everyone is vulnerable and con men can smell it.

People get lonely, depressed. In this case the 'lover' needed money to get out of the country. He'll find his marks on the Internet. Put somebody else's photograph up, create a false identity, the whole bit."

"How could somebody do it in a place like Grovesville, using real estate?" I was eager to know if Vinton was right.

"Scams and cons reinvent themselves according to the con man, the scene, and the mark. I'll tell you about two I worked because somebody got killed and that fell into my purview. A con man got this widowed lady, the mark, to sign over her property, wooed her with roses and chocolate, cheap vacations (which she paid for), and introduced her to a whole new lifestyle, supplied by friends—shills—who vouched for him. When she found out what was going on after she'd lost everything she had, she shot him dead. My case then."

"At least she got even."

"That's one way of looking at it," he said with a shrug. "But she's in jail. Another one I caught. The con woman was working with a partner posing as a contractor, and she convinced the mark to have work done on his house. He thought she was in love with him and took her advice, followed her recommendation, hired her partner. The two of them convinced the mark to sign a lien that gave the contractor rights to the property if the mark didn't pay what was owed. Then they forced him to make payments they knew he couldn't afford because she knew what his finances were. When he missed two payments, they took him to court and got his house."

"Who was killed?'"

"The contractor killed the con woman who double-crossed him. She had a pang of guilt and told the mark what was going on, but then she tried to con him to get more cash. No honor among thieves."

"That's terrible!"

"Then there are phony psychics. A con woman will pretend to have ESP or special gifts, all the better to con some poor sucker into believing that he should sell his home *now* to make a big profit."

"Wow," I said. I wouldn't be telling Lennox Royal about *my* gift anytime soon.

"What makes a person a mark?"

"Anyone who relies on the goodness of the con man, and believes he won't be cheated. They use a victim's compassion against him or her, that and a person's greed and belief he can get something for nothing."

"How can you tell if somebody is a con man?"

Lennox thought for a moment. "There are all kinds of swindlers, but they are usually charming, persuasive, attractive. They need to be in order to rope somebody in. It comes down to making a victim believe in you. Be willing to make you trust him or her with your money. They're also perceptive; they can look at a mark and figure out how he can be taken. Be it for love, money, or both."

I skimmed the newspaper article Lennox had shown me earlier. "This crook took all this money from people he met on the Internet?"

"Yeah, but it's easier done in person. You think your late boss was running real estate cons?"

"Not if charm is what it takes. But he had people working for him who were charming, and he knew what was going on. Allowed his business to be used as a front," I added, remembering what Vinton had said about his brother's suicide.

"He probably kept all records and deeds. That might have been what got him killed."

"But I think he had stopped running it."

"Past is prologue when it comes to crime. Criminals don't forget slights, don't let sleeping dogs lie."

I thoughtfully sipped my tea, saying nothing. If con men

were charming and seductive, Charlie Risko was out of the running. He was about as charming as an eel. Dennis Lane, on the other hand, was charming. And Tanya Risko, and, I hated to admit, so was Harley Wilde. I didn't like to think about that, but he'd admitted as much to me when he talked in jail. Maybe I was as gullible as Lennox thought I was.

"Do you want me to look into this for you, find out what I can? I have friends on the force who owe me some favors," Lennox said. He must have noticed how quiet I'd suddenly become and how far I'd drifted from our conversation. "And that offer is still open to meet your young friend so I can get a look at him." He'd guessed about that, too; I wasn't the only one with a sixth sense.

I hesitated before I spoke. "I don't think he'll meet you, but it would be nice to get a second opinion," I said.

"We all need them from time to time. Like I keep saying, Dessa, you've got a good heart."

"I know," I said, just a bit annoyed. "There's one more thing you can help me with. A name keeps coming up, first from the officers when I had that interview and then from my coworkers. Avon Bailey. Ever heard of him?"

A pained expression settled on his face.

"Yeah. I'd have heard about the father if they had the same name. Avon Bailey Sr. haunted the precinct about five years ago, looking for his son. Said he'd disappeared. Wasn't much we could do, since his body never turned up. Just told the father we'd keep looking and we did. Was he involved with that crew?"

"He was in one of the photographs," I said without thinking and immediately regretted it.

"Photographs?" Lennox, not missing a trick, gazed at me with the eyes of an investigating detective. "You have some photographs of Avon Bailey Jr.?"

Despite everything, I wasn't yet willing to *completely* betray Harley's confidence. But an unnerving thought came and wouldn't leave. What did Avon Bailey have to do with Charlie Risko's murder? Lennox's eyes were still on me, patiently waiting for an answer. I had to come up with something. I went with the truth. Or close to it.

"I don't have them," I said quickly. "But I think they exist."

"If you know anything about them, you'd better tell the police." Lennox's serious voice said he wasn't playing. "Odessa, you don't know where this is going to go. That kid has been missing for a very long time, and if his body shows up, you don't want to be the person who had information you didn't hand over."

He watched me closely, making me feel like a suspect, but then he changed his tone. "I don't mean to scare you. Just don't borrow trouble that doesn't belong to you."

"I already have," I said, as much to myself as to him. There was genuine concern in his eyes but he didn't push it. I was grateful for that.

"Want some more tea?" It was an awkward attempt to change the subject. I appreciated that, too.

"I'd better be on my way," I said, my voice sounding smaller than I meant it to.

"He probably ran away," Lennox said after a moment. "His father threw him out of the house and that's probably what happened. From what I understand, he was a bitter, nasty man who could be violent when he drank. The kid may have run away out of spite."

"Is his father still in town?"

"Last I heard, he died destitute in an old folks' home over in Clifftown. That was a shame because his family owned a lot of property."

"They call them senior citizens' residences now," I said, gently correcting him.

"Thanks. Better keep that in mind. You never know when I'll be needing one," he joked, and things were light again between us. I wondered how long that would last.

Chapter 13

It was Monday morning. Nearly two weeks had passed since Charlie Risko's murder, and the office was still haunted. My skin crawled whenever I walked through the front door. Every now and then, I'd catch a whiff of nutmeg, thankfully not as strong as the day the murder happened, but impossible to ignore—and believe me I tried. Was it the elusive gift "speaking" again—a reminder of what had happened or a hint of what was to come? Whatever it was, I was sick of it, and as I did every morning, I took a deep, calming breath as I settled into my cubicle.

Vinton saw me and smiled. "Morning, Sunshine. Looks like you've seen a ghost," he said, adding an edge to his usual greeting. "Sunshine" had recently become his pet name of choice, and I wasn't sure how I felt about it, but it could have been worse.

"She *always* looks like she's seen a ghost," said Dennis Lane, who got nastier by the day. He'd never been friendly to me, but his words this morning delivered a particularly worrisome jolt following my talk with Lennox. "Hear anything from your buddy Harley? Heard he got out of jail with a lock on his ankle. So much for riding around on his bike." His mocking tone straightened the hair on the back of my neck.

"Leave the girl alone." Vinton came to my defense. "We all know what's going on with Harley. Just drop it."

"If you say so, old man." Passing a sneer off as a smile, Dennis turned back to his laptop, leaving me to wonder why the heck he was picking on me. I figured it had something to do with Tanya. Was he losing his grip on her?

"We've all been through enough," Vinton whispered to me. My pained expression must have given me away. "Don't let him get to you, Dessa." He paused for a moment and leaned closer. "You haven't heard from Juda, have you?"

I smiled to lighten my response. "Vinton, you know I *never* hear from Juda."

"I'm worried about her, Dessa. Something's going on."

"You think something's happened to her?" Was *that* what the nutmeg was saying?

"You never know in this damn place."

"I'm sure she's okay," I said to reassure him, but I wasn't so certain.

I hadn't seen Juda in a while but noticed then that there was something different about her. A lingering shadow surrounded her, not definite enough to be a glimmer, but grayish, almost colorless. Her eyes were empty and her face looked as if it had been hollowed out, all life sucked from it. I also noticed she was letting her hair go back to its natural color, mousy brown speckled with gray. She was the keeper of Charlie Risko's secrets. How long would she keep them?

My instincts (let's call it the gift) warned me to keep what I'd guessed about Charlie's secrets and the involvement of his coworkers to myself until I knew more. Only then would I share what I knew with Lennox and finally the police. Hopefully, it might clear Harley of murder, but I couldn't be sure. I didn't know how deeply he was tied into all that had happened but I knew he was involved. Everyone, including Dennis Lane, seemed to know more than me.

I settled back in my chair, turned on my iPhone, put in my ear buds, and looked for a free meditation app, then got tired of looking for one for which I didn't need to create an account. I closed my eyes and counted, focused on my breath, and asked myself yet again why the hell I kept coming in here. The answer was plain and simple: I had to work. I had two rental deals pending, and the possibility of a house sale (rare for me). It was a short sale, which usually involves sadness and loss, though not as bad as with a foreclosure. I'd never done a short sale before but knew I had to be registered with a legitimate Realtor.

Despite my suspicions about the place, Risko Realty maintained a legitimate presence in the market. This was officially my place of business. Besides that, my office account had been paid for when Charlie was alive, which included the right to use all the office equipment—phones, printers, stationery, exclusive websites, special forms—whatever was needed to do official business. Going to Staples was out of the question. Unless I planned to depend upon Aunt Phoenix's charity every month, I was stuck here; now was not the time to quit. I had to adjust. I pushed back in my chair, avoided looking at anybody directly, and wondered, and not for the first time, about my coworkers. Things had certainly changed yet strangely remained the same.

Bertie sat in her usual place, close to me but not too close. She said very little these days. Her smile was always weary and more subdued than I'd ever seen it. She rarely mentioned Louella or Erika, which had always brought excitement—good or bad—into her eyes. I didn't know what was going on in her family but thought it best not to push her. Sooner or later she'd share her troubles, she always did. But I missed her wisecracking banter with Vinton and sensed that he did, too. A couple of times he baited her, but she ignored his quips, focusing instead on whatever lay on her desk. I wondered if she still wanted me to come by with the pound cake, but she didn't mention it again and I knew she hated surprises. Bertie was, as my aunt might put it, a well you could easily drown in. I'd leave it to Aunt Phoenix to explain what she meant by that.

Ever since our chocolate-chip-cookie-gin-and-tonic soiree, Vinton had claimed me as his long lost sister. He greeted me each morning with some good-natured remark and had become oddly protective. On more than one occasion, he walked me to my car as if he feared for my safety. Except for the coffee and grin, he almost filled the space Harley had left, yet I still missed Harley's smile and good nature.

I kept a suspicious, wary eye on Dennis Lane. I was growing more afraid of him by the day, and hoped he didn't notice. I sensed it would feed his ego, making him grow stronger. I knew now I was in the presence of a con man, a good one, and whenever he glanced my way, I touched my mother's amulet for protection; even without chewing the cloves, it made me feel safer. He studied me curiously from time to time but mostly ignored me. I'd once seen him as attractive and charming but now saw and heard nothing but manipulation when he "charmed" his clients in his quiet, seductive voice.

I was also worried about Tanya. She thought she was tough but was actually a naïve young woman with money and a business. An easy mark for a smart con man who was trying to edge his way into her heart. I suspected that Dennis saw me as a possible threat to whatever long con he was planning to run, and I knew that would put me in danger.

Yet, day by day, Tanya was growing stronger. Free of Charlie Risko, she was winging it on her own. For one thing, she stopped wearing those clinging turtlenecks, willing to let the world witness her fading bruises. Her black leather motor-cycle pants had been replaced by jeans, still tight as a snake's skin but softened by bright-colored tees, well-tailored jackets, and stylish, expensive heels or sneakers. One morning, a fur-niture mover had noisily hauled out furniture from her office. Later that day, painters had come to "freshen up" the place, as she put it. She must have had a major delivery of office furni-ture overnight. When she called me into her office at noon, I was pleasantly surprised.

"Well, how do you like it?" She stood up and gestured around the room, her eyes big as they waited for my approval. "I've made some changes. I've been keeping the door locked because I wanted to surprise everyone after all the work was done. If you don't have plans, can I take you to lunch?" she added in the same breath, then sat back down in the new chair covered in pink damask.

Signs of Charlie Risko were nowhere to be seen. Gone was the heavy mahogany desk where he used to rest his gun beside his helmet and expensive leather gloves. There were no more tacky velvet armchairs or behind-breaking, hard-backed chairs meant to intimidate and torture those sitting before him in judgment. The room was now blazingly white, and she'd headed back to her favorite decorating source (Pot-tery Barn) for tips on office furniture. Her desk was a sleek, economical wonder of glass and steel. A white china vase waiting for a bouquet of fresh flowers was now where the helmet and gloves once sat. A chic, comfortable sofa, covered with the same fabric as her chair, was in front of her desk, inviting coworkers to lounge and chat. A matching one stood against a far wall. There was no trace left of the back door that had led to the alley. Sealed, primed, and painted, it was as if it never existed.

"Have a seat," she said, pointing to the sofa in front of her desk. "So what do you think?"

I sat on the comfortable sofa across from her, too stunned to speak.

"Cat got your tongue? What do you think?" she asked again, like an eager child.

"Took my breath away," I truthfully admitted.

She grinned, obviously pleased to hear it. "Nope, nothing left of him. He's gone for good."

"This is quite a change, Tanya, and done very quickly."

A shadow came over her face. Not quite a glimmer, I decided, simply a change that I didn't know how to interpret. "I'm glad he's dead," she said.

"Don't say that too loud," I said as neutrally as I could.

"Why not? It's the truth, and my grandpa taught me not to lie. I told you about Pa Nettie and what a good man he was. Everything Charlie wasn't. Why shouldn't I say the truth?"

"Because it's in . . . in bad taste," I said finally. I sounded like somebody's prissy aunt. "Your grandpa would probably agree."

"Talking about taste, you ready to have some lunch?" she said, gracelessly changing the subject. "When we come back, I want to show it to everybody, but I wanted to show you first," she added, like a grade-school girlfriend sharing a secret.

We ended up at a diner down the street, one of Grovesville's better-known twenty-four-hour spots. Darryl and I would come here late nights if we'd been in the city for a show or he was late getting home from work and we didn't feel like cooking. It was one of the few places where we regularly ate. The décor was classic Jersey diner. Shimmering aluminum and colored tube lights on the outside, jukebox, shiny Naugahyde seating, and bright fluorescent ceiling lights that gave everything a greenish cast on the inside. But the food was surprisingly tasty, though heavy on fat and salt. You could order a drink, which we always did. A dry martini for Darryl, a glass of red wine for me. Salad and burgers were our usual fare—reassuringly familiar. It all came back in a rush when we walked into the place. My breath stuck in my throat.

"You okay?" Tanya asked when we were shown to our seats.

"Yeah, just memories. My husband and I used to come in here nights. It makes me remember again how much I miss him."

"I wish I had someone to miss like that, good memories of a true love like that." Her wistful voice turned hard as she continued. "Me and Charlie used to come in here, too, after he'd have me out on one of those damned motorcycle rides until all times of the night."

"I thought you liked to ride!"

"No! Give me a Mercedes-Benz or BMW. We could have afforded both, but he was too cheap."

"Well, you can afford it now," I said, taking all judgment out of my voice.

"I'm selling that stupid motorcycle. If you know any-one who's interested let me know. All his motorcycle junk is gone now. That dumb helmet, his funky jacket, all of it." She paused for a moment and her lips parted in a slight, wicked smile. "I already dropped it off with somebody who actually might want his crap."

"Juda?" I took a chance.

"How did you know?"

"I'd heard that she and Charlie were together once and—"

She interrupted, another wicked little smile parting her lips. "Well, now Miss Juda Baker can have something to re-member him by. Our office is full of nosy tale-telling folks, isn't it?" she said as she went through the menu, avoiding my eyes, then put it down and looked across the table at me. "What did you hear?"

I picked up my menu, slowly went through it, pausing before I answered. "The usual stuff."

"Like what?" She glared at me now, daring me to answer.

"That they were together before you-all were."

"According to her, they were still together. At least in her head."

"You sound jealous."

"Come on! In a minute, you'll be saying I killed that fool out of jealousy. So now you think maybe I killed Charlie Risko?" she said teasingly, mocking me more than anything else.

"I don't know about that, but there was a lot of stuff going on between him and you and everybody else that I don't understand," I said, telling the truth.

"Why don't you ask Juda? She thinks she knew everything about Charlie Risko there was to know."

"And you weren't jealous?"

"Of . . . Studebaker?" She spat out Charlie's derisive nickname. "Ask her, when you get a chance."

"I think I will," I said, turning to the menu again and ending the conversation.

I ordered a tuna fish sandwich and a Diet Coke; Tanya ordered a Cobb salad and a Bud Light. I've never been good at small talk and, apparently, neither was she; we ate our meals in silence. She turned talkative on the way back to the office.

"I haven't heard from Harley, have you?" She was walking at a breakneck pace, obviously anxious to get back to show off her new office; it was all I could do to keep up with her. "After I got him that lawyer and all. You'd think at least he'd have the decency to call me, see how I'm doing. He's not answering his phone, if it's still on." She stopped for a moment, waited for me to catch up, then pouted a little pout.

"I haven't heard from him either. I need to get in touch with him about his bird," I said. I hadn't heard from Aunt Phoenix and hoped everything was okay.

"What kind of a man keeps a stupid bird, anyway?" she said, regaining her pace.

"One who loves his mama."

"I really don't give a damn about him anymore one way or other," she said. "Don't tell him I said that, though."

When we got back to the office, Tanya called everyone into her "new" space for a toast. She pulled out a bottle of surprisingly good champagne that she had on ice in the sink in her bathroom and poured us all a generous glass.

"To new times," she said enthusiastically.

"We'll wait and see," muttered Vinton, downing a second glass.

Dennis Lane gave her a mysterious smile, tossed back his drink, and headed out without saying anything else. Bertie sipped hers in thoughtful silence.

At the end of the day, Vinton walked me to my car, despite the fact that I assured him I could take care of myself. I suspected that this walk was more for him than me, his hedge against the loneliness I now knew stalked him.

"Nobody seemed too surprised by her changes," I said, making conversation.

"Nah, we all poked around in there when she took you to lunch. That office wasn't a surprise to anybody. You-all best friends now?"

I detected a note of envy in his voice and shook my head to reassure him. "She doesn't call me Sunshine," I said, and he smiled. "I wouldn't say we're friends. She's young, Vinton. Probably reaching out to me because I've had a loss like hers."

"Her loss is nothing like yours, like mine. Just watch your back. Don't trust her as far as you can throw her. You don't want to end up like her late dearly beloved."

"I don't think it was her."

"Dessa, you don't know who it was or is or might end up being. Don't take any chances. Listen, do you mind stopping by Juda's with me? I called her last night and all day today. She's still not answering her phone, and I'm worried about her."

"I don't think she'll welcome me. You-all are friends, but I don't think she likes me. She hardly speaks to me, and I'm about ready to give up on her. What's her problem?"

"There's a lot behind that, believe me. I'll make us all a gin and tonic when we get there and maybe she'll loosen up. I brought her a bottle of gin when I saw her yesterday afternoon. Good stuff, something called Ransom Old Tom. It cost a king's ransom. She promised we'd crack it open together. How about it?"

Maybe one of Vinton's powerful gin and tonics would loosen her tongue. Charlie was dead and maybe Juda would finally give up some of what she knew. It was worth a chance, especially if Vinton was mixing the drinks and urging her on. I agreed and followed him over to her place.

Juda lived in a small, plain, two-family house built in the 1930s that had probably been a one-family house once upon a time but, like so many places in Grovesville, had been divided into apartments. It wasn't grand, like some old houses, but plain and cheaply built. If her family had had money, it hadn't been put into the property. Her apartment was on the first floor, with stairs leading up to a smaller place on the second. Vinton rang the bell, then took out a set of keys when she didn't answer. When he opened the door, I gasped and stepped back. The place stank of nutmeg, but only I could smell it.

Chapter 14

"Juda? You in there?" Vinton couldn't control the panic in his voice as we stepped into Juda's first-floor apartment. He glanced from side to side in the narrow, tidy living room. "Maybe she's in the bedroom? Maybe she's still asleep. I'm going to check."

"I'll wait here," I said. Juda was dead; there was no doubt about that. My question was how did she die? Had she been shot like Charlie Risko, or was it something else? Was the same person responsible, or was I imagining more than I should, jumping ahead of myself? The smell of nutmeg was everywhere, but not as strong as it had been when we entered. Was it waiting for us to find her body, acknowledge that she had left this world? Juda was Vinton's friend, and he needed to find her. I sat on her couch, waiting for him to scream. He stumbled out of the hallway instead, his face ashen, his hands covering his mouth to keep his scream inside. "Juda's in the bedroom, Dessa. She's dead."

He slid down on the couch beside me. I took his hand, held it without speaking, and he began to cry.

"What do you think happened?" I waited a while before I asked.

"She didn't wait for me." His tone was solemn; my heart stopped.

"What do you mean, Vinton? Tell me what you mean." Did they have some kind of suicide pact?

"I should have known how sad she was. I gave her that damn bottle of gin, and she promised she would wait, crack it open with me, and I'd make us some gin and tonics." He stopped, caught his breath, and went on. "Those pills she was always taking to sleep, even before Charlie's death. I should have known after Stuart that it was more than she could handle. I let her down like I let him down. I should have known."

"Do you think she killed herself?"

"Of course she did! That bottle of gin I gave her was nearly empty. Her pills were gone. With booze and pills, just like Judy Garland. Juda loved Judy Garland. Always trying to be dramatic, like some kind of damn singer or something. With booze and pills!"

"Judy Garland died from an accidental overdose, she didn't kill herself," I said, as if that might offer solace, but it did no good. He rolled his eyes and cried again, for Stuart and Juda. Tears came to my eyes, too, because that kind of sadness touches everyone who is there. When he was finally able to speak, I suggested he call the police and tell them what had happened: That he and a coworker had come to visit his friend and found her dead in her bedroom. The two of us sat there weeping and waiting for the cops.

I was grateful they weren't the same officers who had interviewed us after Charlie Risko's murder. That would have been a mess. God only knew what they'd make of another sudden death. They were women this time, the older one around my age and the younger a rookie just hitting her twenties. Both were polite and sensitive, patiently taking our names and addresses, briefly interviewing us separately to determine our relationship to the deceased. The older one, a lean, no-nonsense woman with a hairstyle she didn't waste time on, was in charge and introduced herself bluntly: "I'm Doyle," she said. It was a down-to-earth delivery of a name that suited her well.

After thoroughly surveying the bathroom and kitchen, Doyle told us to avoid touching anything if we had to go into those rooms, but declared the bedroom strictly off-limits until her "crew" had time to go through it. When Vinton went to the kitchen for a glass of water, I pulled Doyle aside and asked if she thought it was suicide. She was surprisingly candid.

"Mr. Laverne, he's the one who called it in, right? He mentioned she'd been depressed, and signs in her bedroom point to that. But we need to wait for an autopsy to officially declare it."

"What signs?"

"Half-full bottle of gin, open bottle of Ambien, the pills gone. That combination can do you in. That's what it looks like to me." She dropped her gaze, unwilling to comment further without authority, then changed her mind. "Was the lady involved in a relationship that went sour? There were some photographs of a man in her room. One of him riding a motorcycle. A couple of them riding together. Looked like it had been a while ago. Was he her lover or something?"

"Or something," I said. Juda Baker was dead. Far be it from me to share what came down to office gossip.

"Is there a possibility that he could be next of kin?"

"He's, uh, recently deceased," I said quickly, without going into detail.

"We'll look into that. Meantime, you and Mr. Laverne should sit here on the couch until the ME comes to pick up the body. We'll collect any evidence that's there, ask you a few more questions, then you can be on your way. Okay? Who had the keys to get in?"

"Mr. Laverne did," I said, just as Vinton was joining us.

He was still shaken, his hand trembling as he put his water down on the coffee table.

"Give me your address and telephone number so I can get in touch with you if I need to. You were a friend of the deceased?"

"Yeah. We were very close." I squeezed his hand, reminding him I was there. He acknowledged me with a slight, quick nod.

"Juda Baker lived alone?" Doyle asked.

"Yes."

"You know who the landlord is, and who lives on the second floor?"

"Ms. Juda Baker did," he said, hesitated, and then added, "This was her house . . . as far as I know. She didn't rent out the second floor, kept it for storage."

As far as I know. Had Doyle picked up his hesitation?

"Storage of what?" I asked without thinking. Vinton hit my knee hard with his, like a parent reminding a child to keep her mouth shut. It was too late. Doyle picked up my question.

"Of what?"

"I'm not sure."

"Do you have the keys?"

"To the second floor? Not with me."

"As far as you know, the second floor was *only* used for storage, right?"

"As far as I know." Vinton emptied his face of expression.

"And you'll turn them over to us as soon as you can, right?"

"Of course."

Doyle tilted her head to the side like the wise old bird she was, then added, with a trace of sarcasm, "So, as far as you know, does the deceased have any family?"

Unbowed, Vinton said, "Not as far as I know."

Doyle glared at us both, ordered us to stay where we were, and left the apartment.

We sat on the couch squeezed together like scared kids waiting for the worst to come, and it came—in the person of the medical examiner accompanied by four gloomy assistants who carried away Juda's remains. Since there was no family of record, Vinton solemnly played that role, signing official papers and offering any information they needed.

Despite Doyle's warning about touching things, I went to get a glass of water. As I always do when I wander into a stranger's kitchen, I looked around to find out what I could. As all chefs—and folks who cook—believe, you can find out everything you need to know about a person by her kitchen, but not necessarily the appearance. Overly neat says one thing, excessively messy says something else. (I swing between the two.) It's what's *in* the kitchen that counts. Juda Baker's did not disappoint.

The room was long and rectangular, a difficult space for any cook, and painted an eye-stinging yellow. The appliances—stove, refrigerator, dishwasher—looked older than me, and the black-and-white-checkered linoleum floor was popular in houses built in the 1940s. But by the looks of things, she didn't spend much time in here anyway. There were no cooking tools—spatulas, measuring cups, measuring spoons, ladles—to say nothing of whisks or tongs. I spotted one small pot, a greasy frying pan, and a grilling pan that probably came with the stove. Two forks, spoons, and knives stood like soldiers in a dusty mayonnaise jar on the counter along with two wineglasses, three Rubbermaid plates, and cups with no saucers. What did she eat? Her trash can held the answer.

Grubhub, DoorDash, and Uber Eats had recently made inroads down Grovesville's narrow streets, and Juda was a regular. Nearly every Chinese, Indian, Thai, Japanese, and

Mexican restaurant in town was represented in her overflowing kitchen can. Two Entenmann's cake boxes peeked over the top along with an unopened bag of black jelly beans. Hidden behind a stepladder was a back door, probably a fire escape, which led to both the second floor and outside.

Juda Baker was a lonely soul. I knew that the moment I met her, but many people were, including me. But she'd often made references to family—a Swedish grandmother, wealthy family members, trips she'd made to far and exciting places. She either imagined these things or was lying, plain and simple. Or maybe it was a bit of both. There were no posters, souvenir glasses, or plates from far and exciting places. She had lived and died in this small, dismal space, eating her meals while watching the small TV next to the mayonnaise jar on the counter, always trying to be somebody she wasn't. Shaken at the sorrow that surrounded her, I sat down on one of the two rickety chairs at the kitchen table. Guilt swept over me as I recalled her small, faint smile the last time I'd seen her. Had she been reaching out, looking for a friend in her own self-conscious way? Why hadn't I reached out more?

I knew that loneliness could bring its own solace, reminding you of the good things you had and that may come again. It was unfair to judge her now. After all, if I were found dead in my bedroom, how would my life look to someone wandering into my kitchen? A slight, unwelcome smile pushed itself out as I considered that. For one thing, Juniper would be sniffing around, crying, begging for Temptations rather than my company. His whining would alert Julie, my neighbor next door. Aunt Phoenix would show up before my head hit the floor good. Lennox Royal would miss my cakes, inquire about my whereabouts, and feel compelled to investigate. Except for Vinton, Juda had no one, and maybe that was why she clung to Charlie Risko. He was something to hold on to. Their connection was a mystery that died with her.

"They just took her out. Juda's gone," Vinton said, pull-ing me from my thoughts when he came into the kitchen and sat down beside me. "I wish you'd had a chance to know her. Lots of secrets, lots of pain. But a person worth knowing. She didn't let people into her life easily, except for one. I don't need to tell you who that was."

"I wish I'd had a chance to know her, too," I said, which was the truth. "But she never spoke to me, she was never friendly."

"Friendship is hard for some folks, Dessa. Especially if you've never known love."

"Do you know anything about her family?"

"Like about her Swedish grandmother?" He chuckled. "Who knows? Maybe she did have some rich old family somewhere and a Swedish grandma, but she never told me anything about them. She couldn't accept who she really was. People lie about all kinds of things, Sunshine. You should know that by now." He added the last with a snap that sur-prised me.

Doyle came in to tell us that the medical examiner needed to do an autopsy but that her death was most likely a sui-cide, maybe accidental but not a crime scene, and we could go. Someone would be in touch with Vinton later, regarding what to do with the remains. He promised to look through papers Juda had left with him for information about family. Before we left, he stepped back into Juda's bedroom and lin-gered a while, saying good-bye in his own way. His glimmer was deeper than it had been, which worried me. He didn't need to be alone tonight.

"Why don't you let me take you to my place, and I'll make us something to eat," I suggested as we left the building. I could tell he was too upset to drive.

He looked puzzled. I wasn't sure if he heard me. "Listen, I need to ask you a favor first, a big one," he said.

"Sure," I said. After what we'd both been through, there was nothing I wouldn't have done.

"I need you to go with me back to her place, upstairs to the second floor, before anyone else does. To make sure her things are . . . in order. Will you do that for me?"

I stopped dead, facing him in the dim light from the streetlamp. "To the second floor? The storage area?"

"It was more than that."

"What do you mean, make sure things are in order?"

"I'm not sure," he said, turning back to Juda's place. "We were drunk the night she gave me the keys to her place. It was years ago, when we first got to be close. She said I was the only one she could trust. I didn't know if it was friendship or the vodka, but something was bothering her. She said there was stuff upstairs that was too embarrassing for people to see and made me promise to get rid of it if something happened to her."

"I don't think so, Vinton," I said. This sudden request made me uncomfortable. "You should have told the cops before we left. You shouldn't have lied to them." I headed back to my car; he grabbed my arm.

"Dessa, please. Please. I don't want to go up there alone. I lied to the cops, yeah, and I'll let them know what I find. I'll break that part of my promise to Juda, but I need to know why she was worried."

"But if the building belonged to her, why would it matter?"

"Because I lied when I said the building belonged to her. It belonged to Charlie, which means everything in it belongs to Tanya, and Tanya would be the last person Juda would want sniffing around her stuff when she's dead."

Something didn't seem right. Call it the gift warning me or the simple fear of breaking the law. "Vinton, I . . ."

"I owe Juda this, Dessa. I wasn't there for her like I should have been, like I wasn't there for Stuart. I can't do this twice. I need to know what she had in there, why she was so concerned."

"Let me think about it," I said. We went and sat in my car for a while, and Vinton lit a cigarette as I "thought" things over. I finally had to admit to myself that I was as curious as he was.

Yet I felt like a thief as we crept back into the house and upstairs to the second floor. I knew the cops had left but halfway expected Doyle to jump from the shadows and yell for us to halt or be arrested for breaking and entering. But the house was quiet, eerily so because of Juda's death. I glanced at Vinton, wondering again if I could trust him. How well did I really know him? As well as any of them, I realized.

He stepped into the apartment and turned on a dim ceiling light. The blinds were closed, a good thing, since nobody was supposed to be in here. He stood aside, like a gentleman, letting me enter first, and I stepped into the shadowy room. It was too late to change my mind. For better or worse. I touched my mother's amulet; stroking it when I was anxious was becoming a tic.

An empty bottle of vodka sat on the shabby coffee table next to a shabbier couch. The table, chair, and taped cardboard boxes and a file cabinet across the room seemed to be the only furniture up there. It was a dusty, grimy place, not at all like the stylish woman who appeared each day in her fashionable clothes and trendy knockoffs. Vinton collapsed on the couch, sending up a cloud of dust. He sneezed, then sighed. Picking up the empty vodka bottle, he turned it upside down.

"Listen carefully, Dess, this is what happened," he said, like a professor explaining a difficult theory to a dull-witted student. "Juda sat up here, by herself, drank all this vodka, went back downstairs through that door, had some gin, then took the pills." He glanced at me, waiting for a nod of understanding. "The gin alone wouldn't have killed her. It was the chaser. Something got to her up here. She went back down-stairs to put herself to sleep to forget. Forever."

It was a small, perfectly square room, more like a large attic. A door on the far side must have led to the kitchen of the apartment below. When my eyes adjusted to the dim light, I realized it was a shrine to Charlie Risko. This was Juda's private world, a door into the shadowy places of her mind she didn't want people to see or know about. This was what she wanted to protect, even after death, especially af-ter death. There were several sealed cardboard boxes printed with his name. A wall was filled with large photographs of Charlie, taken at various times in his life. A narrow table lean-ing against another was loaded down with things I quickly recognized: the motorcycle jacket he wore to work, the hel-met and black leather gloves he was so proud of—things that were always together, ready for him to slip on or off.

That dumb helmet, his funky jacket. All of it. I already dropped it off with somebody who actually might want his crap.

Tanya had delivered Charlie's things. The question was when.

"Have you been up here before?" I asked Vinton, but he didn't answer. He tore open a cardboard box and began going through it, pulling out copies of the photographs I'd seen at Harley's place, more provocative than the ones I'd seen, sev-eral nude ones of Louella that made me cringe.

"Must have told that kid this crap was 'art,' and she was young and foolish enough to believe him," he said, tossing them on the floor. He went through another folder filled with compromising photographs of Stuart and a man he didn't rec-ognize. His face twisted in anger as he tore them up, tossing them in a pile on the floor with the others. "This is the stuff he collected on Stuart, left it with Juda. I don't know what he

wanted her to do with it. Show it to me, hurt me even though
Stu was dead. But Juda, bless her heart, wouldn't do it."

A gray file cabinet stood near another wall, and Vinton
headed there next, pulled it open, quickly picked through the
folders, and handed one to me.

"Vinton, I don't . . ." He snatched it back, tossing the con-
tents on the grimy couch beside me.

"Let me tell you what's in it, Miss Dessa, since you don't
want to get your hands dirty."

His harsh tone angered me. I'd had enough. I stood up,
brushed the dust from my clothes, ready to stumble out of this
small, sad space and go home. He grabbed my hand, his touch
a marked gentle contrast to the anger in his voice.

"Dessa, I'm sorry I brought you in here, and I apologize
for that, but I don't have anyone else to share this with. Juda
was the closest person I had after Stu, and you're . . ." He
paused but didn't have to finish it. I knew what he was going to say: that I was the closest person he had now, the only
friend he had, and the only one he could trust. I sat back
down. I was here now and had to ride it through to the end.

"You need to know some of what was going on. I told
you about the scams; he got some things legal. The cops asked
you about Avon Bailey? This one." He held up a fragile docu-
ment and waved it in my face. "This is a deed to one of the
places belonging to old Avon Bailey, the father. Charlie got
his house like he got so many others.

"Scamming folks out of their property, taking advantage
of their weakness, using young pretty girls to fool them into
putting their hearts above their heads. Left that old fool nothing. This place, where we're sitting, this was his, too. May
have been one of the houses Avon Bailey used to own. Juda
didn't own it, just lived here, along with all these cabinets
filled with secrets that belonged to other people."

I sat back down, too curious to leave. He pointed to another file cabinet next to the one he'd just been rifling through.

"That one, too. The one marked with Charlie's name." He went over and tore it open, tossing more deeds and documents onto the floor. "Everyone he touched was dirty, and he kept something on everything and everybody. Everybody."

"Even you?" I asked because I needed to know.

"Even me. It doesn't matter anymore. He's dead. Juda's dead. Stu is dead. Nothing can touch me now. I don't know what's in there, and I don't want to know."

We sat there for a while without saying anything, tired and silent in this room haunted by death and filled with ugly things. Charlie Risko was still here. And Juda, and Tanya.

"It all belongs to Mrs. Tanya Risko now. Whatever it is, whatever secrets he had, whatever he had on other people, including her," Vinton said, as if he could read my thoughts.

"Do you think she knows what's up here?"

"I doubt it. Charlie Risko kept these women separate for a reason. Tanya was one thing, Juda was another. He probably had stuff on Juda, too, packed in here somewhere. Maybe that's why Juda wanted me to come up here if she died. She said once she was a wild, crazy little thing when she was a kid, around the time she met Charlie. Her secrets are in here, too. Maybe those are what . . ." He didn't finish the sentence because he didn't need to.

In the distance a dog howled, always a scary sound in the middle of the night, and it was going on midnight. I touched my mother's amulet. Vinton watched me, an amused smile playing on his lips.

"What you got around your neck that you keep touching? You're as bad as Stuart with that kind of stuff. As if charms can protect you from evil."

"It belonged to my mother. Sometimes charms can protect you from evil."

"If you're a witch," he said with a half-smile.

I left that alone; it was a secret for another day.

Quietly and deliberately, Vinton returned the folders to the file cabinets and sealed them up as best he could.

"What did Juda want you to get rid of?"

Vinton looked around the room and shook his head in exasperation, his shoulders slumping with exhaustion. "Everything, I guess, but I can't throw this junk away tonight. Or even tomorrow night. Wherever my dear Juda is, I hope she will forgive me for not being there for her yesterday, for letting her down again tonight. Going through this stuff will kill me as sure as it killed her."

"When do you think the cops are going to get in here?" I asked. He shrugged, offering his hand to pull me up.

"Cops being cops, they'll get here when they get here, find this stuff when they find it, and that's when Mrs. Tanya Risko will get what's due her."

"You're not going to say anything to Tanya?"

"We'd best be on our way, Dessa. Like Mr. Ray Charles used to sing, don't let the sun catch you crying," he said, without answering my question.

Chapter 15

Despite Vinton's warning, the sun *did* catch me crying, long and hard before I fell asleep. I cried for Juda, for Vinton, but most of all for me, and that I was as alone as Juda had been, and this loneliness would always be part of my life. I cried about how unhappy she must have been, surrounding herself with other people's secrets, tying herself to a man who didn't love her. My first impression had been right: She was a liar, but mostly to herself.

I woke up the next morning with the sun in my eyes, and Juniper's rough little tongue licking the side of my face. It was time for breakfast, and he wasn't about to let me forget it. I shoved him off the bed, pulled the cover over my head hoping he'd go away, yet at the same time grateful he was here. He could be a pain in the neck, but he was *my* pain in the neck.

The previous night felt like a nightmare. When I dropped Vinton off, he looked as beaten down as I'd ever seen anyone look. His gait was unsteady and so tottering I feared he wouldn't make it to his apartment. I waited until his lights went on before I left. I sat in my driveway when I got home, too tired to get out of the car and wondering if Juda's suicide had really been that. Could murder be mistaken for suicide?

Vinton had been alone when he went into Juda's bedroom, then insisted that I go upstairs with him. Was there something he didn't want me to know? Could he be more involved with things than he let on? His wounded spirit and sense of humor made it easy to like him, but maybe I was too trusting and as gullible as Lennox Royal believed me to be.

Was Vinton the last person to see Juda alive? Or had that been Tanya, dropping off Charlie's "crap"? Or had there been someone else? My errant gift gave me no help, of course. For a moment, I considered reaching out to Aunt Phoenix, and then remembered she and Celestine had headed down to Atlantic City to "try their luck," as she put it. I doubted that they were back. There wouldn't be much they could tell me anyway.

Juniper jumped on my stomach, nipped my big toe, and began his woeful, wounded mewing, which always got my attention. I stumbled out of bed, blindly poured cat food onto his plate, tossed him a few Temptations, and made sure his water fountain was full. I made some coffee and toast, watched a half hour of *The View*, and tried hard to chase the night before out of my head, but it was no use. The last place I wanted to go was Risko Realty, but I had those short sales to follow up on and a meeting at 3:00 with a mysterious couple who had called the office and specifically asked for me. That had *never* happened before, and I couldn't miss that.

Before I left home, I called Vinton to make sure he was okay. His voice was hoarse and scratchy; he'd probably spent the night crying, too. He told me he'd called Tanya earlier that morning to tell her about Juda and that she'd taken her own life because he didn't want Tanya to think there had been another murder. Tanya told him she was sorry about Juda's death, and that she'd let the rest of the staff know about her. She also said to let her know when Juda's family made arrangements because she wanted the company to contribute. "Nice gesture, since the company killed her," Vinton had

said. "I'm Juda's family now. I really am all she had." I tried
to reassure him that somebody from her past was bound to
show up sooner or later, but we both knew that wasn't going
to happen. "I'm sorry I dragged you into this, Dessa," he said
before he hung up. I didn't say it, but so was I. After talking
to him, I was ashamed I'd suspected him of having something
to do with Juda's death. If it was suicide, it had been Juda's
decision, I reminded myself, no matter who had seen her last.

It was noon by the time I got to the office. Tanya's door
was closed, bringing back memories of her late husband.
Dennis Lane was chatting up some unsuspecting client in his
charming, seductive voice. He put down the phone when he
saw me, rearing back like a predator prepping for attack. I
touched my amulet.

"Too bad about Juda Baker," he said, his voice betraying
what he really felt. "Guess she couldn't take it. How did she
do it? Gun? Pills? Rope? Man, there's something about this
place that sends folks over the edge. Better watch yourself,
Mrs. Jones. But that Juda Baker was an odd bird. Never understood what Charlie saw in her."

"Go to hell!" Bertie said, with a quiet rage that seemed to
come from nowhere. "Someday you're going to pay for your
meanness. You truly are an evil man!"

Her words didn't seem to bother Dennis. He chuckled,
as if taunting us both. "Not in this lifetime. You know what
they say, Bertie. The good die young, and I'm not that young
and you can ask ladies who know me about my goodness."

A slow, cruel smile spread across his lips. "Stare at me all
you want, Mrs. Jefferson. I know more about you and your
family than you think I ought to know, and that's the truth."

He was talking about Louella and we knew it. Bertie
looked as if she'd been struck. I wished again for the skills of
my distant cousins.

"Leave her alone," I said, protecting her as Vinton had when Dennis was picking on me. "Just be quiet, out of respect for Juda if for no other reason."

"Juda? She didn't respect the two of you. And by the way, Tanya's upset, in there crying. Juda doesn't deserve any of your sympathy. The woman took herself out. Just like Stuart Risko did. You can't feel too sorry for folks like that."

I was glad Vinton wasn't there to hear him. He was carrying too much guilt about both Stuart and Juda to have to listen to Dennis Lane's vicious words. Those who love suicide victims often blame themselves, and Vinton already did. I moved closer to Bertie, reached over to hug her, but it was as if her anger had created a barrier around her. I could feel her rage inside me, like I had that day she fought with Louella, and it was frightening.

"Juda's not supposed to be dead. She's not one of those who should be dead. She didn't do anything to deserve to die," Bertie whispered, more to herself than to me.

"She was just very unhappy," I said, even though my words meant little; she barely heard them.

The last week and a half had taken a visible toll on Bertie. A heaviness, not unlike a glimmer, was weighing her down. She'd always been an optimist, picking me up when I was discouraged, teasing Vinton when it suited her, but that was gone now. She was stuck here at Risko Realty, more so than the rest of us, and maybe that truth was affecting her. It would be hard for her to find another job, and as far as I knew she was the sole support of Louella and Erika. Everyone depended on her. She came here every morning, working as much as she could, doing the best she could do, despite Dennis's cruelty. He seemed strangely unaffected by all the things that had happened.

I wondered why he just didn't leave and go somewhere

else. He had more commissions than anyone else and would be welcomed by any company looking for a top-notch salesman. Yet he came in here every morning, chatting seductively to his female clients, seeming to take pleasure in picking on those more vulnerable than he. I was even more convinced that he was running what Lennox called a long con on Tanya—unless she was more involved with Charlie's death than I knew.

If you ask me, the wife had something to do with it. It's always the spouse. Lennox's words came back again.

Before my clients came, I knocked on Tanya's door to check on her. She had been crying like Dennis said, her eyes swollen and her nose running. Every time I saw Tanya I changed my mind about her, as if she were an optical illusion that changed shape the longer I stared at it. But that was nearly the case with all of my coworkers. Bertie had been easy when I met her. She'd worn her pain like an old sweater and I felt sorry for her, but now her flashes of rage puzzled and alarmed me. Dennis probably was a crook running a con, but what did I *really* know about him? I could be as wrong about him as I was about Juda. I hadn't seen how lonely she was, how much pain she was in. Vinton I thought I knew, but sometimes it was just for the moment we were in. I'd had my doubts after the previous night yet believed in him again that morning. And Harley, well, that remained to be seen. As usual, I could blame the failings of the gift, which showed itself through nutmeg only when death was in the air. I'd stopped using the spice altogether these days, to the detriment of spice cake, French toast, and hot cocoa.

I thought about all those things and the part the gift played and didn't when I sat down on Tanya's couch, watching her dab her eyes with a paper napkin. When she saw me, she sniffed and started right in.

"I took all that stuff over to her on Sunday, and she must have killed herself that night. I thought she'd want it. Do you think it was my fault, Dessa?"

She hadn't shed a tear at Charlie Risko's memorial. Who could forget that red pantsuit or her confession to me that she'd never loved him? These tears were real, despite the dramatic dab with the napkin. Or was it guilt?

"No, I don't think you had anything to do with Juda taking her own life, if that's what she did. It may have been an accident, nobody will really know until they do an autopsy."

"She wasn't upset when I saw her."

"Tell me what happened."

"Well, I went over there to her place, rang the bell, gave her all Charlie's stuff in a black trash bag."

"Did you go upstairs?"

"Upstairs? Why would I go upstairs?" she said, sounding surprised.

"But you know what was upstairs, right?" I said, deciding not to take her at her word.

She shrugged. "Her tenant, I guess. Charlie told me she owned the building. I assumed she rented out the top floor. Were they there when she did it? Maybe they could have stopped it!"

"I don't think so," I said quietly.

"Why did you ask if I went upstairs?" she said again, puzzled.

I shrugged. "Something Vinton said."

"What did he say?"

"Nothing much. You know Vinton."

She smiled slightly when I said that. "Vinton and Juda were good friends. They didn't talk to me all that much, but I could tell they were close. When he called me this morning, he was really broken up. I feel like I want to do something for her. Charlie and she were together for a long time. I don't know much of what was between them now, except that she knew stuff about him I didn't know. I want to pay for a memorial service if her family will let me. I feel like Charlie owes her that."

"Yeah, he does. But it's not your debt to pay."

"I was never that nice to her. I should have been."

"We all should have been," I said, saying the truth as I saw it now. "I'll remind Vinton to let you know about a service."

She nodded and wiped her nose. There would be plenty of time for her to find out who really owned that house and what was in it. That would have to play out in its own time.

"Dennis said I shouldn't do anything for Juda, but I want to anyway. He said it wasn't my place," she said after a minute.

"Dennis is still giving you advice?" Her expression said he was. "Don't trust him, Tanya. He may be taking advantage of you, and he doesn't mean you any good."

She smiled a tight, weary smile. "I can handle Dennis Lane the same way I handled Charlie Risko."

"We both know that didn't turn out that well, don't we?" I said, which seemed to surprise her.

"You know what's funny? Bertie said the same thing to me this morning, about not trusting Dennis. Said he meant me trouble, just like you, and that sooner or later his stuff would catch up with him, and that I didn't want to be around him when that happened."

I understood now where Bertie's rage came from. It must have been left over from her conversation with Tanya.

"Have you heard from Harley?" Tanya asked out of nowhere, surprising me the same way she had when she'd taken me to lunch. "He's been out and nobody has heard from him. I've been calling him, leaving messages, but he doesn't answer his phone. What do you think about that?" She searched my face, looking for an answer that I didn't have. "Do you think Harley killed Charlie, like the police say he did?"

"No, I don't."

"Then why hasn't he called anybody?"

"Maybe he needs time to himself," I said as convincingly as I could.

"I don't know who to trust anymore." Her voice turned into the little lost girl. "I used to have so many people I could trust. Dennis, my grandfather, Harley, even Charlie."

"Yourself. Learn to trust yourself, Tanya," I told her, passing on a homily that I only half expected her to believe. I stood up, getting ready to leave. "Well, Tanya, I have an appointment in a few minutes and I . . ."

She stood slightly and grabbed my arm from across her desk, her grip stronger than I expected it to be. "Do you think somebody killed Juda, like they killed Charlie? What if it wasn't a suicide or accident?"

I sat back down to listen; the desperation in her voice wouldn't let me leave.

"That's ridiculous, Tanya," I said firmly, even though the thought had crossed my mind that morning. "Don't let yourself go there."

"I don't know. Something about it, her dying like she did."

"The medical examiner told the cops it was probably suicide or an accident, not a crime scene," I said, repeating what I'd been told.

"I hope they're right," she said.

I do, too, I said to myself, but left her office, more disturbed than I should have been.

My mystery couple canceled at the last minute, which annoyed me. But it wasn't a sudden craving for barbecued ribs, chicken wings, or a slice of my 7-UP cake that sent me to Royal's Regal Barbecue too early for dinner, too late for lunch. It was the need for normalcy and comfort. Darryl used to call Royal's Regal Barbecue a clean, well-lighted place. He always said it with a wink because it was a reference to a Hemingway story he loved and a reminder that he'd been an English lit major in college. I smiled now as I remembered it. Royal's Regal Barbecue was what I needed—a place safe and free of craziness. I needed familiar barbecue smells and the comfort that comes with a plate of good food and a cheerful friendly welcome. I had a wide grin on my face when I walked into Royal's, but my grin turned down when I settled into my usual spot at the end of the counter. Georgia's attitude and suspicious eye hinted that I just might be better off at Risko's.

I wished there was a way to let this woman know I had no designs on a man she was obviously interested in, but I could think of no tactful way to tell her. I gave up playing games with folks—male and female—twenty-odd years ago when I left my early twenties. I had no designs on Lennox Royal. He was a customer and I was his baker. There was nothing between us, and probably never would be. Georgia wasn't buying it.

"Mr. Royal is in the kitchen, if that's who you're looking for," she said with a touch of malice. "If not, what can I do for you?"

I smiled sweetly. "I need to talk to Mr. Royal about his order. I'd also like a cup of coffee and the last slice of that delicious 7-UP cake," I said, tooting my own horn. I was sure she knew who baked it. "I'm always in here for one thing or another, and I don't think I've ever introduced myself. I'm Mrs. Dessa Jones," I said when she brought my order.

"Georgia Wickham. *Just* Georgia Wickham," she said, still eyeing me suspiciously. "Didn't you used to come in here with a man?" she added after a moment.

"Yes, that was Darryl, my husband. He passed away about a year ago." I stared at the coffee swirling in my cup because I didn't want her to see the pain in my eyes.

When I glanced at her again, I noticed a glint of sympathy. Maybe she wasn't as bad as she pretended to be. "Sorry to hear that. He seemed like a nice man."

"Yes, he was."

She studied me, summing me up. She struck me as the kind of woman who checked out, for better or worse, every woman under fifty who talked to her boss.

"So how long have you worked for Mr. Royal?" I asked.

"After Pearl, his wife, left. I stepped in to help him run it. Pearl was, is, one of my best friends. I'm still helping him run things."

I was curious how long that had been, and why his wife, Pearl, had left and why she'd left her best friend to cover for her. But Georgia didn't volunteer any information, and I certainly didn't ask. I wondered if she and Lennox were partners—of some sort or another—and if he knew how possessive she was. I doubted he did. Like most men when it came to women, he probably didn't have a clue. He probably wasn't sure how to handle his feelings, if he had any, or hers, if he knew about them, so he kept them to himself. If he wanted me to know more about his life, he'd tell me sooner or later. Whatever was between them was their business, not mine. I just hoped the woman didn't put salt in my food.

Lennox's eyes lit up when he made his way in from the kitchen. I hoped Georgia didn't notice.

"Hey, good to see you. You're in here just in time for this week's order. A big one," he added as he pulled out the stool he kept behind the counter and slid onto it.

"I got errands to run; I'll be back in time to help out with dinner," Georgia said as he sat down.

"I think I'm covered, Georgia, but thanks anyway."

"What about Lena?"

"She's good! See you later. Speaking of Lena, I've got something for you," he said, turning to me. Georgia's eyes fastened on us both before she headed out the door. Lennox pulled the cookie tin off a shelf and handed it to me. "Do you mind?"

"Of course not. Chocolate chip okay?"

"I'd say yeah, and two yellow cakes with chocolate frosting, and another pound cake, if it's not too much trouble." He wrote me a check for more than he owed me. "Small down payment on the next order."

"It's way too much money but thanks," I said. Being in the business, he knew that the price of eggs, sugar, and good chocolate were no joke. I was glad they were just plain yellow cakes. "Thursday afternoon okay?"

"Sounds good. Want some more coffee? Unless you thought my coffee was too strong."

"I'm getting used to it. But tea would be good. Have anything herbal?"

"Constant Comment, is that okay? I should get some herbal teas around here, chamomile, peppermint, something like that. Cool folks out when they need it."

He brought a cup of Constant Comment and we sat in easy silence, each of us lost in our thoughts, Lennox possibly making a mental note to add herbal teas to his grocery list or wondering how to deal with Georgia Wickham. I was wondering how to bring up murder versus suicide. Finally, I just asked.

"Is there a way you can make a murder look like suicide?"

Lennox chuckled. "You've decided to apply to the police academy? Good idea, you'd probably make a good cop. What's up with a question like that?"

"A lady in my office committed suicide over the weekend, and I'm wondering if it's something else," I blurted out.

Lennox put his cup down so quickly his coffee spilled on the counter. "Odessa, you're not serious."

"Yes, I am," I said, suddenly realizing that Lennox called me Odessa when he thought he had something important to say. Basically, though, we had become Dessa kind of friends, which was great because I didn't like reminding him of his grandmother . . . or myself of Aunt Phoenix. "So can you tell a murder from a suicide?"

"Your boy is still the main suspect, right? But they can track him so it wasn't him. You know who I suspect? The wife and her boyfriend."

"What about murder masked as suicide?" I asked again, not willing to condemn Tanya yet and trying to bring him back to the main subject.

Lennox mopped up his spilled coffee with a sponge, taking his time before he began to speak. "Depends on the suicide. If the victim left a note, where the body is found, stuff like that. Drownings or hanging, it's usually the way the body is positioned. If the rope is found in a certain position, or when the water entered the lungs, is a giveaway. A shooting death, that depends on how the person is shot and where they find the gun and the residue. A poisoning is similar. But most suicides don't use poison, they use pills or alcohol. Where was the body found, who found it, and how did she die?"

"Coworkers found it," I said, leaving out the role I played. "Her body was found in her bed. She drank a lot of alcohol and took some pills. Gin and Ambien, and I think she also had some vodka."

"When did this happen?"

"Over the weekend."

"How did you find out so much, so soon?" Lennox said, regarding me with a hint of suspicion.

"The coworker who found her was really upset and told me about it," I said with as straight a face as I could manage.

"What did the ME say?"

"He has to do an autopsy, but said it could be suicide or possibly an accidental death."

"Then that's probably what it was. If she was in her own bed, and they found the liquor and pills, that's what happened. Somebody would have to get her drunk, ply her with pills, and put a pillow over her head when she passed out. That's the only way it could be done if it was murder, and he or she would probably need to have the key to the apartment. Was there a note?"

"I don't know," I said, which was the truth, yet knowing that Vinton had keys to Juda's apartment made me uneasy.

"Was the woman involved with that Charlie Risko guy?"

"Yeah, an ex-lover," I said, leaving out the juicy stuff.

"You know what I would do if I were you, Odessa? I'd get out of that damn place while you still have a heartbeat," he said, only half joking.

I smiled but it wasn't real, and he could tell, and he wasn't joking when he continued. "If you need me, call me. You've got my number here, and here's my cell. Promise me you'll use it if you need to, okay? Day or night. If you feel scared or worried that something doesn't feel like it should."

I nodded and wrote down my home number and cell for him. It might just come in handy.

The dinner folks were trickling in by then, and Georgia wasn't there to help. Lennox went to check on his kitchen and Lena in her place. I left with more troubling doubts about *all* of my coworkers than I came in with. My clean and well-lit place was certainly clean, but not as well lit as I'd hoped it would be.

It was a merlot night. A double one, at that. I watched the news, trying to take my mind off the day, and ignored Juniper mewing loudly for his evening snack. He'd recently taken to nipping lightly at my pant legs when he didn't get what he wanted—a "gentle reminder," since he did it without drawing blood. I stood my ground. I'd recently seen a show on the news about obese pets, and although Juniper wasn't there yet, his round body bore enough of a resemblance to the featured cat to make me cut back on his treats. After a while, he gave up and settled down in the chair next to me and purred himself to sleep.

I can't say I wasn't expecting the call when it came, thanks, in part, to the gift. I was owed a call, and the person on the other end knew it, which was why it took him so long to answer when I finally said his name.

"How are you doing, Harley?"

"How did you know it was me?"

"Who else but somebody with no place to go and no one to talk to would call me at this time of night?" Of course, there was one other person who I didn't bother to mention.

"I haven't been able to call anyone, Dessa. I don't want to talk; I'm too scared. Especially after what happened to Juda. That really freaked me out."

"Didn't you just say you were too scared to talk to anybody?" I said skeptically.

"Tanya left a message, but I didn't call her back."

"Juda wasn't murdered. It was a suicide or accidental death," I said for the third time today. Who was I trying to convince?

"They don't know that!" I couldn't see his face, but his voice told me everything I needed to know. "I want to ask you for a favor." I rolled my eyes, grateful he couldn't see me.

"What do you want this time?"

"Can you bring Parker home?" A request for Parker was the last thing I expected, and then he added, "I've been doing a lot of thinking about that night, what really happened, about all the stuff I forgot. I need to run it by somebody I trust. Will you come by? Please, Dessa. I'm losing it. I really don't know what's going to happen to me."

I waited for a minute before answering, and finally did because he was clearly in need of company, human and bird. "Okay, I'll come by tomorrow after I pick him up."

"Pick up Parker? You mean he's not living with you?" he squealed in alarm.

"No, and I'll see you when I see you," I said and hung up.

Chapter 16

I was annoyed with Harley and didn't hide it. Although I hadn't admitted it to Tanya, I was surprised I hadn't heard from him. By morning, I was feeling more charitable. After all, the man had been in jail for two weeks for a murder he *said* he didn't commit and confined to his apartment until his trial. God only knew how that would go. Yet I couldn't forget that glimmer of belief I'd felt so strongly when I visited him in jail. It had convinced me of his innocence.

I'd promised Lennox his order by Thursday, so I decided to get Lena's chocolate chip cookies out of the way early; cookies keep better than cakes. If you're going to bake two dozen cookies, you may as well bake four dozen, so I threw in some for Harley; he'd probably need them. Always timely and in touch with my life, Aunt Phoenix sent me a text as I pulled out the last batch.

Celestine gone. Come get this damn bird.

Are you referring to dear little Parker? I joked when I texted her back. *Be there in an hour.*

Aunt Phoenix was in a testy mood when she opened the door. Parker was squawking like crazy in the living room. I hadn't come a moment too soon.

"When did Celestine leave?" I asked as I gathered up Parker's belongings.

"Last night, after we got back from the casino." Aunt Phoenix opened her flask to take a nip of cherry brandy as she settled down in her rocking chair to watch me work.

"How did you all do at the casinos?" I asked, as if I didn't know.

"Cleaned up, of course," she said with a sly smile. "Check your bank account when you get home."

"Aunt Phoenix!" I stopped packing, ready to scold her even though I knew it would do no good.

"'Thank you' will suffice. Give Celestine a call, too. She racked up almost as much as me. Almost," she added with a wink, then turned to glare at Parker in his cage. "He was fine last night, then started up his mess when he realized Celestine was gone. Nasty little thing!" she said, scrunching up her face in disapproval. "Where's he going now?"

"Back to his owner."

"He's out of jail?"

I didn't remember telling Aunt Phoenix who Parker belonged to or that his owner was in jail. But that was neither here nor there.

"You got Rosie's charm?" she asked, concern in her voice.

"Always." I pulled it out so she could see it.

"Keep it close," she said.

I piled Parker's belongings into a garbage bag, put it in my car, and then returned for him. "By the way, did you get a call from the Weatherbees? They're new in town and looking for a house," Aunt Phoenix said just as I was heading out.

I stopped to warily study her. "These people aren't distant relatives, are they? I can't take any more gifts, glimmers, ghosts. . . ."

"We don't do ghosts," she said firmly. "Just nice people I met at the supermarket who I'd like to help out."

"They made an appointment, then canceled at the last minute. You sure they're not connected to us somehow?"

"No."

"I'll take you at your word," I said, still suspicious and wondering exactly who these people were.

"My word is all you've got," said Aunt Phoenix, taking another nip from her flask, which left me wondering.

Parker was quiet on the drive to Harley's place; I was grateful for that. He must have sensed we were getting close because he started squawking—big-time. I left him in the car and rang the buzzer. Harley opened the door on the first ring.

I was shocked to see the state of his apartment, how dark and stuffy it had become. The blinds were pulled down and the lights were so dim it seemed as if he was hiding from somebody. Maybe he was.

"I don't want anyone to know I'm here," he said. "I'm scared, Dessa. Of everything and everyone."

"Harley, that thing you have on your leg cuts both ways. It will protect you from anyone who means you harm," I said, trying to reassure him as I studied the heavy contraption strapped around his ankle. It looked as if it weighed ten pounds, and although he could walk, it dragged him down. "How far can you walk in that thing?"

"Around my place, to my mailbox, the end of the driveway. If I go outside, like to the store or to work, I need to let them know ahead of time. They know where I am every minute, but that's okay with me. But, Dessa, I'm desperate. I know they're going to do me in. There was a story on the news about a guy who served twenty-five years for a crime he didn't commit. I don't want that to be me."

"How does the monitor work?" I asked, eager to change the subject.

"It tracks you from a satellite. It's waterproof; you can't

cut it off. Some people say you can get it off if you try hard enough. But it's on till you go to trial." Just saying the word *trial* seemed to affect him. "Where's Parker?"

"I left him in the car."

"Do you want me to help you bring him in?" he asked, keen to see his feathered friend, then looked at his ankle and sighed. "I almost forgot that I'm stuck in here."

"Don't worry. I can bring him into the lobby."

I hauled Parker's cage and the rest of his paraphernalia out of my car and into the building. When the bird saw Harley, his screeching took on a milder, sweeter tone, close to a melody, which was new to me. Harley carried the cage into his apartment, and after it was positioned, opened the cage door and the bird flew out, landing freely around the room. Apparently, this was something he did on a regular basis. After ten minutes of freedom, he perched on Harley's wrist and began to "talk" in a language that only Harley seemed to understand. The scene between the two was strangely touching.

"How you doin', man? How you been?" Harley asked, as if expecting an answer that Parker actually gave by dropping his head to one side and tweeting softly. Harley grinned as if he understood. "Sorry I haven't been around, man. Thank Mrs. Jones for looking out for you. Here, Dessa, you want him to fly to you?" He pointed the bird in my direction.

"No, I'm good," I said, not eager to feel those sharp little claws on my wrist. The two of them "spoke" a while longer until the bird flew back into his cage. Parker's presence had a visible effect on Harley, and I was glad I'd brought him.

"You need to meet my aunt Celestine. You two have a lot in common," I said as he closed the cage door. He looked puzzled. "Ask Parker," I added.

"You want some tea or a drink or something?" he asked, after making sure Parker was settled. "I have plenty of food.

My mom's reading group, the Aging Readers Club, brought me over so much food I can't eat it all. I didn't tell them that, though."

"You need to eat something to keep your health up."

"All I want is junk food, like chips and candy, stuff with fat and sugar."

"Well, these will be right on time," I said, giving him the bag of chocolate chip cookies I'd brought. He took one and gobbled it down, savoring every crumb, jamming another in his mouth as soon as he finished the first.

"You're definitely into sugar and fat, but you better broaden your palate to get through what's going on."

"I've been drinking a lot of water and tea. Calms my nerves. Not coffee, though. Reminds me too much of work. You want some, I can make you a cup."

"No, I'm fine," I said. He nodded and disappeared into the kitchen and came back with a small teapot and a cup and poured himself some tea after it steeped.

"My mom always served tea like this," he said, probably noting my surprised interest. Harley had never struck me as a tea connoisseur. "Before she came to live with me, I'd just put a teabag in the cup, then take it out, but my mother liked stuff like this. Said it was how tea was supposed to be served, in a teapot after it steeped. She and her club would sip it for hours when they had their discussion. But I'm pretty sure they added a little something to it."

"Sounds like you and your mother were close. How come you never told me about her?" I asked, reminded again of how little I knew about Harley and his life outside of Risko Realty.

"I was so disgusted by working at that place, I didn't want to say her name in there," he said.

"Things were that bad."

"Yeah. Sometimes." His expression told me he wasn't ready to say much more about his life, his mother, or anything else, but I tried again.

"It seems to me that your mother is still looking out for you."

He smiled the smile that lit up his face. "She and her earthly angels," he said. "I don't deserve everything, all these gifts. I hate for Mrs. Grace and those ladies to see me like this, like I'm some kind of a criminal. They dropped off all their favorite dishes. Arroz con pollo, corn beef and cabbage, chicken soup with matzo balls. Comfort foods from every-where, that I don't deserve."

He stuffed three cookies into his mouth all at once as if burying the thought, washed them down with tea, then ate another one. "I'm okay, Dessa. Please, I'm okay," he said as if noticing my concern. But I knew he wasn't. He'd lost weight, his skin was dull, and he looked ten years older than the spir-ited young man I'd known. He wasn't yet ready to share any thoughts he'd had about Charlie's murder, and for the next hour we talked about how to bake cookies, his mother's love of books, and Parker's annoying habits. It took him another hour to tell me what was really on his mind.

"Do you know how many men end up in prison for things they didn't do?" he said, his voice beginning to tremble. "Dudes plead guilty when they're innocent because they don't want to go to trial. Sometimes cops are sloppy or corrupt and put folks in jail who have no business being there. Ever heard of the Innocent Project? There was something about it on TV a couple of nights ago, and they said more than twenty thousand innocent people are in jail. Most of them are poor and black, and that fits me. I'm scared I'm going to be one of them."

We both knew what he'd said was true; neither of us spoke until he began again. "I didn't do this, Dessa. I didn't kill Charlie Risko!" he said, breaking the silence.

"I believe you," I said, because I did.

Harley took in a breath, letting it out so slowly I thought it was caught in his throat. "I keep going back to that night, Dessa. I told you what happened, right? How I went in to confront Charlie, and picked up the gun, which is how my prints got on it."

"They were the only ones that were on it," I said, reminding him of what I knew to be true, turning skeptical again and wondering where he was going with this.

He leaned back on his couch, then rocked forward as if ready to share something I needed to know. "But I didn't kill him, so somebody else had to have picked up that gun after I left. He or . . . she . . . wore gloves or something to make sure the only prints on it were mine."

"What do you mean?"

"I've been over that scene so many times in my mind, Dessa. What was there, what wasn't there. Trying to remember what was on that desk." He paused for a moment, reasoning something out. "He kept those fancy motorcycle gloves on his desk, remember? Next to the helmet, laid across the edge like they were something special. He was always bragging about how much they cost. Two, three hundred bucks. Deerskin, I think he said. Were they still there when the cops came? Did somebody test them for gunshot residue? Maybe somebody slipped them on, shot Charlie, then put them back where they were or took them with them after he or she killed him."

I thought about what he'd said for a moment, then asked, "If the gloves were there, wouldn't that have been the first thing the cops tested?"

"Then maybe they weren't there! The cops wouldn't know about them unless somebody told them. They were there when I left." He must have seen my doubts because his face fell. "You don't think that could happen?"

I searched for words to let him know I wanted to believe him and finally said, "You think that somebody came into the office after you left, put on Charlie's gloves, shot him, then took the gloves with them?"

"I know it doesn't sound like it could happen, but that must be it."

"Maybe you should mention it to the police," I said, for lack of anything better to say. He continued, as if he didn't hear me.

"Something else, Dessa, that I remember from that night. It came to me last night before I went to sleep, almost like in a dream."

A dream? Sounded like he was heading into glimmer territory, which gave me pause. He studied my face as if he wasn't sure he should share it but then he did.

"Remember when I told you what happened? How I called him on his BS, slammed the gun down on the desk, left through that back door? But it didn't quite close. It never did when you first closed it. It always popped back open. When I was halfway down the alley I heard something. Remember I told you about those ghost whispers I heard? I heard him talking to somebody else. It came to me last night what he said. He wasn't being mean, just like he was puzzled. 'What the hell are *you* doing here?' he said, like he was surprised."

"Did anybody answer?"

"I wouldn't have heard it. I was on my bike by then."

"And you think that person who surprised him must have killed him?"

"I don't know who it was. I tried to think about who had been there earlier before everyone left. Vinton, Dennis, Bertie, and Louella were there earlier, and then there is something else, somebody I saw last week. He was with Louella, but he'd changed so much I didn't recognize him." He paused again, as if wondering if he should tell me.

"You think that person may have had something to do with Charlie's murder?"

"I don't know. He might have. He was with us in those old days. Maybe he came back for some reason. He was connected to Louella. They were close. I just don't know, Dessa."

"Who did you think you saw?"

"I don't want to say because I don't want to accuse him of being involved in something. He could end up the same place as me. He had changed so much, Dessa. It couldn't have been him. The guy I'm thinking of is probably dead. After what we did to him and his family."

"Avon Bailey," I said.

"How did you know?" I couldn't read what was in his eyes. Was it shame or fear?

"I've heard his name before."

"Where?"

"Just around," I said, leaving it at that.

I hadn't spoken to Harley since I'd found those photos, now neatly packed back where they had been, and I knew more than he thought I did. I decided to keep it to myself for now. I didn't say anything for a while. The only noise in the room was Parker swinging back and forth on his perch with an occasional chirp. Harley glanced at Parker, then dropped his head to look at his hands, tightly folded in his lap. He needed to tell me whatever was haunting him, haunting all of them, and I knew if I sat there long enough he would. It finally came out, all in a rush.

"It was about his old man's houses. He owned three that had been in his family for a couple of generations. Landed gentry, Avon used to laugh about him. His father was mean to him, used to beat him, beat his mother. Maybe he loved him in his own way, but Avon never felt it. But you never know about fathers. Who they are, who they think they are."

I wondered if Harley was remembering his own father,

thinking of the man who stood beside him on his bike and what memories he still had; they would have to come out sooner or later.

"How did Avon Bailey and his father get involved with Charlie Risko?"

"The land his houses were on was worth a fortune. Charlie knew it, and wanted to get them as quick and cheap as he could because prices were going up fast and he wanted to tear them down and make big money. You know the places I'm talking about, over there where they built those condos that cost more than most folks can pay. Over there on the border of Bren Bridge. That was Avon Bailey's daddy's land. Remember when Dennis Lane was bragging about buying his place over there? You'd think he would have been ashamed, but that's not Dennis."

I nodded that I agreed. "So how did Charlie get them?"

"If I'd known what was going to go down with my friends, I never would have brought them into it." Regret, embarrassment, and humiliation—everything was in his voice at the same time. I gave him a minute, then pushed him with the little bit I knew.

"You're talking about Louella and Tanya?"

He nodded. "They were nice girls, well, a little what my mother would call 'fast,' but nice. You could say they both had an edge. They liked to play dangerous games, make fast money, go around the boundaries. I had just started working with Charlie, and he told me he had a way for us all to make some money because there were a lot of old guys with property and houses and they liked pretty young girls, and I knew pretty young girls." I could see the shame in his eyes when he finally looked into mine. There is a word for men who use young women like that and we both knew what it was.

"I'm not making excuses for myself, but my mother was

sick and I needed some money, and they did, too, and it all seemed okay. Once Charlie got that land and sold it, we'd all make some money. We'd be out of it, and it would be over. Everybody enjoyed it for a while. Avon Bailey wasn't the only one. There were other old men we took in. Lots of them."

I thought about those pictures with the empty bottles and the cash. They may have thought they were into it, but Charlie Risko had the last laugh and they all knew it, and maybe that was why he was dead.

"So how did it work?"

"Just how it sounds," he said. I remembered the scams that Lennox described, swindling foolish old men out of their property, hiring a "contractor" to work on problems that didn't exist. There were a dozen ways to fool an old man with more heart than head and a libido fueled up by Viagra or other means. Charlie Risko knew how to play it all.

Harley got up then and walked around the room, stopping to talk to Parker and finally coming to sit back down with me. Maybe it was because he didn't like thinking about what had happened or talking about it. I let him have the time; he needed it, and I waited a bit before I spoke.

"Avon Bailey was your friend, too?" I asked.

"No, he was Louella's friend. And that was the worst part about the whole scam. I brought her in. She brought Avon in. He brought his father in, and then he disappeared."

"The father or the son?"

"I heard he was dead," Harley said, more to himself than to me. He hadn't answered my question but it didn't matter. I already knew which one because Lennox had told me. The younger one must still be alive. He must have been the one the cops were asking about.

"Are you saying you saw Avon Bailey with Louella the day Charlie died?"

"Yeah, I think I did," he said. "And I'm wondering if he had something to do with Charlie's death, or maybe somebody else did."

"Like Louella?"

"Her story isn't mine to tell," he said.

"Whose story are you talking about? Charlie and Louella? Louella and Avon? You and Louella? You and Tanya?" I threw the last one out to see his reaction, but there wasn't one. He opened Parker's cage, allowing him to circle the room, then cut up an apple to lure the bird back inside. He put on the kettle for more tea. I considered asking him about the photos but thought better of it. Someday, after everything was over, I'd ask him, but now was not the time.

When I was ready to go, he asked if I would bring his mother's Bible when I got a chance, and I said I would. I left him sitting in the dark with his bird flying around his stuffy apartment and a refrigerator packed with uneaten food. I prayed this wasn't the end of the Harley Wilde I once knew.

Chapter 17

When I left Harley's apartment, the sunlight caught me by surprise. I was so captured by Harley's mood I'd forgotten it was midafternoon. It was sunny and warm for late October, yet I felt chilled to the point of shivering. This was how I felt the day Charlie Risko was murdered when I'd been so incensed by the casual indifference of my coworkers, I'd had to leave the office. The pain between Bertie and Louella overpowered me, and I'd taken their emotions inside of me. Only sitting in the park listening to Darryl's playlist had brought me back to myself.

The only real support I could offer Harley was kind words and chocolate chip cookies—and that was sad. Even a good lawyer was no insurance he wouldn't spend the rest of his days in state prison. Every convicted felon is an innocent man, Lennox cynically observed. He might consider me naïve, but I knew Harley was innocent although I couldn't—and wouldn't—explain exactly how I knew. Harley's fears were becoming my own.

This would be the time when Darryl would run down his concern about my empathy: how quickly I absorbed people's feelings, became overwhelmed by people's troubles, took on more than I should. He tried to protect me from those he felt sapped my energy—folks who talked too much about nothing, came with too much drama, lied because they couldn't tell the truth. He always found some gentle way to keep them out of our orbit. I wondered what he'd say about Harley, and if he would feel he needed to protect me. Would he agree with Lennox that Harley was just another "innocent" person who actually belonged in jail?

Darryl was gone. I had to protect myself now. I thought about going to Royal's barbecue to sit and chat with him, but he was probably busy by now. I'd see him tomorrow when I dropped off his cakes. I considered going to the office to check the list for possible sales, do some cold calls. Vinton and Bertie might be there to keep me company, at least keep my mind off Harley. But I needed to be outside; when things got overwhelming, feeling the sun on my face or the wind whispering past, and even a light drizzle of rain, could be soothing. The park had strengthened me the day Charlie Risko ended up being murdered, and when I drove past I considered stopping there again, sitting on the bench, watching kids play on the jungle gym. But I needed to go home. I had cakes to bake.

When I climbed out of the car, the sun felt so warm I couldn't go inside. Next week would be November, then December, then winter with its shadowy, cold days. I should enjoy this warmth while I had it. Truth was, I wasn't yet ready to cook, despite how easy it was to lose myself when I did. Experience has taught me never to cook unless I want to. If I force it, bread won't rise, gravy will burn, grease will splatter wildly. Besides that, I wasn't ready to face Juniper demanding cat treats and noisily chasing his toys around the living room. I needed peace and quiet. Calmness to collect my thoughts. I needed sun shining on the darkness that Harley had left me with, to bring me back to myself and away from his sadness.

I made my way around my house to my overgrown backyard and sat down on the long wooden bench we bought two summers ago. We had great plans to paint it then, but something always got in the way: It was too hot or rainy; we were too lazy. So here it was, waiting for me to fulfill our broken promise. *I'll do it in the spring,* I said to myself, then smiled. I'd probably say the same thing next year when I came out here looking for peace.

It was late afternoon, and my block was quiet, the streets empty except for a few kids riding bikes home before dinner. Our neighborhood was a peaceful one. The houses were close together and similar in age and architecture—classic Cape Cods, each with its own distinguishing feature or color.

A single mother with two teenage boys lived in the white one on my left side. The backyard was nearly covered by a rectangular cement slab that served as a basketball court; a torn basketball net was fixed on the garage door. Darryl would routinely toss the ball around with the boys when we first moved in. They were ten and twelve then, and in the last five years their interests had switched from basketball to video games to girls. Once, when the older one was in the yard laughing with friends, I caught a whiff of marijuana wafting over the fence, but it had only been once, thankfully. I didn't mention it to their mother because I hadn't smelled it since.

She worked two jobs, worried constantly, and had her hands full with two growing boys. I worried about them, too, as I do about all black boys growing into manhood, but my worries were nothing compared to hers. They were sweet, polite kids, who always offered to carry my groceries, mow my lawn, and rake leaves after Darryl died. They were growing up so quickly I hardly recognized them. The previous summer, they had a barbecue, and the block was filled with teenagers laughing, dancing, and cutting up, as teenagers do. I felt my age, wistful to see how quickly time had passed, and how life can pass you by. Overnight, it seemed.

Julie Russell lived in the gray house on the other side and made a point of reaching out to me after Darryl's death. She'd invited me to Thanksgiving dinner, but I turned her down. It was too soon after my loss and I felt like being alone. I regretted it, though, when I ended up eating takeout Chinese food with Aunt Phoenix, who doesn't believe in Thanksgiving. On Christmas Day, Julie dropped off a hand-knitted shawl. I was embarrassed because I didn't have anything for her until she confided she'd actually made it for her daughter who already had two. We'd chuckled about the joys of re-gifting and shared a glass of heavily spiked eggnog. We hadn't spoken since, but it was nice knowing she was next door if I needed her.

The sun was fading, and I made another promise to attend to my neglected yard. Come May, I'd *force* myself to paint the bench—no matter what. I'd plant red-and-white impatiens under the trees and replant Aunt Phoenix's herbs that had faded into weeds. I'd invite Julie or Vinton or Bertie over for lemonade or sparkling wine, and we'd sit on my bright yellow bench in my pretty backyard, talking about nothing and savoring the beginning of spring. Just thinking about my plans made me smile and shake off my worries about Harley. Right on cue, Aunt Phoenix texted me one of her Maya Angelou quotes:

"If you don't like something, change it. If you can't change it, change your attitude."

Like the gift, texts from Aunt Phoenix often missed their mark, but when they hit it, they hit it good. This one was right on time. I didn't know what would become of Harley, but there was nothing I could do about it, and it was time for me to change my attitude, just like this text suggested. I picked myself up, finally ready to go inside, talk to my cat, start my baking, and be grateful for the blessings I had.

"Dessa, is that you out there enjoying the last of this sun?

You got a minute?" Julie called out from her kitchen window just as I was standing up. The gift had summoned her, I figured, so I sat down and she joined me.

Julie had been a librarian before she retired, and had the quick, sharp attitude of a woman who loves books, donates to public TV, and keeps up with everything and everyone—locally, nationally, and globally. Darryl loved talking to her because she knew a little bit about everything. My own personal Google, he jokingly called her, which always made her grin. She was a tiny woman, not quite five feet, and probably weighed less than a hundred pounds, even with the two heavy chains with two sets of glasses always around her neck. Her dark brown Afro streaked with silver was cut short, and the training suits she loved to wear always looked freshly pressed. When she sat down beside me, I caught a whiff of lilac, and as lilac tends to do, I felt immediately at ease.

"Forgive me, sweetie, for not stopping by to check on you," she said, grabbing my hand and holding it for a second. "I've been neglectful of everything. Trying to get myself together. This being single again is no joke, I'll tell you that."

She took a quick breath. "I'm sorry, I didn't mean to put it like that," she said, apparently realizing that being single again for me was a far worse situation. "And I hope you don't mind me calling you sweetie. That's my default name for everybody, including the guy who fixes my car, who spent a couple of years in the joint and is nobody's sweetie."

"Sometimes it's good to feel like somebody's sweetie," I said, and meant it.

"So how are you doing these days; how are you coping?"

"Okay, most of the time," I said, which was the truth. "How about you?"

She chuckled deep in her throat. "Well, after being married to a man for forty years, it's a real kick in the butt to have him walk out on you for a girl forty years his junior. But I'm better off without him. I just didn't see it coming. I should have seen the warning signs, but according to him, I always had my nose buried in some book. He didn't like to read. He was *that* kind of a man, which was the sign I should have seen," she said, with an exaggerated shake of her head.

"I have a friend at work who had a similar experience," I said, thinking of Bertie. "And she lost her job nearly the same week."

"How is *she* doing?"

"Well, she found a job at the real estate place where I work, Risko Realty, and she's okay now," I said, a generous exaggeration.

"Risko Realty, isn't that the place . . . ?"

"That's it," I said, not eager to discuss it.

"Her name wasn't Bertie Jefferson by any chance, was it? A young woman whose last name was Jefferson and said her mother worked with you stopped by here earlier. She rang my doorbell by mistake, and said she needed to talk to you. Something about a pound cake."

"Oh Lord!" I said. Bertie had mentioned she wanted a cake but that had been a week ago. She hadn't mentioned it since.

"Did she say if she was coming back?"

"She didn't say much, just kind of gazed at your house for a while looking disappointed, which struck me as odd. I thought she was going to cry. I asked her if she was okay, and she said she was. Do you think I should have asked her in?"

"No," I said, too quickly. Julie, sharp as she was, picked up on something in my voice.

"She's not dangerous, is she?"

"No, I don't think so," I said, trying to sound convincing, but after talking to Harley I wasn't so sure. "Was there anyone with her?" I said, thinking about Avon Bailey, if that was who Harley had seen.

"I didn't see anyone. Are you sure about this girl? Do you think we should call the police?"

"No. I'll bake her mother's cake, take it to work tomorrow morning, and find out what's going on with her daughter." I had momentarily forgotten I had other cakes to bake. But a pound cake was nothing to make, and it might make Bertie feel better, pick up her spirits as she always had mine. I was uneasy about Louella, though. Was it just the cake or was she reaching out to me for some other reason?

"You look worried," Julie said, her eyes lingering on my face.

I tried to reassure her with a confident smile. "I'm fine, and I know an ex-detective I can call if I feel uncomfortable."

"Oh, a protector!" Julie said with a naughty wink.

"Nothing like that, he's a client," I said more firmly and quickly than I needed to.

"Sweetie, you must be some kind of baker," Julie said with an amused chuckle as she left to go inside. "You take care of yourself, Dessa, and if you need anything, yell loud enough so I can hear you," she added, not entirely joking. "You know if you ever just need to talk, I'm always here."

"Thanks, Julie." Julie had a calm, reassuring way about her that made me glad we'd taken the time to talk. It was good to know she was nearby. I wouldn't wait until my bench was painted to take her up on her offer.

When I got inside, I "chatted" with Juniper for a while and then took two dozen eggs, three pounds of butter, and a quart of milk out of the refrigerator so they could reach room temperature. I greased and floured all my cake pans. Six for the layer cakes, two tube pans for the pounds. The 7-UP cake was basically a pound cake with fizz, so I'd double the recipe and bake Bertie's in my fancy fluted Bundt.

It was smart I'd had the foresight to make Lena's cookies

yesterday. Thank God those were out of the way. Between the baking, cooling, and frosting, I'd be in bed before midnight with luck. Lennox's cakes were basically the always depend-able 1-2-3-4 Cake, a four-egg yellow cake—a safe bet for gen-erations. Buttercream chocolate frosting was easily whipped up—butter, confectioner's sugar, cocoa, splash of milk, touch of vanilla, beat and done—*boring*. Like the 7-UP cake, I could make it in a trance. Nothing like caramel icing, and the memory of that difficult frosting made me pause—just for an instant—reminiscing about the burnt sugar pleasure of it.

I hadn't made it since Darryl died and didn't think I'd make it again. It was a special-occasion kind of frosting. I hadn't had a special occasion in a while. There was too much stirring, and waiting, and melting of sugar—and if you didn't get it on the cake soon enough the whole syrupy mess turned into candy. But it had always been worth it to see Darryl grin when he bit into that first slice. It wasn't his favorite (he was partial to coconut) or I would have made it more often, yet it was worth the trouble.

Cooking calmed my nerves as it always did. When the layer cakes were out of the oven and cooling to be frosted, I made myself a quick tuna fish sandwich with mayonnaise, onions, and pickles and then made the buttercream frosting, helping myself to generous tablespoons. In a sugar-induced daze, I finished the 7-UP cakes—butter, eggs, flour, lemon zest, lime zest, 7-UP—in a heartbeat and placed them in the oven, and sat down with a cup of chamomile tea. They'd been baking for nearly an hour when the front doorbell rang.

"Mrs. Jones, you in there? Are you there?" Louella Jeffer-son yelled at the top of her lungs from my front porch. It was late. I decided not to answer it. I dug the paper with Lennox's cell number from the bottom of my pocketbook and stuck it under a magnet on my refrigerator, just in case. I waited for five minutes, hoping she'd left. No such luck.

"Please. Please let me in," she called out again, her voice so loud and desperate I couldn't ignore her.

"Are you alone?" I asked, standing at the locked door, then regretted my words. If I'd kept my mouth closed, she would have assumed there was nobody here. It was too late now. She hesitated just long enough to make me worry.

"Why do you think there is somebody with me?"

"I need to know before I let you in," I said, cursing our thrift in not buying a front door with a window that allowed you to see outside. I had to believe whatever she said.

"I'm by myself. I just came . . . for my mother," she said, her voice suddenly low. "I need to make peace with her. I'm worried about her."

I wondered what my baking her mother a cake had to do with her making peace, but she sounded so anguished and in such despair, I couldn't find it in my heart to tell her to go, and she stepped inside—alone, thankfully.

Louella's worn green coat was too warm for that night, too big for her small frame, and had probably belonged to half a dozen people before it found its way to her. Her hair was messy and needed the touch of a strong comb and stronger brush. The smell of industrial-strength disinfectant followed her inside, which told me she had probably come from a women's shelter. I recognized that smell from my volunteer days. (I was grateful it wasn't nutmeg.) Her eyes were swollen and red, yet surprisingly, that terrible glimmer that had followed her around for so long had completely disappeared. I touched my amulet, despite Vinton's cynical take on charms offering protection. I didn't think this girl posed a threat but couldn't be sure.

She stood in the middle of the living room for a moment,

pulling in a long breath as if inhaling the lemon cake scent that filled the house. "It smells good in here," she said. "Erika told me when I saw her this afternoon that my mom said you were baking her a cake. I want to bring it to her tonight to surprise her. To make her feel better, get on her good side again, make her happy again."

"It's a little late at night to be taking somebody a cake," I said doubtfully.

"If I go there with the cake, ring the bell, and she sees it, she'll let me in and we can talk. There's some stuff we still need to get straight. I need to find things to make her feel better."

I studied her face, trying to figure out what the girl was up to, what she really wanted. Bertie had always been kind to me, and I owed her daughter a courtesy. She needed to talk and if it was about her mother, I needed to listen.

"I just happen to have one ready," I said after a moment. "You're really in luck tonight."

"Then luck is breaking my way tonight, Mrs. Jones. I wished hard for it and it came true."

Her magical thinking threw me, and for a moment I had my doubts. Bringing somebody a cake in the middle of the night was a nutty way to get on somebody's good side. Had I made a mistake letting her in?

"I'll buy it," she said, misinterpreting my hesitation. She pulled a folded twenty-dollar bill out of a well-worn wallet. "Is this enough?"

"Don't worry about money. Just come into the kitchen, and sit down. The cake's ready to come out," I said, following behind her, thinking about what Lennox Royal would say.

She sat down at the kitchen table and gazed around the room in what looked like wonder. I snuck a quick look at Lennox Royal's number tacked on the fridge.

"I've never seen a blue kitchen before," she said.

"Neither had I." I was softened by her sincerity and my memory of why I'd chosen the color.

It had been Darryl's idea, and we'd argued about it, long and hard. Blue is a bedroom color, I told him. Nobody can cook in a blue kitchen; there are no blue foods. Kitchens should be yellow, white, even light purple—think of grapes or eggplant. But blue? How about blueberries? he'd said, and I laughed and gave him five. We'd trekked up to Home Depot and bought something called Celestial Blue, which was soothing, soft, and heavenly, and every time I stepped into this room I felt like I was in heaven. Shelves, as white as clouds, were stacked with dishes and cups, cookware and containers, in varied shades of blue that we collected over the years. The one spot of red, a whistling teapot, was always filled with water and kept on the stove. I filled it now to make myself another cup of tea.

Louella, closing her eyes, seemed to draw in all the smells, colors, and memories at once.

"It's nice here," she said after a moment.

"Yes, it is. Now, you need to tell me why you came here. Why you really came."

My question took her by surprise, and her answer came quick, with an edge of defiance.

"But I already told you why. You promised my mom a cake, and I want to surprise her . . ."

"What do you *really* want from me?" I said, interrupting her, not hiding the mistrust in my voice.

Her sigh seemed to come from the bottom of her heart and told me she might be telling the truth, or most of it. "You're my mother's only friend. She doesn't talk to anybody anymore. Everything is bottled up inside, and she won't let out what's bothering her. I'm worried about her. I was hoping you could give me some advice. Maybe talk to her for me. Maybe see what's bothering her."

I was surprised to hear that Bertie considered me her only friend. I was flattered but it made me sad. "You know that giving her a cake is not going to solve anything."

"I know. I . . . I just need to talk to somebody, about everything that has happened. But you need to tell me something, too, okay?" she added, eyeing me suspiciously. "Why did you ask me if I came alone?"

"I was afraid Avon Bailey was with you," I said.

"How do you know about Avon Bailey?"

I checked the cakes and took them out to cool before answering. "The cops who interviewed me after Charlie Risko's murder asked if I knew him. Then a friend told me he knew his father, and Harley mentioned him again this morning. He said he'd seen him with you. I've been hearing his name all over the place, and I want to know who he is."

When I sat back down, there were tears in her eyes.

"Why are you crying?" I asked her.

"No reason," she said, wiping them away.

I knew that wasn't true but didn't push it. "Who is he?"

She didn't say anything at first, then finally broke her silence, her voice low and empty.

"The first guy I ever loved, even though I couldn't love anybody back in those days. I did a lot of stuff I'm ashamed of now. I destroyed a part of my soul. Do you know what I mean?" she asked, looking me directly in the eye for the first time since she'd been here.

"Yeah, I do." She had pretty eyes, dark, wide, and long-lashed, and made me wonder where Erika had gotten hers. Everything about Louella had been so swallowed by the glimmer I'd never noticed her eyes before.

"It seems to me you're getting your soul back," I said.

"I'm coming to terms with stuff."

"What kind of stuff?"

"Stuff about Erika. Tanya, Harley, and what Charlie and

Dennis Lane did to all of us. How they played us. Took advantage of us."

It struck me then that maybe Charlie Risko was Erika's father. When I asked her, she spat the answer out.

"Hell no! I slept with Charlie after Erika was born. Yeah, I slept with men before she was born and after she was born. I did a lot of nasty stuff when I was younger. My mother never knew everything I was doing and why. She just knew I wasn't the daughter she raised, she knew that. She baited me, too, saying I had no right to raise Erika. Maybe she was right once, but she's not anymore. Can I have a piece of that cake?" she said, swerving in a different direction.

"Don't you want your mother to get the first piece?" I said, halfway joking because we both knew it wasn't about the cake.

"But it brings back so many memories of when I was a kid, when everything was good and made sense."

You're still a kid, I wanted to say but didn't. "What kind of memories?"

She leaned back in her chair, a sliver of a smile on her lips. "My mother used to bake cakes like this. She was happy then, always smiling and laughing. Just smelling that cake makes me think of how things were. Before my father left, when they were still together. Before I made my mother ashamed. Before everything."

The cakes were still warm but cool to the touch, so I cut her a generous slice.

"Do you have any milk?" she asked, hinting that she was trying to recapture something from her childhood. I got my blue cobalt glass pitcher and a matching glass (which I never used) off a top shelf, filled it with milk, and settled back to hear what I suspected she was ready to share. She drank the milk quickly, and I thought about Tanya, even though the cakes were different: decadent chocolate for a widow who didn't grieve, wholesome pound for one who couldn't stop, both caught in a past that still held them tight.

"Why do you suddenly need to make peace with your mother?"

"Because of things I told her. Things she didn't know before, didn't want to hear."

"What did you tell her?"

"You were there the day Charlie Risko died and heard what I was saying," she said with a slight, teasing smile.

"Why don't you tell me about Avon Bailey?" I said.

She sighed, and took a long swallow of milk. I knew then she wouldn't stop talking until everything was told. Even though it was going on eleven, I needed to hear whatever she had to say.

Chapter 18

"I called him Red," Louella began. "He hated the name Avon because he hated his father. Said the name didn't suit him, said it sounded like something some woman would put on her face." She took a sip of milk and another bite of cake before she continued. "Harley called him Ave; Tanya called him Bailey, but Red was my name for him because of that light, bright skin he had, his reddish hair, those freckles that dot his face like they do Erika's."

I should have guessed what was between them. It was in the way he gazed at her in those photographs, love, sorrow, and jealousy all wrapped up together.

"Everybody thought he was dead, disappearing like he did, and when I saw him I thought I was seeing a ghost, but it was Red in the flesh."

"Did he know you were pregnant when he left?"

"I didn't know I was pregnant. I was playing ball then, even though I was doing stuff for Charlie and Dennis. I worked out regular. I was in good shape, thin and fit, like when I was a teenager. Then I hurt my back. Charlie knew a guy who had some pills that helped, and I ended up taking them for everything. Headache, sore knees, whatever, I took those pills."

"That was about six years ago?"

She nodded. "I left Erika with my mother as long as I could, going to get her back when I was able, caring for her the best I could. Then things started falling apart, and my mom kept her. She wouldn't let me see her, asked me to leave, said I wasn't fit." Her face crumpled in what I assumed was shame, and she changed the subject—to me.

"You live alone here? Your husband left you, right? Men do that, like Red did to me, like my daddy did to my mom."

I wasn't about to share the details of my life with Louella, so I told her the short version: My husband didn't leave me. I was a widow. I lived here by myself because he died last year. We bought this house five years ago, right after we got married.

"Five years ago? The stars were lucky for you. Things turned bad for me right around then." I offered a tepid smile of agreement; she was right about that.

We sat there for a moment, me considering just how bad that turn had been, wondering if maybe she was thinking the same thing. But I wanted to hear the rest of her story and keep her talking while she was in the mood to tell it. "What happened between you and Red?"

She jumped right into it. "Charlie came up with this plan to rob Avon Bailey, Red's father, and I played along with him. I got close to the old man to fool him into trusting me. I was close to Red so he did whatever I told him. He loved me deep like that, but Red didn't know what was going to go down and that I would lead that old man on like I did until it was too late. Or maybe he did know. Men are like that sometimes: They see what they want to see. Charlie used our feelings against us both. I made some money and so did Red. Then he disappeared. It got so we couldn't look each other in the eye. Maybe he was as ashamed of himself as I was."

She stopped looking me in the eye then, too, and dropped her head.

Between what Harley and Lennox had told me, I understood the con game they'd run yet I was surprised to hear her tell it so plainly. I pulled away in disgust, but just for a moment before asking myself who was I to judge her. I touched my mother's amulet to remind myself of my mother's kindheartedness.

"It's in the past, now," I said. "Don't let it ruin your future." She nodded, lifting her head to look at me. "How did you meet Charlie in the first place?" I asked her.

"Through Tanya. Harley knew him, too. She and Harley used to go together. She was, like, his first love, like me and Red, until she started seeing Charlie and they brought me into it and . . . well, the rest I don't really want to talk about."

I nodded that I understood. My guess was that it was the scams as much as the pills that took her down. There was no use in pushing things any further.

"When did Red come back?"

"A week or so before Charlie was killed."

"Where had he been?"

"He didn't say much, just that he'd been traveling here and there, finding himself. Most people didn't know this about him, but he is a sensitive man. What first attracted me to him was that he was gentle, even though he was built big, like a linebacker. I loved that about him, too, that he was strong; he could protect me."

"Why did he come back?"

"This was his home, even though there was nothing left of his family or what they owned. This is where he was from. Charlie took everything. Him and Dennis. Red said he was about to leave town again, but then he saw Erika in the Shop-

Rite with my mom. He said he took one look at her and knew something was left, after all.

"My mother was always saying Erika doesn't look like family, like she could have belonged to any man I slept with, but Erika looks like Red's mother, and when he saw her he knew she was his daughter and he had to find me, and he did. Do you believe in miracles?" she asked after a moment, gazing at me with an intensity that was startling.

"I believe in lots of things people can't see, hear, or understand," I said, telling the truth.

"Red coming back is a miracle. Him showing up like he did, him finding Erika, wanting to be part of our lives. Forgiving me for all the things I did. It's all a miracle."

"That was what you said to your mother that day you two fought, about something being a miracle?"

"Because it was," she said, with the conviction of a true believer. "Red said he had some money saved, and he was renting an apartment over there in Clifftown, and he wanted to get to know his daughter, and me."

Juniper chose that moment to make an appearance. As usual, he nosed around the kitchen looking for treats, then made his way to Louella, who jumped when she saw him.

"Bad luck," she said. "That's what they say. Black cats are bad luck."

"Not true!" I said, genuinely offended. "Actually, it's the reverse. Black cats are *always* good luck. I can vouch for that." As if to prove my point, Juniper rubbed against my ankles, purred, and stared benevolently at Louella, trying to show his worth.

"I'm bad luck," she said, petting Juniper on the head. "That's why my mother told me to stay away from Erika. *You'll just bring her bad luck,* she told me. That hurt me more than anything else she could say because it's probably true.

"She told me the other day she thought Tanya Risko

would be a good role model for *my* child. She and Tanya are getting close these days; she's like a replacement daughter."

"A daughter is always your daughter; no one can take that away from either of you," I said, thinking of my own mother. "Erika belongs to you."

"And Red," she added defiantly.

"And Red." I gave her that. "Was Red what you and Bertie were fighting about that day in the office?"

"It was other stuff, too." She hesitated, a puzzled expression on her face as if just remembering something. "I thought Tanya had told her about all the stuff we did, but she hadn't. I told her because I needed, like, you know, absolution. Is that the word?"

"Yeah, it's a fancy word for forgiveness," I said. "Red forgave you, and you wanted to forgive yourself and for your mother to forgive you. Is that about right?"

She nodded that it was. "My mom didn't believe me when I told her, said she was going to talk to Tanya about it to find out the truth."

"Did she talk to her?"

"Whatever Tanya told her, if she told her anything at all, she made sure she came off as the innocent one. Tanya is always the victim. Ever since we were young. Tanya Risko is never what she seems, not then, not now."

"Nobody is what they seem," I said. She looked surprised, then hurt.

"I'm who I say I am."

"I'm sure you are," I said but doubted she knew herself that well.

"Do you think I had something to do with killing Charlie Risko?" she said, raising her voice slightly. I pulled back from her, suddenly wary. "You think Red killed him, don't you? Red didn't have anything to do with that, and neither did I. It could have been anyone, like that lady who killed herself.

Or that guy my mom was always arguing with. Mom said his boyfriend died two years to the day Charlie got offed. Maybe he was getting even. Or Dennis Lane. Or even Harley. It wasn't Red. He doesn't have the heart," she said, not giving me a chance to answer. Everything spilled out of her in a stream of words.

I nodded as if I agreed, but I wasn't so sure. Harley was right about having seen Red that day, and that was probably why the cops asked if I knew him. They had his name and knew he had a motive, but his fingerprints weren't on the gun, and anyone who came in that night had to have had a key or gotten one from somebody else.

My cell phone "honked" then with that ridiculous duck sound I kept forgetting to change. Julie Russell's name came on the screen, and I stepped into the living room to speak to her.

"Dessa, I hesitated before calling you, but I did want to check to make sure everything was okay. I heard that young woman yelling like a maniac on your front porch, sounding like she was unhinged. Do you want me to call that friendly cop you mentioned? If she's there and you can't talk say, 'Thank you for the cranberry sauce,' and I'll call the cops right away."

"I'm fine, Julie, but thanks for caring. She's just a troubled young woman who needs to talk."

"Maybe I've been watching too many crime shows on the ID channel, one of many guilty pleasures, but keep in mind that a troubled young woman who needs to talk will put a knife in your back as fast as one who doesn't."

"It's okay. Thanks for checking on me. I think I'd sense if she meant me harm," I said and hung up. I knew I was trusting the gift on this one, and Julie, bless her heart, didn't push me on it. Ended up I was right.

Louella *and* her cake were gone when I went back into the

kitchen. The back door was unlocked, and there was a note attached to the refrigerator under one of the magnets.

Thank you for listening to me. I'm taking Mom your cake. Thank you for baking it. My mother said you were an angel. She was telling the truth.

"Hear that, Junie, I'm an angel!" I said to Juniper as he jumped up on the chair where Louella had been sitting. He purred loudly, in what I assumed was agreement. Too tired to make a fresh cup of tea, I sipped what was left of the luke-warm chamomile as I packed up Royal's cakes for delivery. Then I fell out, dead tired, on the top of my bed.

I called Harley first thing in the morning to tell him I was dropping off his mother's Bible. I also wanted to find out more (as subtly as I could) about Red and Louella and everything else that had gone on between them and Charlie. There was no answer, so I tried again half an hour later, with no luck. Harley had been right when he said that Louella had her own story to tell, and I was flattered that she trusted me enough to tell it. I'd suspected that there was more to Harley's relationship with Tanya then he'd let on, and I was right. Both Louella and Tanya had told me as much. It was, of course, his business, not mine, but I'd misread him, and he was probably holding more anger toward Charlie than he let on. Tanya had been his first love, and he had seen those bruises, too. I called him a third time when I got to work. Still no answer. One thing was for sure: He couldn't get far with that ankle bracelet.

Vinton was hard at work, talking on his cell, sounding cheerful and sure of himself. He'd filled a vase with pink roses and put them in Juda's cubicle and stuck one in a water bottle on top of my desk with a note taped to it. "For Bringing Sunshine Back into My Life" it read, which was giving me more credit than I deserved but made me smile. I blew him a kiss, and he stopped working long enough to blow one back.

Tanya's door was closed. I knocked, but when she didn't answer, I went back to my desk to do some work. I read through some lackluster listings, made a dozen cold calls, which amounted to just about nothing, then headed out to Royal's Regal Barbecue to make my delivery. It was 1:30 and the lunchtime crowd was thinning out. The perfect time to drop off my cakes.

"Hey, lady!" Lennox called out an enthusiastic greeting when I walked through the door lugging an overstuffed shopping bag. "Hey, let me help you." He carried it inside and placed it on the counter. "Well, let me see what we've got here," he said with obvious pleasure as he took the cakes out of their boxes and placed them on cake stands.

"Thank you. This was a lot of baking."

"It was . . . relaxing," I said, avoiding his eyes. "And you paid me."

"I'm really grateful. I know you have a lot on your mind," he said, cutting us both a slice of layer cake. He sat down across from me and closed his eyes when he took a bite, sighing as if it was the best thing he'd ever eaten. "Dessa, each one is better than the last." He eyed my piece and grinned. "If you don't want yours, I'll gladly eat it for you."

I pushed my plate toward him. "To tell the truth, Lennox, I ate so much of that frosting last night, I don't want to look at chocolate for a while."

"I know how that goes. I'm that way with my chili. Ate so much of it one Saturday I just about made myself sick. Then, the next week, I was ready for some more." He put down his fork, went to the counter, and pulled out a box of mixed teas.

"Got these herbal teas for you, for the place," he added, handing them to me to look through. "I didn't know they had so many kinds. What would you like? Peppermint, orange blossom, jasmine, chamomile?"

"Peppermint is good," I said, deciding to keep my chamomile tea ritual to myself and not mention that jasmine wasn't herbal.

"I tried some jasmine the other day, and I liked it. It tastes like the flowers smell. That's the kind they serve in Chinese restaurants, isn't it?"

"Yeah, I think it is." I hadn't had peppermint in a while, and breathed in its restful, calming scent.

"A good friend of mine just opened up a Chinese restaurant down the street and wants me to come by. Would you like to, uh, well, check it out with me? I'd love your company."

It took me a full minute to realize Lennox was asking me for a date, another to decide whether to accept, and a third to come up with a tactful way to turn him down. It took me so long, Lennox answered for me.

"Listen, if it's too soon after Darryl's passing . . ."

"I think it might be," I said, not looking him in the eye. "I don't think I'm ready yet."

"Hey, I understand, believe me. Hopefully that place will be around for a while. Give me a call, and we can meet for lunch, no big thing, no pressure, just good food, hopefully. How's that?"

I nodded that it was fine, wondering if I'd ever be ready— or if I wanted to. How long was long enough to wait? Forever?

"What's going on with your murder case?" he asked, as eager to go on to another subject as I was. "Your friend still wearing his ankle monitor?"

"As far as I know. Why did you say *still* wearing it? He can't take it off, can he?"

"Well, that's what they tell you anyway."

I felt a pang of anxiety. "What do you mean?"

"It depends on the restraint and how serious the accused is about getting it off. Some are so cheap you can cut them with kitchen shears. Most, though, are tough like they're supposed to be. But people do escape. I heard of one guy who got his off and went back for a second chance at the victim. Luckily, the cops caught him in time."

"That's not reassuring to crime victims," I said.

"Besides that, there's all kinds of videos on YouTube about how to get them off. Amateur crooks sharing their knowledge. A guy would have to be pretty desperate to try it, though. Desperate and dumb." Lennox saw the expression on my face and quickly added, "From what you've told me about your friend, he's not dumb."

"But he's desperate," I said.

"Let's just hope he's not *that* desperate."

I didn't answer him. I just remembered what Harley had said the last time I saw him.

When my cell phone "honked" (I was used to it now—a bad sign), I hoped it was Harley; it was Tanya Risko, her voice breaking up so much I couldn't understand her.

"They asked if I had somebody to call and you're the only person, Mrs. Jones. The only one."

She'd slipped back into Mrs. Jones; I wondered what that meant.

"I tried to call Bertie, but she didn't answer. Harley didn't answer his phone either. Maybe they're dead, too. Maybe everybody else is dead except me and you. Everybody. Please come. I need somebody here with me. They told me to call somebody. I found him, Dessa. I found him, I . . ." She stopped and began to cry.

"Tanya, slow down. Tell me what happened. Where are you? Who did you find?" I shouted into the phone, interrupting her.

"He's dead!" Tanya screamed.

"Who is dead?" I screamed back at her.

"Dennis is dead. I'm here at his place. The police are here. I'm scared. I'm so scared. Can you please come, please?" she said, begging in her best little-girl voice.

Chapter 19

I knew where Dennis Lane lived; we all did. When he signed the deed to his new condo, he wanted everybody to know that he could easily afford to live in the most expensive property in town. Bertie and Vinton were annoyed by his braggadocio. I just shook my head in disgust. The development was on the border of Bren Bridge, that notorious sundown town, and there was no way I would live there. Yet the place did have every amenity—pool, gym, clubhouse, and a bus that took residents to the nearest train station so tender feet never touched the street. When they conned Avon Bailey out of his precious property, they got paid in spades. It was a gated community, so only residents, guests, or Realtors showing the property had access keys, and that included everyone from Risko Realty.

They might have done this thing together. He might have killed the husband out of jealousy or because he didn't like the way he treated her or she convinced him to do it. I don't know, and neither do you.

Maybe Harley had been involved, and I just didn't want to admit it. If he'd managed to get out of his restraints, he could have murdered Dennis, too.

An officer stopped me at the gate. I explained that Mrs.

Risko had called me, and that she had discovered the body and she was the owner of the firm where Mr. Lane worked.

"You knew the victim?" the patrolman asked.

"Yes. I worked with Mr. Lane, and Mrs. Risko discovered the body and then she called me," I said like a mantra, as a senior officer approached us. I parked my car in a visitor's space and realized with a start that the approaching officer was Larkin, the older of the two detectives who had interviewed me after Charlie's death. I hoped he didn't recognize me. Of course, he did. There just weren't that many murders in Grovesville, and as a ranking detective he'd grabbed them both.

"I'll take her up," he told the patrolman. As we headed out of the parking lot, he turned to me with a halfhearted smile. "This doesn't seem to be your month, does it, ma'am? You have a knack for showing up at murder scenes. Sure you're not Jessica Fletcher in Technicolor, always somewhere around when a murder takes place?" He winked then guffawed at his own joke. "You trying out for a role on *Murder, She Wrote?*" he added, in case I didn't get it the first time.

"I knew the victim," I said somberly, hoping to remind the detective that although this might be funny to him it wasn't to me. He got the hint.

"Sorry, miss," he said. "We don't get a lot of killings here, and sometimes it gets to you, especially one as gruesome as this. Come on, I'll take you up so you can comfort your friend. But I do have to tell you this: I won't be buying any houses from Risko Realty anytime soon," he said, with a fleeting grin. One more stab at gallows humor at my expense.

But the man had a point. This was the second time in less than a week that I'd comforted one of my coworkers in the discovery of a "loved" one, though I wasn't absolutely sure if Dennis Lane was all that to Tanya Risko. Whatever he was, she'd found him dead the same way Vinton had found Juda, and for an uncomfortable moment I wondered if the detective was right. Was the gift responsible for this, putting me in places I shouldn't be? At least, there was no nutmeg this time, so I should count myself lucky.

"Mrs. Risko, your friend is here," the detective said as he knocked on the office manager's door and led me into the stylishly decorated office. The furniture and décor befitted the upscale nature of the place. I could only imagine what Dennis's apartment had looked like. No wonder he was always quick to grab his laptop and work from home. The night Charlie died he must have come back for it. He must have known more about Charlie's murder than he was letting on. Or somebody thought he did.

"You okay, miss?" That thought disturbed me, and Larkin must have noticed the slight shift in my body.

"I'm Mrs. Jones," I said. "I'm fine."

"No ghosts this time." He delivered a last, parting shot.

Tanya sat at the manager's desk, the chair turned away from the door to face a large picture window. She didn't turn around when we walked in. I wasn't sure that she knew I was there. Her cell phone was clasped tightly in her hand, and her arm hung off the edge of the chair. I sat down in the chair beside her, putting my phone on vibrate. The last thing we needed to hear was the duck.

"Tanya, are you okay?"

She turned to confront me, eyes swollen, all color gone from her face. Her voice was so low I couldn't hear her, so I leaned forward, touching her hand. She jumped, as if startled. I wondered if she recognized me. Her eyes were wide and she gazed into space, slowly shaking her head in disbelief.

"What happened?" I could see the lost girl with no pretense, the child her Pa Nettie loved and cared for, Harley's first love. I could see the frightened eyes of all the battered women I'd comforted during my volunteer time in the shelter, when there was nothing to do but listen. She started from the beginning, telling her story in a halting voice.

"He called me this afternoon. We had this, uh . . . Thursday afternoon thing where we'd meet sometimes. Started when I was with Charlie, and we hadn't met in a while, but he said he wanted us to get together today because he wanted to share something with me that might come in handy one day. He didn't say what, just something."

"He didn't say who it was about?"

"No, just that I might need it to protect myself from someone who I shouldn't be trusting."

"Did he sound worried or scared?"

She made a sound that was supposed to be a laugh, then shook her head. "Dennis was never scared. Not even of Charlie. He could be a big bully, too. Just like Charlie. Using stuff against people, just like Charlie."

I nodded that I understood; nearly everybody else had said it, too.

"So I called Harley to see if he knew what Dennis was talking about, but . . ."

"Why would Harley know?"

She shrugged. "I just thought he might, and I'd been trying to call him, but he wasn't answering his phone, and I wanted to see if he knew. But he didn't answer. Do you think he's okay?"

I was beginning to worry about Harley, too, but not for the reasons she thought. Old doubts were creeping in. Like everybody else, he had a passkey to this place.

Or maybe I was going in the wrong direction. The police weren't treating Tanya like a suspect, not yet anyway. But you could never tell with cops. They always knew more than they let on, always kept the important stuff to themselves. Lennox came to mind and what he'd say if he knew "the widow" had been in such close proximity to another murder victim, maybe her lover.

"Do you think they let you smoke in here? I have an e-cigarette. You know, like a JUUL. It's grapefruit. It takes my mind off stuff. Do you think they'll let me smoke it?" That took me by surprise, reminding me how young she was.

"If I were you, Tanya, I wouldn't do it now," I said, which was the best advice I could give her. "What happened next?" The detective said Dennis's murder was brutal. How brutal could somebody Tanya's size be?

"Like I said, I called Harley, and didn't get him, so I left him a message, and then I drove over here. I called Dennis from downstairs but he didn't buzz me in."

She leaned back in the chair, as if trying to remember or too tired to tell the rest.

My phone vibrated. Vinton's name came on the screen, and I answered it.

He sounded as if he was out of breath and could hardly get the words out of his mouth. "You okay, Dessa? I've been scared out of my mind. There was this report on the TV, about another murder of a local Realtor. A real smart-aleck news guy said it like it was some kind of joke. I was scared it was you."

"I'm okay."

"Bertie? You think it's Bertie? I—"

"No, it's Dennis Lane, Vinton. I'm here at his place with Tanya."

"Tanya killed Dennis Lane! Didn't I tell you . . . ?"

"I'm not sure what happened." I glanced at Tanya, but her mind seemed somewhere else.

"But you don't know, do you?" I could imagine Vinton squinting his eyes with suspicion. "Thank God Harley Wilde can't leave his house. One less suspect we have to worry about!"

"I'll call you later, Vinton," I said and hung up. Tanya covered her face with her hands and slowly spread her fingers apart, gazing at me like a child playing peek-a-boo. I smiled slightly like you might with a kid, letting them know you can be trusted, and she dropped her hands back in her lap.

"You called Dennis from downstairs," I said, beginning where she'd left off.

"When he still didn't buzz me up, I thought I'd better check on him myself. I wanted to know what he was talking about, why he sounded like he did. I took the elevator to his floor and let myself in. I have a key." She took a deep breath, letting it out slowly, then her words poured out in a rush.

"Everything blanked after I saw him. I don't even remember calling the cops, but I must have because they came quick. There was blood everywhere. The gash in the back of his head was so deep I couldn't look at it. They say head wounds bleed more than anything else and they're right. He was in the living room in front of the bar, lying on that fluffy white rug I helped him pick out when he first moved in here, and there was blood all over it, and he was dead. There was glass there, too, all around him, and the cops said that was what killed him. That stupid bottle."

"What stupid bottle?" I said, trying to put together what she was talking about.

She looked at me as if I was the one not making sense. "That bottle he kept with all the others on his bar. He had four of them. Somebody took one and bashed in his head."

"The cold duck?" I asked in amazement.

She nodded her head with a slit of a smile. "You'd think if the killer was going to kill a guy like Dennis Lane, he would have picked up a bottle of Moët," she said.

As had happened before with Tanya Risko, her words left me speechless. She'd said "he." Was it just a chance choice of pronoun or did she know more than she was letting on?

There were three men who held a grudge murderous enough to kill both Charlie and Dennis: Vinton, Harley, and Louella's "Red," who "didn't have the heart." I had assumed that none of them had the heart. But of course, that was the gift, whispering false glimmerings and fake truth.

Vinton could have shot Charlie from pure and simple revenge. He could have made it over here today, come up behind Dennis, surprising him and swinging that bottle with such rage it could have killed him. Or Harley, whose first love, Tanya, had been "dirtied," then abused by Charlie. Tanya could have told him in her message that Dennis knew something about Charlie's killer. Could he have gotten out of his apartment? And there was Red, built like a prizefighter, who would have had the biggest motive of all. They had destroyed his family, robbing his daughter of her legacy. Could that have been the real reason he came back?

"Why did you smile when you said that about the cold duck?" I asked her. "The man is dead. It's not funny."

"Don't you think it's kind of funny, in a non-funny way?" she said.

I understood for the first time why this girl had no glimmer. I wondered if that meant she could be a killer, too, a sociopath who gave nothing out and took everything people had to give. She looked straight ahead, avoiding my eyes.

"He was starting to hit me, too. Dennis was, but I didn't kill him," she said, as if reading my mind. "Do you think I killed him, too?" she asked, her voice incredulous.

My vibrating phone saved me from answering her. It was a text from Aunt Phoenix, a new quote from Maya Angelou with the words in quotation marks followed by a flower emoji.

"Bitterness is like cancer. It eats upon the host. But anger is like fire. It burns it all clean."

I shook my head in bewilderment. Sometimes Aunt Phoenix hit it out of the park, but this was a sure enough ground ball. I had no idea what she was talking about.

Better stick to the Pick 4, Aunt P. And give that cherry brandy a rest. I texted her back with a smirk.

Listen to your mama's gift was her swift response, making me wonder what gift she was texting about: the amulet that didn't talk, or the gift my mother didn't give?

Tanya grabbed my hand to get my attention, sensing that I was ready to leave, holding it so tightly I didn't think she was going to let me go. "You are the only one I could call. Thank you for being here. I don't have anybody else," she whispered before releasing me.

"I'm happy I came," I said, hiding my doubts about this puzzling young woman and glad to be leaving.

I was getting into my car when a text came through, displaying a number I didn't recognize. I thought it might be Lennox checking to make sure everything was okay, and I called back. It was Harley Wilde, calling from somebody else's phone.

"Bertie!" was the only word he muttered before he hung up.

I called her cell, then her home number. There was no answer on either. Something bad had happened, I was sure of that. I backed out of the parking lot and made my way to Bertie Jefferson's place, driving as fast as I could.

Chapter 20

I was scared for Bertie, Louella, and for myself as I headed somewhere I probably shouldn't be going. Fear had turned my stomach into a knot. Under good circumstances, I'm not the best driver in the world: My mind wanders. Darryl used to scold me about it, but it didn't do much good. My mind was wandering now, racing with so many questions I felt dizzy.

I pulled over to the side of the road, took a deep breath like they tell you to do when you're anxious, and tried to get myself together. Should I call the police? What would I say? *Bertie!* The name Harley had uttered. It would sound like a crank call and get the attention it deserved, which was none. Did he want me to go to Bertie's? Was he there himself? If he was, he was free of his ankle restraint, which said more about him than I wanted to admit.

They might have done this thing together. Lennox's suspicions hit me again, along with Tanya's question asked with disbelief. *Do you think I killed him, too?* I simply didn't know.

What if it had nothing to do with Tanya or Harley? Maybe Louella had called Harley and told him to reach out to me. Or Bertie had asked him herself. And there was the matter of Avon Bailey. Could he have killed Charlie, then Dennis, and showed up at Bertie's to lay claim to his daughter? Did Bertie try to stop him? But then how would Harley know?

I got back on the road and found Bertie's house on a poorly lit block of single-family homes. She lived in an older neighborhood that had seen better times, a struggling street filled with struggling folks working hard to keep what they had, like Bertie did. A child's pink bike lay on the sidewalk in front of Bertie's small one-story house; Erika's, I assumed. I remembered how excited Bertie had been when she bought it on eBay, like with those hot-pink gloves she was so proud of, despite Vinton's criticism. I felt a pang of sympathy and affection toward my friend, with her quick temper and kind heart. What had happened to her? Was she okay?

I parked down the street from the house, midway between a gray Ford, about the same age as mine, and a black Chevrolet. A late-model Mercedes sitting in front of the stairs to her yard got my attention. Fancy cars like that weren't usually found in this part of town. Most folks here drove cars like mine, always secondhand and often on their third owner. This one looked new, as if it had just driven out of a car wash. It belonged to somebody with money or power, and that wasn't Bertie. I peeked into the car as I walked past. The two well-dressed women talking and sitting inside looked vaguely familiar, but I couldn't place them. I must have seen them at some posh spot where I rarely went and they'd made an impression.

When I walked up to the house, my breath caught in my throat. Harley Wilde, agitated and weeping, sat on the stairs, his head in his hands. He pointed to Bertie's place. I didn't think I could move because I knew the worst had happened.

Yet there was *no* trace of nutmeg.

Out of nowhere, a police cruiser—lights flashing, sirens blaring—pulled up behind the Mercedes, and two officers jumped out. One was short and plump with red hair and freckles, the other lanky and tall with cocoa-colored skin. Guns drawn, they rushed over to where Harley sat and surrounded him. Harley raised his hands above his head and slowly stood up, tripping over the restraint attached firmly to his right ankle. The redhead shoved him toward the police car and pushed him down on the hood.

"He's still got it on," said the lanky officer to his partner, who glanced at the restraint with a puzzled look.

Neither noticed me standing off to the side. They did, however, see the two women sitting in the car and turned to confront them, the red-haired officer demanding to see a driver's license, which the driver promptly gave him.

"Oh, crap," he said, loud enough for me to hear him. He handed it to the other officer, who shook his head and gave it back. Then he turned to the driver. "Mrs. Grace, are you all right?" he asked, his voice tightly polite.

"Of course I'm all right," said Laura Grace from the Aging Readers Club, mink coat tossed carelessly around her shoulders. Hands above her head, she climbed out of the car. Margaret Sullivan, in a blue peacoat, hands held high, followed suit.

"This man is a felon. Were you ladies aware of that?" stammered the redhead.

"He's not a felon yet because he hasn't been tried and convicted," snapped Laura Grace, hands still up. "And if you knew the laws you're enforcing, you would know that." She paused to stare intently at the other officer. "I know you," she said, smiling sweetly. "You were in my sixth-grade Bible study group at St. Mark's. Please give your mother my best."

"We're the ones you should be arresting," said Margaret Sullivan, looming over the short policeman. "We kidnapped *him*. We ordered *him* to get into the car. We're responsible for him being here, not the other way around."

"Maybe we should call Chief Grace," the tall policeman said in a low voice.

"And say what? We just pulled over your mother for kidnapping a prisoner?"

"We got to do something!"

"I should be treated like everybody else," said Laura Grace. "The law is the law."

"I guess they can put their hands down," said the short officer, which the ladies did.

The officers exchanged quick glances, neither knowing what to do. The short one stayed to guard the "prisoners" while the other put a call in to the precinct. Between arresting Harley and the ladies of the Aging Readers Club, they paid no attention to me. I looked around the side of Bertie's house and saw the back door was ajar. I quickly slipped inside.

Everything was still, and too quiet. Was this how it sounded when someone's life was gone? I stopped, listening for any sound, anything that moved.

"Bertie!" I said softly, afraid to speak too loudly, though I wasn't sure why. "Bertie, are you here?"

"Mrs. Jones?" Louella stepped into the kitchen. Her eyes were wide with fear. "Can you come back here? My mom is in the living room."

"Louella, the police are outside. Do we need—"

"No. Harley came over because my mom told him to. She needed to talk to him, to say what she needed to say. We knew the cops would follow him here. I'll get them soon. But she wants to talk to you first." Her voice was filled with an emotion I couldn't identify.

I followed her into the living room, still wary of nutmeg, but there was only the leftover smell of rotisserie chicken, green beans, potatoes boiled, then forgotten, on a back burner. It was a small, sad room, everything about it worn and tired. The walls, once white, had faded to the dull color of evaporated milk. A big-screen television, long broken, had been pushed into a corner and a smaller sat in front, a sign that nobody had the strength or energy to move either one. A coffee table, stained to look like mahogany, was in front of the couch, which was upholstered in yellow and green and spotted with tufts of cotton peeking through tears. A vase of plastic tulips, hot pink, was in the middle of the coffee table. Bertie's gloves, the same color and covered with blood, lay beside the vase.

Bertie was on the couch, face grim, eyes filled with terror. Louella sat beside her, holding her hand. I sat on the other side. Bertie reached for my hand, and I squeezed it gently, letting her know I was on her side, whatever she said. I was here for her for all those times she'd been there for me.

"It's my fault," Louella said, her voice low and filled with anguish. "All of it is my fault. It is because of me and what I did."

Bertie shook her head, a faint, halfhearted smile on her lips.

"I made my choices. I did what I did. I guess I just couldn't take any of it anymore. None of it! It had to come out like it did.

"I never told you this, daughter, but my father was a batterer. You had a good daddy, I had a bad one. Maybe that was how it started, him beating me and my mother until we were bloody, me tucking that pain and fear away inside of me so deep I didn't know it was there until it came out. Charlie brought it out."

I recalled what she'd said about her father at that bar after the memorial. I hadn't paid much attention then and I should have. She continued speaking, her tone gentle, a mother speaking to a child she loved, wanting her to understand.

"I knew what I had to do when you told me," she began. "Then seeing how he was beating on Tanya, getting worse every day, like my father did on my mother, and then thinking about what he had done to you. All of them ruined you: Charlie, Dennis, even Harley in his own way."

"I thought you went home, Mom, after our fight I thought—"

Bertie gently put her fingers on her daughter's lips, silencing her. "I didn't want to believe it. I went back to the office, sat there for a while. Got sick to my stomach. Went into that nasty bathroom just crying, then went back to the office. I was looking for Tanya. I wanted to talk to her. I heard him yelling at somebody, screaming like he was out of his mind. I sat there listening. I thought it might be Tanya, then maybe Dennis, because his laptop was still there. I sat there, thinking maybe I should go home. I didn't know what to do. Seems like I always ended up doing nothing but feeling ashamed. I put on my coat, hat, and new gloves, all ready to leave, then changed my mind when the yelling stopped."

She paused for a moment, as if remembering something she'd tried to forget, and then spoke in a tone filled with regret.

"There is something hard in me, Louella. You know that better than anyone." Louella nodded that she did. I'd seen glimpses of it, too. "After being fired so close to retirement, after Ronald left me like he did, and all the rest of it. All the kindness in me was gone."

"Like me, Mom? *I* was all the rest of it."

"No, never you," she said, but we all knew that wasn't the truth.

"I went into his office. He was nasty as always, yelling at me in his ugly way, 'What the hell are *you* doing here?' he said, like I didn't have a right to live. 'What they hell are *you* doing here?' after what he had done to my daughter, to me! He turned his back on me like I was nothing. I picked up that gun and shot him dead."

Her words were casually spoken, emotionless. I wondered how I could have sat next to her for so many months and not sensed the rage she held inside. Her devil had been poked for years and none of us knew it.

"I realized Harley was the one he was yelling at, but I didn't know he'd picked up the gun and left his prints on it till later; that was luck, I guess. I had to tell Harley I was sorry because I knew he didn't do it. He needed to know the truth. He didn't deserve to do time for something he didn't do. I told him I was sorry when he came in here.

"But Dennis? He was beating up on Tanya, so it felt good to hit him hard with that bottle. I didn't think there'd be so much blood, though, ruining my pretty pink gloves," she said with the barest hint of a smile.

Louella's eyes filled with horror at her mother's words. Her gaze followed mine to the gloves on the table, then returned to her mother.

"You okay now, Mom?" she said quietly, like any child worried about her mother's well-being. Bertie smiled, full and bright, showing just the glint of a gold tooth like she had so many times when she made me feel better.

"Yeah, baby. I'm just fine now," she said.

Aunt Phoenix's text about anger burning it all clean came back to me then. As usual, she got it right.

I left the two of them sitting together, Louella still holding her mother's hands, Bertie rocking back and forth as if comforting herself. I stepped outside to get the police, who were puzzled, then surprised by my sudden appearance. Harley, locked in the squad car, nodded when he saw me, letting me know he was okay.

"Officers, the person who killed Charlie Risko and Dennis Lane is inside her house," I said, my voice shaking so hard I wasn't sure they understood me. They glanced at each other, and then at Harley. Hands on holstered guns, they followed me into Bertie's place to hear what she had to say.

It took a while for things to get back to normal at Risko Realty. We'd been through two murders, a suicide, and shared a work space with a "nice" lady who shot one man in cold blood, bashed in another's head with a bottle, and we'd never suspected a thing. Juda's despair and Bertie's quiet rage haunted us all; none of us had seen the depth of their sorrow. Tanya closed the place for a while because too much had happened. But after two weeks she opened it back up. She owed us, she said, because we were her family. We were Louella's family, too, and each of us reached out to her in our own way. Like a family, we needed to heal together until we were strong enough to set out on our own.

And as it usually does, life eventually fell into place. Louella became a Realtor and joined the company. Vinton visited Atlantic City, stayed for a while, and had lost most of that gray glimmer by the time he returned. He told Tanya about Juda's files and they burned them, which was good for them both. (I still harbored some doubts about Tanya, but for the time being tucked them in the back of my mind where they could do no harm.) The influential ladies of the Aging Readers Club (Harley's angels in high places) kept their word—and faith— and continued to look out for him. As for me, I felt stronger, too, and was finally able to meet Lennox Royal for lunch.

"You know you were the key to solving all this," he told me as we were finishing our shrimp in oyster sauce. "You were everybody's best friend, everyone depended on you, from that kid Harley to enigmatic Tanya to that crazy murdering woman. You know what you are, Odessa Jones? You are the rainbow in everyone's cloud," he added with a grin.

I recognized the words as one of Aunt Phoenix's favorite Maya Angelou sayings, twisted a bit to work for me. I thought about telling him, then decided not to. It is no small thing for a man to love the name Odessa and quote Maya Angelou even if he doesn't know he's done it.

"Thank you," I said, and finished my jasmine tea.

Dessa's Go-To Cake

I call this my "Go-To Cake" because I can bake it quickly, take it anywhere, and count on folks to ask for second and third helpings. It's basically a pound cake with a down-home twist, also known as a 7-UP cake. That humble soda (Aunt Phoenix calls it "soda pop") is a main ingredient. Truth is, any lemon and lime soda will do—but why take a chance?

Here's what you need:

(First, take out the butter and eggs so they're room temperature—it makes things go quickly!)
1½ cups softened unsalted butter
3 cups granulated white sugar
5 large eggs
3 cups all-purpose flour
1 teaspoon vanilla extract (Don't be cheap. Use real vanilla extract.)
1 teaspoon almond extract (If you like a lemony taste, use lemon extract instead of almond—or use all three if you dare.)
¾ cup 7-UP
Confectioner's sugar for dusting, when the cake has cooled

1. Preheat the oven to 325 degrees F.
2. Grease and lightly flour a 10-inch tube pan (or fancy Bundt pan) and set it aside.
3. In a large bowl, cream the butter and sugar. Add the eggs one at a time and beat well each time you add one. Add the flour and the extracts. Beat well. Gently fold in the 7-UP, ¼ cup at a time. Pour the batter into the prepared pan.

4. Bake for 1¼ to 1½ hours. You'll know it's done when you poke a toothpick into the cake and it comes out clean. Transfer the cake from the oven to a wire rack and let it cool for 15 minutes. Unmold it on the rack and let it cool completely, and then, and only then, dust it with as much confectioner's sugar as your heart tells you to.

Connect with U(s)

Visit us online at
KensingtonBooks.com
to read more from your favorite authors, see books
by series, view reading group guides, and more.